Praise for *The Good Negress*

"Truly extraordinary."   —Toni Morrison

"A knife-edged, poignant debut . . . Both the vitality and perils of life in divided families—as well as the larger conflict between a woman's duty and desire—receive deft, honest handling here, revealing a vibrant new voice in our midst."   —*Kirkus Reviews*

"In a particularly accomplished debut, Verdelle imbues her ambitious novel with a confident style, finely realized characters and a strikingly original first-person voice . . . Consistently absorbing and beautifully detailed, Verdelle's novel brings universal truths to an affecting study of adolescence."   —*Publishers Weekly*, starred review

"To find a truly unique and resonant work is exciting. In this company, A. J. Verdelle's first novel resounds, her vibrant prose ringing clear . . . The language and sensibility remain true, and the story spills forth in a broad cape, its prose filled with the enchantment of Denise's telling. Haunting, at times mystical, this novel has all the dimension and beauty of song. To read *The Good Negress* is to fall under a spell, to open a window, to fly."
                    —*Los Angeles Times Book Review*

"A. J. Verdelle weaves jolts into this strong, plain story until it teeters on extraordinary . . . [*The Good Negress*] is deftly crafted and sweetly fought out. A. J. Verdelle shatters perceptions quietly and Denise stays with us, as she should."   —*The Boston Globe*

"In this fascinating debut novel, language becomes both a cause of oppression—and a metaphor for it . . . To watch this girl take control of her life is an amazing and rewarding journey—no doubt the first of many from this first-time novelist."   —*The Seattle Times*

"I've never used the word 'genius' in a book review before, but in the case of A. J. Verdelle's first novel, *The Good Negress*, no other word will do. It's a virtuoso performance at the level of craft, and at the human level, totally real and absorbing . . . Verdelle's diction, idiom, syntax, spelling, and punctuation make her narrator's speech jump off the page: the sound of the language, its rhythm and intonations, like a rich music, fill your blood . . . The author's depth of feeling is as great as her verbal skills . . . Writing like this doesn't come along very often."
                           —*The Raleigh News and Observer*

"The complexity of the novel is in its rich, evocative language, a recreation of sights, sounds, and smells so keenly observed that they infuse the narrative through memories of a grandmother who is sadly becoming an anachronism. But the wisdom in the advice dispensed by the 'good negress' lives in Verdelle's powerful pages."
                           —*American Way Magazine*

"The musical sensibilities in Verdelle's imagination make *The Good Negress* sing. Out of Verdelle's—and Denise's—combination of passion and wisdom, of sophistication and struggle, has come a novel as soundly structured as any classical symphony but as fluid and easy as a Louis Armstrong solo."   —*The Independent Weekly*

"Verdelle deftly moves back and forth in time. As the girl matures into a woman and becomes a student with much improved communication skills, the way in which she tells the story also evolves. It is an ambitious undertaking that makes this first novel even more accomplished . . . Verdelle's bittersweet tale offers . . . honest emotion, respect of culture and appreciation for innocent discovery."

—*The Detroit Free Press*

"A remarkable first novel . . . Lyrical and evocative."

—*Greensboro News and Record*

"Like *Their Eyes Were Watching God*, here is a novel about a woman's voice, and a woman's coming-of-age, and a woman gaining her own power. Intelligent, sorrowful, warm, and intimate, this portrait clearly marks a powerful debut into a long and proud tradition of American letters."

—Randall Kenan, author of *Let the Dead Bury Their Dead*

"With plain sounds like that of a tin kettle banging on an iron stove, Verdelle creates worlds we have rarely read about before. She renders character, suspense, subtlety of insight, and poetry by knocking together—in unprecedented ways—the simple words of everyday life."

—Melissa Fay Greene, author of *There Is No Me Without You*

Awards

The Harold D. Vursell Memorial Award from the
American Academy of Arts and Letters

Black Caucus of the American Library Association
Literary Awards Honor Book in Fiction

Whiting Award for Fiction

Finalist for PEN/Faulkner Award for Fiction

THE GOOD NEGRESS

A. J. VERDELLE

THE GOOD NEGRESS

ALGONQUIN BOOKS OF CHAPEL HILL
2016

Published by
ALGONQUIN BOOKS OF CHAPEL HILL
Post Office Box 2225
Chapel Hill, North Carolina 27515-2225

a division of
WORKMAN PUBLISHING
225 Varick Street
New York, New York 10014

This is a work of fiction. Names, characters, places, and incidents are
either the product of the author's imagination or are used fictitiously.
Any resemblance to actual events or locales or persons, living or dead,
is entirely coincidental.

Library of Congress Cataloging-in-Publication Data
Verdelle, A. J., [date]
      The Good Negress / A. J. Verdelle.— 1st ed.
      p.   cm.
      ISBN 978-1-56512-085-3 (HC)
      I. Title.
   PS3572.E63T48   1995
   813'.54—dc20   94-40889
                                               CIP
      ISBN 978-1-61620-527-0 (PB)

10 9 8 7 6 5 4 3 2 1

Algonquin Books of Chapel Hill gratefully acknowledges the involvement of the Center for Documentary Studies at Duke University in the publication of this novel.

Many are due thanks for their support in the times when this book was still a whisper. Patricia Howell Jones, my mother, and Jimmie Verdelle Williams Howell, her mother, both had expectation. My two sisters, Brenda Jones and Adrienne Semidey, had faith.

Appreciation to my mother-figures, both mythic and real: Patsy Washington, Janie Small, Mamie Washington, Goldie Washington Rikard, Viola Williams, Sadie Aikens, Louise Young, Mabel Jones, Dixie Moore, Marcella Pope, Betty Howell Henderson, Marjorie Jackson, Pat Robinson, and Jackie Shearer; to my father and his father, A. Y. Jones, William Jones; and to my grandfather, Ted Franklin Howell, and to Dr. Charles G. Adams and Dr. Henry C. Gregory, III. Some people have just insisted that I write and I thank them for pushing me along: Beth and Beloved Sutter of Philadelphia, Sauda Burch of Oakland, Alecia Sawyer of Albuquerque, Lynda Parker of Austin. Our niece and nephews danced Clara for me: Mariah Birdsong, Miles Ballew, Alexander Semidey.

Professionally, the people who have helped me get this book to market have been a huge encouragement: Alex Harris and Iris Hill of the Center for Documentary Studies at Duke University; Rob Odom, my editor; Wendy Weil; Shannon Ravenel and Elisabeth Scharlatt at Algonquin Books of Chapel Hill; Marie Brown; and two of my legion of teachers in life, both teachers and good friends, Tom McDonough and Archie Rand.

Alexa Birdsong has been *sotto voce* reassuring. She plays jazz for me. Aché.

THIS BOOK IS DEDICATED TO BABY ALEX AND HIS GRAMMY.

THIS RAIN COMING

I KNEW I was sleepin too long. And as I have come to know myself, I think I felt her leavin, the door closin behind the belly at the end of my rope. When I did finally shake myself awake, I was at Granma'am's house. I got out of bed, tiptoed down the hall, and peered around the door frame into the quiet front room. Nobody there, or in the front yard. I walked back toward the kitchen, and, there at the line where the floor planks got wider, I had to stop and take a look: one boiled egg, bacon, and glass of brown juice, all sittin so orderly in one place on the table. I dragged a chair over to the open window and climbed up on it. I hung my neck through the window and looked out to the backyard. Granma'am was outside in the bleachin sun, bent over, pullin tomatoes off the vines.

I stretched farther out the window to see where Mama stood. She would be standin more in the shade, havin conversation. Or maybe foldin clothes she was takin off the line. I reached farther out to see her feet underneath the long white sheets. No feet. Granma'am must have heard my elbow slip. She turned as if I called. "Well, good mornin, sleepyhead," she said, and she was inside, the screen door slappin, before I got down off the chair.

"Hi, Granma'am. Where's Mama?" I answered.

Granma'am had red and green and yellow-orange tomatoes stretched out in a dip in her upturned house-dress. "Well, hi is *you*, Baby Sister? You ready for some breakfast?" She has turned her back to me before I can nod my head. One at the time, she lays the tomatoes on the wood board by the sink. Then she brushes off her dress front with her hand and goes over to the big black Vulcan stove that anchored the kitchen's back wall. Her cotton stockings were thick, and she had them rolled down below her knees. There was a bulge on each right side, a knot she had twisted to hold her leggings up.

"Sit down to the table, Baby Sister." My place at the table was set directly across from the stove. In time, from that place, and that kitchen, I will know all the Vulcan's dents and injuries. I will cause some more.

Granma'am lifted warm bread across the table and onto the white plate with the yellow-green flowers round the edges. She pushed the plate closer to the egg. And then, in one of the wide chairs with beige and brown flecked vinyl seats and backs, the one to my right, Granma'am sat down. "Say your blessin, and have your break-fast, Baby Sister." Her hand stretched out and pressed down my hair where sleep had rumpled the edges up. That was the end of the sentence.

"Where's Mama?" I was screaming; my voice was qua-very, wild, quick. I jumped up. The chair legs scraped against the kitchen floor. I stood as tall as I could on the floor. I looked directly at a face and mouth that did not move, eyes that looked surprised but ready too, somehow. The whole situation answered, with a shudder and a sucking sound: she's gone.

I tore away from the table, my arms heavy like they was wet and wrung out. They swung very late behind my hurly-burly hurt. I upset the neat breakfast place with my wet rags for arms. Off the plate and the table went the swiped boiled egg, it landed in the chair, it rolled off onto the floor. The shell crumpled at the compact hit, and the egg rested there, displaced and on its side. The cracked pieces of shell hung together; it was that tough-but-thin inside skin. One boiled breakfast egg, preserved through the fall.

I ran out to the front yard again, in just what I had slept in and in my bare feet. I wrapped my fingers around two of the boards on the gate. I looked in one direction down the what-they-called road. I didn't recognize the place or its colors. It had no blocks or corners or streets, no other two-families with shutters. No traffic lights, no pavement. No Detroit. Disbelief is an emotion, you know. Like an ocean and its major pulse, it can overtake you. It can blind your eyes and block your ear canals. It can knock you to a depth.

Both my hopefulness and my faith in my mother went flat. I felt so completely betrayed.

After many choked breaths, I collapsed at the gate. Left by Mama second and by Daddy first, now I was sent away. My behind on the dirt was naked, and the soil wasn't dry or rich. It wasn't grainy or rocky under my skin. It wasn't cold, but grass wasn't growin. It was in between everything, that's how ordinary it was. Ordinary, just ordinary dirt.

When I finally started to see again I noticed that the dirt in the yard had been raked. Overtop of the lines of rake teeth were two crazy curvy paths. My dashing feet —yesterday in shoes and today without. Down the middle of all that dashing hurly-girly were two other lines. The little small ovals of my mother's high heels. I stayed there and looked hard a while, my mouth hanging open, my tongue drying off.

I had this tantrum at Granma'am's front gate, where I had run to to look for my mother. This was my down home coming-out scene, a slow motion moment when I got left where Mama grew up, in history. This was when the years started to yawn. I opened my mouth wide, and I roared. Anybody could hear knew I was there. I stomped, and I wailed. Some people walked by, nobody I knew, and since I wasn't seeing so well at that moment, it all went by me, their slowing and staring and shared looks with my granma'am.

She stood behind me, calm as her age, in the yard near the front of the house.

I wanted to take to bed, in the spirit of my mama, but Granma'am's ideas did not allow that. Granma'am didn't rush me to be happy, but she didn't permit no aimless layin round. She let me sleep until the sun was high up in the middle a mornin, as she was prone to say. I got up about eight, and then I helped her with things.

First, we made dinner. We washed and seasoned meat, cut up onions, cooked vegetables. We set out ingredients for a cake or pie so they would warm while we cooked. We mixed dessert last, and put it in the oven or the icebox to set.

We had breakfast sometime in the midst of all this. Granma'am would heat up milk for me, and pour a little taste a her coffee in it. Then after breakfast, while I did the dishes, Granma'am would start to fry or roast, whatever the day's meat called for. Seemed like I washed dishes all morning. Time the first set a dishes was done, Granma'am would have flour or cornmeal all over some others, and she would need the table cleared in order to roll out her dough.

I came to like bein in the kitchen with her. Anywhere else in the house, I was by myself. We talked as much as any two strangers, one who knows and knows she knows, and the other who is young.

"Hi you feelin this mornin, Baby Sister?"

"Fine, Granma'am."

"You ain't got nothin else to say this mornin, Baby Sister?"

"How you, Granma'am?"

"I'm jes fine, thank you for astin."

"You ever made a pumpkin bread?"

"No, Granma'am."

"You ever ate pumpkin bread?"

"No, Granma'am."

"You like pumpkin?"

"No, Granma'am."

"You ever had it?"

"No, Granma'am."

"Then you cain't say you don't like it, now can you?"

"No, Granma'am."

"What else you got to say besides no, Baby Sister?"

"Nothin, Granma'am."

"We gone cook the pumpkin first. You know how to peel it?"

"No, Granma'am."

"Here, lemme show you. Look in that second tray there and hand me one a those lil short knives."

"This here knife is dull. Go out back and sharpen it on that rock by the door. You know how?"

"No, Granma'am."

"Here, lemme show you." Her hollow screen door

slapped shut behind us. She stoops down to the rock, and I sit and watch. She shows me how to slice the knife, one side at the time, against the rough stone. It is a white–gray rock; it has edges and a few points. It is almost big as my head, and so I know this rock will not be moved. It will stay right where it is. I wonder how many years it's been there.

Granma'am watches me slice the knife once or twice, then she goes back in. "Fi'teen times both sides," she says, "and den bring y'knife on in."

The little knife wasn't much bigger than my hand. Had a dark brown wood handle. "A *parin* knife," Granma'am said it's called.

"NOW, FIRST YOU cut de pumpkin in half downa middle." Granma'am used a much bigger knife. The round little pumpkin divided in one swipe.

"And then you scoop out de seeds and de stringy part. You watchin, Baby Sister?"

"Yes, Granma'am."

"And then you take and cut the flesh in whatever kinda pieces you want, but small enough so it'll boil in good time. Like this here." She held up a neat, orange cube.

My turn. I swiped at the pumpkin flesh, stabbed it, broke it apart, used her parin knife like a pick. Granma'am stood and watched me and told me to keep my fingers out from under that knife. Since she was gone look, and not correct me, I went right ahead and mauled her pumpkin.

"I wanna know why my mama lef me here!" I crossed my arms hard cross my chest.

"Lay dat knife down, Neesey, fore you cut y'self."

I had let the pumpkin go abruptly, so it teetered

between us on its ridges and curves. I put the parin knife down beside it, which stopped the sway, and I crossed my arms again.

"Baby Sister," she started, "everybody cain't know *why* bout everything alla time. Ain't no reason why, lease none that matter a bit right now. Now lissen, y'mama lef you down here wid me. And that's because you gone be fine, right down here wid me." She took a breath and went right on. "I raised y'mama. All she know bout raisin is on account a what I taught her. So you gone get the same raisin whether you home here wid me or up in Detroit wid y'mama. You gone be all right, little pumpkin, don't you worry y'self."

I didn't say a thing at first, didn't look at her, and didn't uncross my arms. I tested the tear ducts, but thanks to all the sleep I'd had, and all the days that had passed, they were dry as the dirt in the yard.

"I wanna go home," I whined.

MY MAMA AND me, we had been down home at Granma'am's most a two weeks, which was a long time. Mama went out to see people and took me with her, and we had fun. But when her and Granma'am were in the house together, Lord have mercy, I was the meat on the plate. They looked at me and around me. Wanted to see how the light blue shift look on, wanted to see the mud cups I made, wanted me inside until the storm let up, wanted me outside to get some fresh air, wanted me to stay near the house now, wanted me to come back in now, wanted me to rest now, wanted me to listen now, wanted me too, wanted me.

I liked their attention, mostly, although it would have been better each one by herself. There was too much "we" in them this time; it made me nervous. They kept me too close, and they asked too many questions. They looked at each other over my head. They didn't answer me much. I could almost feel their plannin, but not a word to me.

"YOU CAIN'T GO home," Granma'am answered. And then after she picked up the parin knife and started again to cut the pumpkin, she went on, "And Neesey, I done told you, you home right here."

In the face of that pronouncement, I ran back to the bedroom where I had slept. It had been my mama's room when she was young. I leaped across the bed and buried my head. I just wailed into the bedclothes since I was all cried out.

Granma'am didn't call or come after me. The time passing got to be way too long, so I got up and went back to the kitchen. Didn't have one tear track to show, but I didn't care. I wanted company.

The pumpkin and the parin knife waited on the table. Same few pieces cut as when I had left. Granma'am stood workin at the sink, and she didn't turn around when I came in. I stood in the doorway until she spoke to me.

"Neesey, I know you upset. I know how lonesome you feelin, cause when I came here wid my husband James, I didn't know nobody. Wasn't a animal in this state would recognize me. But you let Granmama tell you somethin. The best way to make y'self feel better is to get y'hands to workin. When you put y'hands on somethin and make it somethin else, that will heal you lower places than you cry from. We be jes fine down here us two. Time might come when you like it.

"Now I lef that pumpkin on the table for you. You go on and cut it up. And watch y'hands. That knife is jes the right size, so ain't no need a you cuttin y'self."

I couldn't make any other decision then. I was too far from any other body I knew. I had got tired of my new bedroom and the front-inside-the-fence, so I went dry-eyed to the table, and I did what she said.

I HAVE TWO brothers: David and Luke edward. David is my oldest brother. By the time I get back to Detroit, he's nineteen. He was fourteen when I left. Luke edward, my brother closest to me, is two years behind David.

We used to all go down home together in the summers. But when Mama dropped me off, it was fall, not summer. And David and Luke edward stopped coming regular, that very year. So, I didn't see my brothers much in the four or five years before I left Granma'am and went back to Detroit. But even I knew about those years, the teenage ones. Years like riots, when boys groan and strain and struggle and grind their teeth in the effort to pass to men.

The young and hopeful in them both seemed to have given way, the way thriving succumbs to flames.

I tried to do what Granma'am had said, get my hands to workin.

BIG JIM—MARGARETE'S new husband—was a big house of a man. Since this was the first time I had seen him, I looked as close at him as I could. I only stopped cause Margarete said stop starin. His feet crossed five or six of the slats on Margarete's front room floor. His hands seemed big as plates.

He was brand new to me, and for a much longer time than I was new to him. He got to know me pretty quick, mostly through the food I cooked. Ain't much food cain't show you bout people. In three or four weeks time, I had made enough meals to index. So, me and Big Jim got to the place where he might say when he left the house, "Neesey, I put three dollars on the table for you to go down and get some neckbones and whatever you want to cook alongside." He would close the door behind that remark, and that was how I would know what he wanted to have for dinner. I might ask Margarete what else I should fix, and in the beginning she would tell me. Later, after she finds out how good a cook I am, she just says, "Neesey, you the one like to cook, just get what you want. It'll be good, Jim'll be happy." So that's how I got to the place where when I left for school in the morning, I would take whatever money Big Jim left on the table, and then on the way home, I would stop at the butcher and get what I thought best. I made all the meals.

ONCE THERE IS a Wednesday night when David will be somewhere celebrating. It is Serena's sister's birthday, and David is going with Serena to have cake and ice cream. Serena is David's girlfriend, and Serena's sister is in her twenties.

Big Jim and Margarete are going to a card party with his friends. Big Jim says on his way out the door that they will all be out this evening and that maybe I want to get some potted meat for dinner.

"Who gone be out?" I ask him. He stands at the front table collecting his keys and his pocket change.

"Me and your mother, and David is going to Serena's."

"Luke edward gone be home?" I want to know.

"Your guess good as mine," he says, and he goes on out the door.

Why would he think Luke edward would want potted meat? And why would he think I want potted meat either? I know Big Jim does not plan for Luke edward's feeding. Luke edward, though, is my brother, and Big Jim is just the boss.

BIG JIM COMES to complain about how I cook meat. He says I cook like a old woman, somebody been cookin twenty years. That was the good part. He complains I make my meat too soft. I do put gravy on almost everything.

Now, gravy is not easy to make. Plenty people—good cooks too—cain't make good gravy. Fact, when I first started to cook in Margarete's kitchen, I had forgot how to make gravy. It was a sign a my homesickness for Granma'am and Patuskie, I decided. Nobody knew it but me. And Luke edward.

"Luke edward, you like gravy?" I ask him this one day when he got up. He was sittin dressed up at the table with sleep still in his eyes, and I was standin at the sink lookin at cabbage leaves for worms.

"Yeah," he said, drinkin his coffee.

"I don't see how you drink that coffee, been sittin here three hours," I said to him. And that was so. Either me or Big Jim or David made a big pot a coffee early, when we got up. Actually they got up before me, but not because I was sleep. I just didn't much like to run into those two—David or Big Jim—while they was so dedicated to gettin ready. They both had to go all the way cross town to work. To get there on time, so early in the day, they made some fast turns round the house. So I let them have all the mornin space. I usually just stayed on my cot where I was out the way and tried to think good things until they left. In the first months while I was tryina get my own routine, I prayed: Lord, let it be all right. Lord, don't let me get mad. Lord, help me feel better. Granma'am, send for me.

Luke edward don't care about drinkin old coffee, which probly was not a good sign for his opinion bout my gravy. I ask him do he know how to make gravy, and he say no. I told him I forgot how, and he ask me if I forgot since last night.

He talkin bout that juice I served over them meatballs. I said, "Luke edward, that juice I poured over them meatballs wasn't no gravy."

"Tasted fine to me," and he start to pick sleep out his eyes.

BIG JIM SAY he like his meat crisp. He say, "People don't always want gravy, Neesey. For example, like on steak. Now, you grill some onion on top a the steak," he say, "now, that's good."

Me and Granma'am don't eat no steak nohow, I am thinkin. Margarete is lookin straight at me while her husband sayin all this. She sees I have raised my hand to my lip and started to pull on it; I'm feelin disapproved of. She tells me, "Don't worry, Neesey, all the food is good." Big Jim acts like he ain't complainin and puts in, "Yeah, all the food is good." They see me not especially likin it that they say they don't like the food I cook. Seem to me wasn't much cookin goin on before, since if Margarete cooked a meat, she figured she had done somethin. She figured she had done enough. She seemed to feel that each one could get their own bread and mayonnaise. Least I cooked a vegetable and some rice or somethin to go under my gravy I made. Granma'am said that I'm a good little cook, and that I should do my best in Margarete's kitchen, that that would be the best help to Margarete, that that would let her get off her feet some.

I have said what Big Jim thinks about the meat. And I have said Luke edward don't half know juice from gravy. Well, Margarete has remarks too: she think I cook too many greens. She say it take some craziness to slave so hard over somethin that cook way down like that. You start out with a bushel, she say, and end up with a quart.

I believe in greens. Every Sunday I clean and cook five pounds, for Sunday dinner and the week. It takes good eyes and some dedication to cook greens. Maybe that's what Margarete tryina talk about, the dedication part. I felt like I was doin best for the family, cookin greens regular, especially for Margarete. If you gone have a baby, you need to eat greens.

I thought maybe the taste bothered her, so I put in okra one time. Some people cook they greens that way. Margarete said she wasn't complainin about eatin the greens, she just wasn't gone cook none herself. She said she hate okra. So then I went back to plain greens.

I did stop short a makin gravy every meal. Well, truth is, I stopped short a soakin the meat. I continued to make gravy every night I had meat to go with it, but I mostly kept the gravy in a pot on the side. While I was adjustin my habits to fit Margarete's house, I had to wonder why it is that I prefer to have gravy, even if it just sits in a pot on the stove. Me and Granma'am ate plenty leftovers, soft and soaked in gravy. Granma'am had got to the place where her teeth wasn't so strong or so many anymore, so maybe we specialized in soft food to go easy on what few teeth she had left. We ate all our food in gravy, or mashed in butter, or slow-cooked.

THE GREENS AND gravy are only two problems I have with the meals. Breakfast is the third problem, especially after the baby. And then again after Luke edward has gone and

David has moved. I don't want to make breakfast for just Big Jim because that is Margarete's job, I decided. Big Jim don't want gravy, but he do want breakfast. Well, whether I make breakfast just depends. Every Saturday I cain't bring myself to make breakfast, because if I make breakfast, other things happen. First off, I don't get no school-work done until half the day is passed. And second, the scrapple or the bacon smell gets both the boys up, and that means that right away I need more breakfast than what's already cooked. And sometimes Big Jim has the nerve to not want what I make: a few scrambled eggs, some toast from the loaf, some slab bacon. I think that's a real good breakfast! But Big Jim has learned that I can make biscuits and that I know how to keep the lumps out a hominy grits. So he wants biscuits and grits, and for a while, while I was still confused about refusin to be cookin all this breakfast, he took to bringin the breakfast meat he wanted home with him from work on Friday nights. He would bring enough meat for both Saturday and Sunday, and I would make sure to add enough— fried potatoes, stewed apples, biscuits or breakfast cake— so that it fed everybody. But like I said, his Saturday and Sunday special breakfasts seem work for Margarete to do.

Lucky for me I had stopped with so much on the breakfast on the weekends, anyway, once the baby was born, and before Luke edward left. So Big Jim cain't say that I don't make breakfast for him because I am mad about him runnin Luke edward away. I stopped makin breakfast because I need that time to take care a his and Margarete's baby.

If I did all the things they got accustomed to, and did all the things their baby needs too, then I would be mad all the time. And with me mad all the time, I would be teachin the baby all about bein mad, before she could even talk. That would not be good. So I give the baby a full breakfast, a bottle, and a washrag bath afterwards. And I let the grown folks in the house get breakfast for themselves.

Saturdays, after breakfast time, about ten, Big Jim goes out to meet his buddies. I don't know what they do, but he will stay out until the evenin, when Margarete comes home from the shop where she works.

ME AND MAMA have always had a time with the men and the meals and what they want to eat and do. It used to be my job to get the boys in the house. At dinnertime, dark, when it was time to change activities. This started when they were little and so was I. Many a day I would stand ten minutes, and holler their names out the window. Not a bobbin brown head would come runnin. I would get on Mama's nerves with all that, and then Mama would send me out to the schoolyard, where I would chase them down. I been walkin to the schoolyard by myself since I was four years old. I would call their names from our front door until I got right up to where all the boys would be, playin ball. *David, Luke ed-ward. Da-vid, Luke ed-ward. DA-VID, LUKE ED-WARD.*

"Don't you hear me callin you David? Luke edward, why ain't you answerin me?" I would not start to ask questions until I was a foot, at most, away from either one. I might stomp my feet, for effect.

They would keep playin, like I wasn't talkin. I would tug on their coats and pretend like I could drag them home sometimes. If they were out runnin in their shirts and sweaters, I would go on my own and pick out their coats from the coat-and-jacket-mound piled high at the end a the field.

"Come on, David, Mama wants y'all to come in now."

" 'K, Neesey, get my coat."

"I already *got* y'all's coats, David." I might be cold, hands full a their things. But I had to stay till they came with me. Otherwise, I would be in trouble.

I cannot understand how they don't move when you callin them. Sometimes I wanted to let them starve. Or leave them out there till night fell, hard and black and brutal onto them. Course, when they was ready, they'd come runnin in, stickin their hands in anything that smelled like food.

No washing, no consideration, no restraint.

"Why don't y'all answer when I'm callin you, David? I called y'all all the way here." They were not really listenin to me, what I said. I don't know what they were thinkin. Oh, one time David did manage to answer, *Aw girl, you ain't callin nobody, you just walkin round singin.* David always was the one to honestly name a thing. When I examined the sound of my memory, I had to admit their names did make a sing-song for me. That was how I paced myself, going from home to where they were.

Well, I still learned as a little girl to make a mess a their game. An important little sister skill: stand stubborn in the middle and refuse to let them play on. Then they would come.

Unless I did all a that, they might just keep on playin, ignorin me. Be outside till Kingdom come, raisin a rowdy ruckus. Coats tossed to the ground, sweaters flyin open, things to do forgotten, wind yankin at their screams.

SUNDAYS IS DAVID'S day to sleep late now that he works all the time. It's the one day in the week that six o'clock can come and go without his havin to splash water on his face. So he stays in that bed like a slab; gets up hungry, round eleven or twelve. Sundays is the one day that Luke beats David to the morning.

ONCE I START TO CLEANIN, IT'S HARD FOR ME TO STOP

I HAD MY coffee alone at the table. Drank two cups. In the quiet of the morning after my return, I realize I let Harold Grayson go without saying goodbye. Without findin out when he will see Granma'am again. I decide to begin a letter that I can just sign my name to whenever he stops by on his way. I hope he remembers to stop by.

I take up my cot and collect all the plates and glasses layin round the front room. I wash them up. The kitchen is clean, and I stand starin out the window to the back alley when the sandman loosed his hold on the folks who still slept. David and Big Jim both are gone, I find out. Only Margarete and Luke edward are in the house with me.

They both come in the kitchen wantin coffee, Luke first. We both hear Margarete stirrin round.

Luke edward comes in, "Hey, Dee-Neesey!" grinnin, glad to see me. "How you doin? Did you forget in your sleep where you were?"

"Naw," I answer him. I set a cup a coffee down in front of him. I have figured how to use Margarete's electric percolator and I am proud. "I heard you in here eatin last night. What was you eatin?" I said. "What time did you come back in?"

"Whatever I was eating, it's gone now."

He says everything so flip.

"This is good coffee, girl. I see you didn't have no trouble finding things."

"Y'all disappeared. Where did you and David go?" I stick to my subject. I want to know what everybody does, so I can decide what I will do, now that I'm here.

"We went to look at Harold Grayson's fancy car. Boy, what that mortician money won't buy."

"Dog, Luke edward," I say. I feel like I should discourage him from bad-mouthin how money gets earned.

"Ain't sayin nothin ain't true," he answers.

"Where David?" I ask, as Margarete comes to the kitchen where we are. Margarete and Big Jim's bedroom is the closest to the kitchen and the biggest, off the back of the house. Look like it could of been the dining room or a second parlor room for the use of the whole family at one time.

Margarete and Luke edward both say David is at work.

"Yeah?" I say. "What time he go?"

"He leaves about seven-thirty, with Jim," Margarete answers. She helps herself to the coffee, while I sit at the table with Luke edward, wonderin what is his schedule.

"Luke edward," I return to our conversation, "was you and David just comin in when I heard you in here shakin salt in the tinfoil?"

"Lord, Coyote Ears is back," Luke edward says.

Margarete laughs. "You in trouble now, Luke baby. Got somebody else watchin you come and go. Now tell your baby sister you stay out half the night, every night." She sips after this.

It's easy for me to look at Margarete while she talks to

Luke edward. She always looked at him intently, her eyes full of challenge and amusement. She's been looking at him that way since we were kids, when Miss Lena used to chide Margarete and say he was gone be rotten and wrong. I can't figure anymore about her eyes and how she looks at him these days, because she looks at him and not at me, so there is no face for me to read. She looks different, older, though. I notice that her veins in her hands have risen above her flesh; this from age, and work, I suppose.

"What time David come home?" I ask, turnin my back to them to refill my cup. I don't really want any more, I'm just nervous. I pour in the muddy coffee, I empty the can of milk.

"David and Jim both come back around seven," Margarete answers me as her chair scrapes back from the table. In my mind, I practice, "Luke edward, you workin?" When I turn around to say it out loud, I see that it's Luke edward who left.

I don't have a choice but to sit down at the table with Margarete. I cain't think of anything else to do in the short space between the stove and the table, where Margarete sits. It seems to me the humor has mostly evaporated from her eyes. I ask Margarete if she slept all right, and she answers me Yes. I ask her if there is any more canned milk in the house for coffee. She tells me we have to buy some. She goes on as if I have asked her all the questions about the house routine that I will ask in time. David has to be cross town to work at eight, so he's up and gone shortly after seven. And Big Jim works in the plant from eight too, so he's out right with or right before David. Luke ain't workin, she tells me, and that's all she says about him. She ask me if I'm lookin forward to school in Detroit.

Before I can answer, Margarete changes the subject again, like she just thought of it, and thanks me for cleanin up the dishes. "Lord, chile," she said, "don't these men leave everything everywhere?"

I smile because she noticed and she thanked me. Everybody's glad I'm here, I decide.

I HAVE TOLD Margarete I don't want to go to school. She ask me what I mean I don't want to go to school. "Yet," I say. She don't ask me much more, since I guess it's only three days after I get there. She tells me she can't let me sit around and do nothing.

But I am not doing nothing—I don't say this part to her—I am cleaning.

She notices my progress. "Oh, Neesey, you wouldn't believe what a time I have keepin this house clean."

I don't answer, because anybody got eyes would believe.

Margarete goes on. "I can get help with the heavy work. I can get David or Jim or Luke edward to get up on a ladder for me. But by the time I pick up all these cups and glasses and socks and things and wash them up, and dust and wipe all the furniture, and sweep the rugs and floors, too, I'm tired, and I still have to go to work. Lord have mercy, I'm so glad you here to help me."

I feel one a Margarete's hugs on the way. It's been a long time, but I still know how she is. Sure enough, she comes over in the midst of her chatter, and so while I'm trying to listen, and I am slow to look, the bauble of her voice comes close. I squeeze the broom handle, it is familiar and hard. She puts two of her hairdresser fingers under my chin. She has shaped her nails. She pulls my head up so she can look directly at me. She smiles. She says again: "You are such a help."

Her mouth is lined with worry. Her eyes seem open but maybe they are not kind. I will have to watch. I guess they do look wary, and may be bruised a little, too. Her skin is fadin some, caramel, and her hair is envy thick. She is thirty-six. I see Granma'am in her features. I hadn't noticed that before. The first time I saw Granma'am in Margarete.

I HAVEN'T SEEN Margarete in more than two years. The last time I saw Margarete was down home, and looking at her visit us down the country was much different than looking at her now, what with me being back to stay. She pulls me and the broom both toward her, and pats me on my back. She smells like bottles and jars: like hair grease, and bath salts, and other things I don't recognize yet.

Granma'am told me things would be strange for a while, but that they would calm down and I will feel at home again. "You and Mahr-greet will be a good team," Granma'am said. "You just be a worker bee, like I taught you."

I PRETEND TO be a doctor to the flat. I try to keep everything clean and organized. I try to keep the meals to a schedule. Mostly we eat one at a time, whenever we come in the house. So I give myself the job of makin sure there's food to eat, when the folks in the house are ready to eat it.

Most of what I did for the first two weeks was clean and sleep.

Didn't have much else in mind to do.

No matter where you are, or in whose house, if you stay there long enough, you can find dust in the corners, a need for hands to straighten the closets. And because Margarete had two boys and a husband, there was no need to look for places to clean and sweep. Just start anywhere.

I HAVE WIPED all the way round the kitchen. I started when Big Jim finished at the table, while he counted his money and left a message for Margarete. It happens to be Saturday and Big Jim is out early, the first of the men to leave the house. When he passes through the front room, he ask me do I need anything else to finish what I'm doin.

I lean back on my heels and shake the can of powder I have almost used up. "I need some more Bab-O," I tell him.

He says, "It's three dollars in there on the table." He says I should get some ground meat for dinner if I want, because he will take Margarete out this evenin.

"Is David gone be in?" I ask him.

"Yeah, David be back, far as I know."

"Is Luke edward gone be in?"

"I don't know," he says.

"OK," I answer; David likes meat loaf.

EVERY MORNING I wake up and the flat still snores. I try to decipher the who's. Recognition comes slow. I still expect to open my eyes to down home. I realize through a thin veil of sleepy that I am not down home. These are new walls.

I put my hand up to the cross Granma'am gave me and hold onto it while I try to point my mind forward. After a few minutes, tears well up in my eyes, and run down into my ears. I get up, and tiptoe round the flat.

Big Jim and David got used to findin me awake, even though they tried to tiptoe round too. They would look at me with two faces: guilt and relief. "Did we wake you up, Neesey?" one of them would say.

Now, how you be a big grown man, and know that there's two of you up, rushin round, makin coffee, runnin water, pullin sandwiches wrapped in wax paper out the Frigidaire, snappin lunch pails shut on those big hinges they have, fillin thermoses, wearin work boots, countin change and rushin back to where you slept to get your watch—now, how you gone keep from wakin up the stranger in the house, she who sleeps on a cot in the front room?

"Naw," I answer, "I always wake up early."

"You makin sandwiches?" the other might say.

"All right," I might answer. Or on occasion, "I put y'all's lunch in tinfoil last night. Look in the box on the second rack."

And then, after they were dressed and gone, there would be a little piece of house for me to move around in. Then I would go on in the kitchen, have myself a cup a coffee, wipe the counters to a shine, look out the alley window, decide what I would straighten up for the day. Granma'am's rhythm was in me.

Once, when Margarete and Big Jim are both out, I go in to sweep out their closet and get under their bed. Before, I had been too nervous to clean in there, but when I walk by their door sometimes, dust dances in their doorway, lit by the sun through their bedroom windows. They have the best room in the house; it gets the afternoon. I am being so thorough everywhere, but I decide not to spend too much time in there; I will not wander or try to get to know their things. I clean quickly, in stages, so that if they come in, I can move out.

Their closet is divided: Margarete gets the left, Big Jim the right. Big Jim has belts and pants and a few shirts. Most everything is black or blue, except the greenish clothes he wears to work. His work clothes are folded, or rolled, into a stack near the front on the floor on his side. Four greenish trousers and three shirts. His dirty work uniforms must be somewhere else. When I was learnin how to use the wash machine, he told me he has two weeks' worth of work clothes.

In Margarete's closet I find a pair of green shoes, with eye-bashin heels and roach-killin toes. The pointed green shoes kick me back to Virginia, to the staccato of Margarete's fast walk down Granma'am's hall, and through Granma'am's front door. Well, all of it drums on my heart and my head. My bucket is stone cold when I put my hand back in it. I lean my head over the bucket, and breathe in ammonia to wake myself up. Granma'am told me never to breathe in ammonia, that the fumes would kill me. I decide not to mop the closet floor.

I reorganize all the clothes, hang them up neat, and I am still home alone. I go back to the kitchen and grab a dustrag from under the sink; I also put clear hot water in the bucket. I go back to their room; I dust off and wipe down all the furniture tops, and the brackets that hold their mattresses. Swipe the night tables, and rub down the lamps, there are three in the room. I wish I could get to that light fixture in the ceiling, but I haven't seen no ladder.

There is a throw rug between the bed and Margarete's vanity dresser. It is dark, maroon and blue. My sweepin might be loosenin up the pile from the rug. I wish for a line so I could beat it, but there is no outdoors line for the upstairs flat. I pull Margarete's and Big Jim's shoes out the closet, sweep the closet out and put the shoes back —Big Jim's on one side near the front, and Margarete's along the walls everywhere else. I tried to do most of my cleanin and handlin of things while Luke edward and Margarete especially are out. I don't want to get caught with my hands deep in other people's things.

Somehow I expect the closets to bring me up to date. To substitute for the things nobody said, and that I wouldn't know unless they told me. Nobody has said much. I don't know what I expected, to come back and find that they would sit me down: *Neesey, this is all that's happened since you lived with us last.* That would have been nice; I could have asked questions. But of course no one does, and I don't really expect it. Fact, more than makin clear what has happened with the family, the closets just tell me that I'm hungry for a place to put my things. That is so like me, to work feverishly in other people's interest, and discover from the work a naked ache of my own.

No one had offered me a closet yet. And there wasn't much room in any of their closets, anyway, even after I had cleaned and straightened and replaced.

I wet the broom tips, so it's easier to sweep the dust from the rug. I drag the rug to the front room to do this wet sweep, and I'm careful not to spread the dirt. The wet broom and sweepin remind me of Lonts. Lonts was Lantene's brother, and Lantene Ownes is my best friend from down home. Her brother Lonts died not long after I came down home. Lantene and I was just gettin to be real good pals. Poor Lantene, her heart near broke. One thing to have a brother, out somewhere near the edge. Another thing to have a brother killed dead by it.

SOMETHING POSSESSES ME to change my mind, to go ahead and mop. I have finished everything, still nobody is home. There is still more time. Maybe I think I won't get a chance to get back in there. I notice that there's not enough fresh smell behind my hard work. That's what it was. So I retie my hair, and go for the mop and bucket again. I roll the rug up to the side this time, and in a big hurry, one that makes me laugh, I mop their bedroom floor, take the carefully arranged shoes back out from the closet, mop the closet underneath all the pants and skirts and sweaters that hang at every length. The sense that I should not be in their room ticks in me like a clock motor, so I move around in there like a wound-up toy.

I am near finished, and it is near five. The window I opened has made the room cool, but it has helped so much to air it out and dry the floor. I remove all my tools to the kitchen, and go back to observe my work. I feel accomplished, and the room smells like bleach and out-side air.

Margarete is ecstatic. I am not surprised. She has always been fond of bleach—bleach for floors, bleach for clothes, bleach for hair (her own hair, not mine). She comes in, as usual, tired from standin at the straightenin chair. Usually, she plops down in the big chair in the front room, but this day she goes into her room, shrieks, and comes back to the kitchen to pull my plaits and give me sugar. I am makin potatoes to go under the meat loaf gravy, and I am surprised when she spends the whole evenin stretched across her bed, lazin through a maga-zine or somethin. When Big Jim comes home, she does not come out, and then the boys come home one at a time, and that's how everybody eats, on entrance. Big Jim takes food in to Margarete and tells me I'm gone make somebody a good wife.

When I finished the dishes, I did not sweep the floor. I went, instead, to sleep on my cot. Not sweepin the floor was hard for me on account of once I start to clean, it's hard for me to stop. But I had done enough for one day.

LUKE EDWARD DOESN'T see me when he comes in because I am under the table. But I hear him: he goes in to the icebox and pulls out the leftover fish I fried. He shakes salt into the pie pan I put the fish away in; I hear the salt tinkle. He stands beside the icebox lookin like a five-year-old—big ears from behind, cheeks movin up and down. He hears my scrub brush rubbin. He turns around and looks and then bends over, and sees me under the table. "Neesey, what are you doing?" he says.

I back out from under the table, mostly because I am not gone be able to hear Luke edward from underneath there. Also I like to stop and talk to Luke edward, so I come out and leave the pail underneath, that way it won't get knocked over.

Luke edward has a piece a cold fish in one hand, and I wonder why is he lookin so surprised.

"What are you doing, Neesey?" If I was standin there with roll dough hangin out my ears and nose, Luke edward would not be lookin at me more strange.

"Whassa matter wit you, Luke edward?" I am alarmed. If I let them, Margarete and Luke edward would have me thinkin I'm nuts. I brush past him to the stove where I check if any coffee is left. None but the bitters. I brush past Luke edward again, because he has not moved. I take the can a coffee out the box, and commence to makin another half-pot. "You want some coffee, Luke edward?"

"What's the matter with you, Neesey?" he says in answer, as if I haven't asked him about the coffee in between. "What are you doing?" He insists that I answer him. He can only sound but so stern, because he has fish in his mouth and bones in his hands. Him bein there with the fish I cooked makes me feel one up somehow.

"I'm helpin Margarete with the house," I say. "I'm just washin down the wallboards before I scrub the floors."

"Mama ask you to do all that?"

I turn to him. "Naw, Margarete did not ask me. But it needs doin, and I'm doin it. Do you want some coffee, Luke edward?"

"Got any ice tea?" he says. He has returned his concentration to the fish. "What's that you got on?" he goes on to ask me, his mouth full again.

I look down at the old dress and apron I got on. "It's a old housedress I found."

"Where?" he says, and then before I can answer, "Never mind. What about those shoes?"

"They some old shoes a Margarete's," I say. "I only got one pair and I ain't cleanin in them."

"Oh," he says. "And what's that you got on your head?"

"Come on, Luke edward. It's a rag I'm usin to tie up my hair. Don't act like you don't tie your own hair up at night."

"It ain't night, Neesey. Besides, where'd you get that headrag?"

"It's a piece a old shirt that I found round here. I tore off the sleeve parts, and I'm usin the square part for a head rag." I heard a proud sound about my industry in my voice.

"Well, you look a sight. You got on more rag than you got hair, don't you? I think you should quit scrubbing and put on some clothes. When are you going to school, anyway?" He is puttin the water glass to his lips when he ask me that. I sat it in front a him cause ain't no ice tea. He look like Margarete the way she scoot her eyes and look out over the cup rim. At you, at me, decidin. Well, he don't have to be so snappy.

I don't say too much else.

Luke edward leaves the fish bones in the empty pie plate. You can still see the shape of the fish, but all the meat is gone.

I CLEANED LUKE edward and David's room too. I learned a few things in there. Luke edward buys new cosmetics when his old ones are only half used. On his side of the closet is a nice wood crate that still smells like timber. The crate is now full of half-empty colognes, beat-down hair brushes, and near-empty yellow tins of Murray's Superior. All these I found misplaced in his room. I wiped each container clean of dust, and stacked them neatly in the crate.

I also find a lamp he made—I remember when—from popsickle sticks. I loved the lamp when he made it, and now I idolize him lookin at it again, here on my knees at his closet door. The lamp was his one pursuit for a time. Aunt Lena, who had a stick lamp of her own, hand-counted the glued-together sticks on her lamp and told him how many he would need. Margarete bought him his ice cream, and he constantly cluttered the sink soakin off the orange stains. Even if me or David ate the ice cream, he handled all his sticks himself. Some he had to rub with bleach, and Margarete helped him with that.

The popsickle-stick lamp was not an easy design. The shade of it has six sides, all arranged. He taunted me then, because he learned the word hexagon. He wouldn't tell me what it meant. The stem of the lamp is narrower and the bottom widens out again. The making of the lamp was a complicated peace: art, geometry, electricity, engineering, curiosity, concentration, vocabulary, boyhood. It took Luke edward a long time to make that lamp, I remember. Now the cord is frayed, and a teeny-weeny section of wires shows through.

Way back in his closet, David has a strongbox. I discover it behind Luke edward's broken lamp. I find it at eleven o'clock, after I have made the beds and put dinner in to roast. I try to guess what's in it until I finish David and Luke edward's whole room. By three-thirty, when I'm done, and the whole house smells like pot roast, I have decided that David has not locked the strongbox; I haven't found any keys. He could have the keys on him, but that's not like David to think his strongbox would need to be locked. I guess: inside must be a picture of Serena—she's his girlfriend—and some money. Anybody know David know he keeps a stash, cash money for emergencies we hope don't happen. He is responsible like that.

Serena is a little bit taller than David and is heavyset for a woman. She is darker than David too: she crosses the shades of difference between thick maple and molasses, between plain hard work and hard work plus religion. Serena is religious and a blessing for David. She is all busyness. She has a job minding children and goes to church Sundays plus two times in the week.

Most of the Sundays, David goes out to Serena's where she stays with her mother and the rest of her family. Sometimes, though, Serena comes by after service to see about David. She stands at the door, dressed in her hat and gloves. I open it. She got one of them faces so honest it's wide, and hands so used to caring that her fingers are spread; she is ever interested in the new piece of furniture, ever ready for holding some little one's hand, ever willing to help an elder by the elbow.

HIS STRONGBOX IS neatly packed with five-dollar bills. Nobody's picture is in there, except Lincoln's. The box is full. Now I have my first secret since I came back to Detroit. David still hoards money, still hides it.

While I finish my work and the roast and rice bake cool, I think about a pie. There in my metal cooking bowl is an inch deep of flour, spread out in the bottom, half a cup. Into that loose white powder add one dollop of binding grease, take a fork and press and press. Add ice water, mix only enough to moisten. Form into a glutiny ball. Texture is correct when your fingerprints are visible. Leave sealed in wax paper until ready to fill. Roll out to one-fourth-inch thick and press again into pie pan. Bake until brown unless filling is hot in which case just pour in filling—the heat of the mixture will harden the shell. Bake pie in high oven. Let set. Enjoy.

IT IS THURSDAY, after I have been there a week. I have gotten all the surfaces clean, and so now I search for deeper occupations. By the time Margarete gets up, I have finished the front room wallboards. I have dumped the water into the commode, and I have come into the kitchen to see about ingredients for the stuffed peppers while I decide what I'll do next. Margarete comes in to the room with me, and my pail is in the middle of the floor. I watch Margarete walk around it.

"Mornin, Neesey, how you?" Margarete's voice is husky from her sleep. She has slept without tyin her head.

"Fine, how you?" I answer her back.

"What are you up doin so early this mornin?"

"Oh, I'm just washin up the wallboards."

She holds a cup to her mouth and is lookin over at me; I see her eyes smile, and her lips turn up a little. I decide she is pleased.

"Big Jim say y'all goin somewhere this evenin, so I'ma make David and Luke edward stuffed peppers for dinner."

"You ain't gone eat none?" she ask me.

"Yeah, I'ma eat some," I answer back, slowly.

After a few minutes, she says, "Well, that'll be fine." Then she goes on, "Neesey, you don't have to wash the wallboards, you know."

"Wait till you see in the front," I say, excited, "all the brown dust is gone."

"Well, I do heavy cleanin round here in spring and again before Christmas. You can help me do it at Christmastime." I guess I look disappointed cause she says, "You already doin it now so go ahead, but you have to go to school next week. Don't think you gone stay round this house and wash wallboards all winter."

She is gone back to her room with her coffee, to get dressed. I go back out front to look at the wallboards dry. They are cleaner. They look much better. I need to push the furniture back against the wall.

MARGARETE SAID THINGS would change for me once I got up nerve to go to school, but I had had enough change already. I did not want any more. What did I want? I had to think. Somethin I knew or recognized, I guess. Maybe that's why the stuffed peppers, the pies. Or maybe I wanted somethin to know or recognize me. Luke edward and Margarete looked at me funny, even David and Big Jim sometimes too. And these were my people.

Shucks, I was gone hafta go on out next week. I sighed and wiped the tiles.

MARGARETE HAD NICE floors. Neat wood slats, placed carefully in a design where the start and finish of the boards were alternated, and every one was angled at a slant. Somebody had thought about those floors, laid down and hammered each slat that way. I loved them; I coaxed dust from every corner. I collected mounds of sweep dust and used a big piece of cardboard for a dustpan. I wanted all the floors to look the same: caressed and neat and pretty, so carefully hammered in.

In the bathroom and kitchen, and on the back sleeping porch, linoleum was on the floors. I swept and mopped those too. First, with the canned Bab-O detergent Margarete kept underneath the kitchen sink. Then I went down to the store one day—Peckway's it was called—because Big Jim had taken to leavin a dollar or two on the kitchen table for me to get whatever I planned to cook, he said. "Since you making the meals and all," he said.

I bought two half-gallon bottles of ammonia. I ran buckets a water to put it in and always the water was too hot for my hands. I don't know how many times I scalded myself. I don't know how many times I winced, yelped, jerked my hand back from the steam. I had had to boil water down home, so this boilin hot water comin out of a spigot took me some time to get used to again.

I look around the bathroom while I wait for some a the heat to escape my second bucket. Steam rises from the pail. There is tile everywhere, back behind the big bathtub and halfway up all the walls. I plan to clean it all. I sit on the commode and wait, and I have pulled Margarete's old housedress up under me so that it doesn't droop down into the toilet water. Big Jim and David have both gone to work.

FINALLY, ONLY THE routine dust came to settle on the flat. I had cleaned up everything that hinted of before I came. The clean was much appreciated: the windows caught this northern sun. No more dullness, no more dust. Big Jim could locate his socks, mated and folded in his top two bureau drawers. Luke edward did not buy new containers of the same pomade because he couldn't find what had rolled far back under his bed, and no, he didn't mind if I used his popsickle-stick lamp. I put it up on the right side of the couch where Big Jim had been sittin when I first come and where I sat in the clean house now.

WHERE I STARTED

THE FIRST DAY I went, Luke edward walked me to school. It was a Monday, round eleven o'clock. I asked him didn't we need to be round there earlier, and he said since it's my first day, I might as well be late, cause after this I won't have no excuse.

Made a little sense, I guess. Luke edward says a lot a different things that somewhere buried in them have truth. He made me wrinkle my forehead, tryina take apart what he just said and find the place in it for what I believe; or just the same, find the place in it where he turned wrong, so I could be clear where I didn't want to go. So, my first day at school started about midday, on account a Luke edward's way with the clock. I was made to stand in the front a the classroom while the teacher wrote my name on the last line in her class book, and then had me turn and say my name out loud to the class. She had me take a chair in the back, next to Josephus Johnson, the boy who Margarete had invited over to meet me. He leaned to me and whispered much too loud that she put all the country people in the back there where we were.

I got myself situated at the desk; ooh boy, it was really

nice. The lid lifted onto plenty space inside, and there was a dip for a pencil at the top. I put the pencil I had brung right in it. The dip kept it from rollin off. I found by lookin at the people round me, that under the seat where I sat was a openin on one side, so books could be slid in. I didn't have no books, but I thought about puttin Margarete's sweater there, when I wore it. I slid my foot back slylike to make sure my desk was the same as the rest.

The windows in the room were big, big enough for me to stand in. The glass in them was clear, and arched at the top, and divided by crosses of wood painted gray. Across the front of the room was the big teacher's desk. Also the long blackboard with the math numbers on it.

The teacher turned back to writin. Cardboard vegetables and turkeys were pinned on brown tackboard, over top a the chalkboard. I kept rovin my eyes round, tryina take it all in. See what I'm in for. When my eyes go over to the right, somethin catchin light behind the windows in the classroom door caught my eye. Lord, there was Luke edward standin there. When he saw me see him, he pressed his face to mutilation on the pane. I chuckled, and my tryina keep it quiet made gurgles in my throat. I waved my hand to shoo him away, and soon as I did that, Josephus from Arkansas was in on the whole thing.

The teacher finished puttin all the numbers cross the board and turned and said, "Deneese, we are multiplying columns of numbers. Just try to follow along with us and if you have questions, I'll work with you afterwards." Her callin my name startled me; I swallowed and tried not to choke. When she finished addressin me and had started to work with some kids on problems at the board, I looked back at the door and Luke edward was gone. He don't see he almost got me in trouble, and I make up my mind to get him good when I get home. Luke edward is not home when I get home, so I make butter beans instead.

MARGARETE AND BIG Jim's friends come over on Saturday nights. This marks their break in the weeks, and gives them chance to talk about gettin paid on Friday. A lady named Miss Tip comes over all the time. She Margarete's friend, but she hang around Luke edward too when she over to the house. Round nine o'clock one Saturday before I'm used to them all, the door bell rings. Margarete and Big Jim are dancin in the hall. Margarete says over Big Jim's shoulder, "Luke, get the door." Luke doesn't budge from loadin records on the hi-fi, so I get up to answer it. Miss Tip is right behind me. She got up same as I did. "Marg'rete, Luke's playin the records," she said. "I'll get it."

We both open the door cause she don't beat me to it. There is a man named Jump with a boy named Josephus standin there. I find this out because Miss Tip squeals: "Jump!" And Josephus—he the boy—speaks right up. "You Deneese?" he ask me from the hall. I shake my head in answer, yes. "I'm Josephus," he tells me, still standin in the hall. Miss Tip pulls both the men through the doorway, from the hall shadow into the light of our clean flat. I can see by his hair he is moved here from farm dirt, like me.

When they come inside, they separate. Mr. Jump goes toward the grown people. Josephus stays with me. He stands so close to my face, I wonder if he think I cain't see. He tells me Jump is his uncle.

Josephus is just up from Arkansas, like I am just up from Virginia. Me and Josephus get to be real close eventually. He explains things to me—some I didn't expect him to know—us both bein from the country and all. But he's almost sixteen and he say he gone go to school for a while and then he gone get a job. Josephus talks a lot. I just listen. Cain't say much anyway on account a the grown folks is talkin one on top of another, and Luke edward is still down on the floor choosin records.

"What grade you gone be in?" That's what I think of to ask him, finally.

"Grade seven," is what he answered.

Ooh, he's behind, I think to myself.

"TELL THE CLASS your name and where you've moved from, Deneese."

I pull off my coat—it's too short. I rather be standin there in my blue Sunday dress. Margarete had let me wear it even though she didn't like it. Margarete does not like my clothes. She say all my skirts and dresses are too short and not new. She say I'm in Detroit now and I cain't be wearin all remade clothes. She ask me who remade my things, and I tell her Granma'am and Miz Evelyn Ownes. She is shocked that I mention Miz Evelyn Ownes on account a the Owneses ain't got a pot to piss in, she say, so how do they think they got clothes enough to remake for me. She ask me where is the rest of the things I wore down Granma'am's, and I tell her I left them because they was even smaller than what I brought.

She lays all my things out on her bed. She holds her right hand to her back where I guess the baby comin is painin her. She say when she get a few dollars she gone buy me some new skirts and sweaters. She holds up my blouses and says they will be all right except that the collars is round like I'm a baby. "In the meantime," she says, and then she goes into her chifforobe, I can wear this and this. She pulls out two skirts and three sweaters and one blouse. Both the skirts is brown—one is dark brown and the other is dark tan. Both the skirts is straight down and, since I am by then tall as Margarete, when she holds them up to me I can see that they will come to the top a my bobby socks. One a the sweaters is white and one is black and one is brown. They all button down. The blouse is cream colored.

I don't like the clothes Margarete give me. They look like I am doin things I ain't got no business doin. Once I put the skirts on, I can see they are too close, and the sweaters sit way up over my behind.

Now, I do like the pants she sent down home for me to travel in, and I secretly wish she would pull some more pants out the chifforobe, but then why would she when I cain't wear those to school.

I asked Margarete could I wear my blue Sunday dress on my first day. She said no.

"Why don't you wear a skirt and sweater? All the girls will have on skirts and sweaters."

"I would like to wear my blue dress first, Margarete." I drop my voice way low on the Margarete part.

She took a deep smoke from her cigarette. "When did you start callin me Margarete, Deneese?"

I had my speech prepared. "I don't mean no disrespect, Margarete," I rushed. Now, this first part was a lie. "I haven't been round you in so long, sometimes I called Granma'am Mama. And, well, when I talked about you down home, I just called you Margarete," I said. Another lie. I only called Granma'am Granma'am. And I only called Margarete Margarete when I was listenin to other people talk about her. But what could she know about how true it was or wasn't. There was no way she could know what I knew, and I knew I did not want to call

Margarete Mama anymore, not unless I had to, not unless she made me.

She looked at me a long time. "Are you glad to be back, Neesey?" she asked me.

I wait a minute to answer. "Luke edward done grown up handsome like Daddy," I said.

"Don't say that to him." She laughs a little, blowin out her cigarette smoke. "He already thinks he's Creation." She looked steady at me.

"You can wear that blue dress if you want to, but you gone look like a little baby. It's all right, you ain't got enough clothes to avoid them skirts for too long. But don't wear that white dress anymore, it's not in season. I'll get you a new white dress Easter," she said. She was walkin out the room when she said, in summary, "I don't know about this Margarete business."

She never said anything else about the Margarete business. And so that is how I came to call my mother Margarete, and that is how I knew that we agreed on a few things: the power of changing subjects, the serious significance of the wearing of clothes, the control we have over the naming of names, and how in truth the change of name can change the person, even if the change is done in secret, or is done by somebody else. And how in the light of day nothing can be done to change the person back, there is no return to the prior name.

"MY NAME DENEESE Palms an I come up from Fuhginia," I said. Snickers from the rows of heads.

"Class," a clip from Missus James, while I stand still up front. "And why have you moved to Detroit, Deneese?" I scratch my leg with my other shoe, and reply, "My mama sent for me." And so from another place in the desk lines: "Cakka-lakky." What does that mean?

"Class!" Missus James tells them to shut up laughin at me. "Do you need to sit in the front of the class, Deneese, or does it matter? Do you wear eyeglasses?"

"Naw," I mumble, head down. "Don't matter," I go on, hardly knowin if she hears.

"Well, all right, we are glad to have you. Aren't we, class?" Nobody answers. "There's a seat in the back next to Josephus Johnson. Why don't you sit there, Deneese?"

I walk down the nearest row and pass by Brenda Greenfield, who Margarete had invited over to meet me at the party. She has eyeglasses. She whispers, "I'm your friend," as I pass her, a voice sweet as bells to my ears.

I get to the back desk and try to disappear, but country sand had trickled from my socks and marked the path I took to the back-desk chair. Missus James starts to talkin again. Josephus leans toward me and tries to whisper. I think everybody heard what he said.

THE SCHOOL HAD books for everybody, but not for each one in every subject. Each desk had either four or three books: the subjects alternated by desks. Between your desk and the one beside yours, there was a complete set. After we figured this out, Josephus and I discovered we shared because we sat next to each other.

Missus James gives me four books to go in my desk. She says I can carry them round with me long as I have them in school every day. I take all four a my books home every night. Geography, English, a history book, and a speller. Geography was my all-time favorite. I commenced to askin Missus James bout maps and lakes and directions, and Josephus, who had got in the habit a walkin me home, would wait by the side a the classroom door while I got some answers.

I WOULD GO to the teacher wantin to know somethin almost every day after the school bell rang. "I wanna ax a question," I'd begin, "bout Lake St. Clair." I bothered Missus James when I said the word ask.

"Ask," Missus James would lean to me and say, "you want to ass-suh-kuh."

Sound like a chair scrapin the floor. "Ass-suh-kuh," I tried, and lo and behold it came out right. Ass-suh-kuh, I had said. But like Granma'am usedta always say: Ignorance is a green switch; it'll hurt you, and won't break. Even though I practiced—ass-suh-kuh, ass-suh-kuh—when I tried to say it normal speed it came out aks, which is close to ax, which is where I started.

I WAS MOSTLY lukewarm about school in the beginning. I thought sure they would shut it down for the winter. The cold was deepening and not letting up. It was only the end of October, the beginning of November. Down home, in Virginia where I had lived, this season would still be cooling off the middays and encouraging the squash. In Detroit, on two lakes and a river, the water hung in the air and the wind was wet. I had outgrown my coat, so that it hardly buttoned over the sweaters I wore to try to keep the wet air off my chest. The days mocked me, blowing my coat wide open.

Margarete was intending to buy me a few things, she had said. When she did I planned to mention that I really need a coat. In the meantime, I had my eye on a coat Luke edward had hanging in his closet that he only wore sometimes. I had to either get warmer, or stay in. Down home, in January and February, I had borrowed Granma'am's day coat and kept it nice.

But the Lord had put Missus James's eye on me. One

Monday she brought in a black coat, outgrown by a girl at her church.

"Deneese, try this on," Missus James said to me, and she held the coat with the inside to me for me to slip my arms in.

I fit into the coat, and had plenty room. I had taken off my sweater for the inside, but once I was in it I could see that I could a left my sweater on.

"Are you warm in there?" Missus James asked me. She turned me round by my shoulders, and shook the coat different places to see how loose it was, I guess.

"Yes, ma'am," I answer.

"Well, now you have a coat to wear," she said. She folded her hands in satisfaction.

"I have a coat to wear?"

"Yes, Deneese, the girl who had that coat doesn't need it anymore, it's yours."

"Lawd, have mercy," I said. I sounded like an old woman, even to myself; but I couldn't help but say it. The coat come down to the middle a my knee socks and buttoned so far down it may as well of zipped. Sometimes God just brings you (clap) exactly what you need.

"Should I bring it back at the end a winter?"

"No, you keep it until it's too small for you," she said. "Just tell your mother I brought it from the church. Wear it every day—wear it home today—and keep it buttoned up. You'll probably get some wear out of it for a year or two," she said.

It had a fur collar that sat high off my shoulders and rubbed at my ears. I loved that part the best. When I got home, Margarete said we needn't accept charity and from the school teacher no less. But Big Jim said to Margarete that it didn't make all that much sense to be refusin the coat. Maybe the woman was tryina help me feel welcome, and the coat was in very good condition, he inspected. I was glad to let Big Jim talk, even though I don't know why he had to call Missus James *woman* like that. I told Margarete that I liked the fur collar, and she said it ain't real fur.

Well, I didn't have to give the coat back, and Josephus said I looked citified and well-off. More important than what Margarete or Big Jim or Josephus had to say was that the outside battled that coat the rest a winter, instead a wagin war on me.

After Missus James gave me geography, and brought me a winter coat, and tried to teach me not to say ax, she stopped being my teacher. She and her husband and her little boy moved back to Georgia. Her husband went to teach at a college.

I WAKE UP very early, especially in Detroit. I am like a old person, I cain't sleep late.

One night early in my stay at Margarete's house, I dreamed Granma'am was hung by a rope that was tied around her waist. Of course, it really wasn't Granma'am at all. She would never hang from anything; her feet were always planted in the ground. But her body and her housedress and her black house shoes made it her image all right. While I was watchin, shears cut the rope. Scared me to death since I had just left Granma'am and I was worried about her care.

Early that morning before it was light, I woke up overwhelmed. I turned my body over on my cot. I opened my eyes, pulled the pillow over my head, and closed my eyes again. I wanted to see colors on the back of my eyelids. I did not want to see Granma'am hangin from no rope.

I got the colors after I changed positions: tangerine and fuchsia and buttercup like a flower field. I love to get colors in my eyes. I fell back to sleep feelin better. And when I was sleep again, the dream dropped back. While I watched Granma'am dangle, the jute she suspended from got thinner and thinner; the cords that made it up dissolved. Finally, there was only the one strand. Since the strand wasn't sturdy enough to hold Granma'am, I started to wonder what in the world should I do. I started to run. There was hay on the ground at my feet. I waded as quick as I could through the hay, and I felt the hard ground beneath. I could not let Granma'am fall on this hard ground. That was what I was thinkin. As I ran back and forth, tryina stay underneath her, the biggest gardenin shears came across the white night.

Granma'am hung by only a strand of thin rope. It had gotten so thin. The huge shears came and cut it, and Granma'am started to fall. I did my best to run under her, so when she hit bottom, she'd fall on me. I figured my bones was younger after all; if the whole situation broke a bone or two I would have a better chance to heal.

I hurt my back in that dream, although in the dream it didn't hurt. Granma'am did come down on me, and she crushed me between herself and the ground. She knocked me down. Like I said, in the dream it didn't hurt. Granma'am was in such a odd position: she was strainin to hold her head up, strainin to talk out loud while all this is goin on. She fell into me back and shoulder blades first, then her backsides came down, then her legs slammed me fully flat.

My back hit the ground so hard I called out. I sat bolt awake on my cot.

I hobbled around all day. Margarete finally asked me what's the matter. I told her I was worried about Granma'am, and then she asked me why. I told her and Big Jim, who was sittin at the table with her, about how Granma'am was on the cord and it got so thin and how she fell in the dream, and so I had run back and forth trying to gauge her fall and catch her, and now my back was angled on account a the way Granma'am crushed me when she fell.

Margarete's mouth hung open. She squinted through the vapors a the story I just told. Big Jim asked me in the midst a Margarete's not speakin if I wanted to call down to somebody to ask after Granma'am.

"Where can we go to call?" I asked, just out like, to them both. I said *we* on account a I hoped they wouldn't send me by myself.

"We can call Miss Macie," Margarete half answered, slow. She looked down, brushin imaginary crumbs off the table into the hand she held open underneath the table edge. They had to be imaginary cause ain't no dust or crumbs on that table, ain't nobody eaten at it since I cleared and wiped it off just a hour ago. I don't know who Margarete is tryin to fool, but I just let it be a trade, since she was gone take me to call Miss Macie.

"What you waitin on, Neesey?" Margarete wanted to know. "Go on in the bedroom, and call Miss Macie."

I walked into the bedroom mostly in a mist myself. There it was, right by the bed. Under Margarete's maroon lamp with the ladies painted one on each side was a large black telephone with the dial of numbers in the middle. Well, I'll be. I had dusted those lamps. Wiped them too, I think. How had I missed that telephone? Had I missed it? How could I not know it was there? I had rushed through Margarete's room. I had not fondled her things and noticed her progress. And I had never talked to her on the telephone from down home.

"Do you know Miss Macie's number by heart?" she said, talkin right in my ear. She had snuck up behind me. How? Margarete has a inside telephone, that's what I'm thinkin.

"Naw," I reply, late, I'm a little giddy.

Margarete goes over to the telephone and turns each number professional-like. Her fingernails are shaped like almonds and may be just as hard. She let the circle roll back between each number; it sound like the scrape a drapes bein opened, rings runnin on the rod.

Margarete talks a minute to whoever answers, and then she hands me the telephone top. It is Belle Eva, Miss Macie's sister, talkin out from the phone from all the way down home. Took us all day plus two hours to get this distance, and now we talkin at the same time. I cain't help but smile at all this, and I have near forgotten about my back, but then it pinches me. "Have you seed my granmama Dambridge today?" I holler to Belle Eva.

Belle Eva is sayin, "Yes, yes I have," and tellin me bout Granma'am havin come out to the front yard first thing every day since I have left. Jes watchin and greetin the children goin to school. That's how she has seed Granma'am, she says, and yes Granma'am is lookin strong and jes fine.

At the same time that Belle Eva starts to talkin, Margarete is sayin to me, "You don't hafta holler in that telephone, Neesey."

Margarete turns on her heel and leaves, and I holler to Belle Eva the other things I want to ask. Then I give her a short list a things to go by and say to Granma'am in the mornin. I tell her to tell Granma'am I dreamed about her but everything is all right and my back is straightenin up.

Belle Eva say she sure will go by. Belle Eva hollers how am I makin out in Detroit, but I have already started to hang up the phone and I don't have the poise or experience to recover and so I end up the conversation by hangin up still hearin Belle Eva talk. Hallo, oh, Neesey, oh, she disconnected. I imagine that's what Belle Eva will say after she hears that I'm gone.

LUKE EDWARD HAD to walk me to school the whole first week. I had to beg him. To this day, Luke edward still hate to get up early. He don't have to, so he don't. But also my not bein able to find my way irritated him. Specially when I was tryina shake him out the bed. He was not happy that I couldn't get directions good. Some days, sometime between the flat and the schoolhouse, he might start to think the whole thing is funny, and be laughin at me. I encouraged him; I rather have him laughin at me than mad at me. Mostly, he was mad.

On the third day of my wakin him up too early, he said, "Neesey, you big enough to be able to get to school by yourself." The first and second day we had talked all the way. It made the walk a lot shorter, but I forgot to pay attention. We talked about Granma'am, and Lantene and her mama, Miz Evelyn Ownes, and I asked him how pregnant was Margarete. He said he thought maybe four months, or five months. That the baby might be comin in February or March.

"Where you goin now, Luke edward?" I ask him.

"Back to bed," he answered me. "Bye."

The next day I have to beg him again. "Come on, Luke edward, don't fuss."

"This is not about my fussing, Baby Sis. I'm not about to keep walking you to school every day. I'm not going to the school—you are," he said.

I promise to make him a dessert.

He smirks. "What you gone make?" he asks.

"Chocolate pie."

He gets up and gets ready. I knew he would. But when we go out and the cold shakes him, he sucks in his teeth.

"I'm tryina learn my way," I answer.

"This is not complicated, Neesey," he says to me. "You just walk down to Warren and make a left, and walk down to Dexter and make another left, and then walk over to Scovel and make a right. The school is on the corner of Scovel and Thompkins. Or, you can walk past Warren down to Grand River, and walk down Grand River to Scovel and then make the right. Go down Scovel to Thompkins. That's the way we went yesterday, but it's the long way."

I don't answer cause already I'm dreamin.

"You better pay attention to where you going, girl. You gonna end up out here lost, and by yourself." He calls me back to the streets we are walkin. "You can see this big old school building from Virginia."

Luke edward is so funny. He was right, though, I should a been payin more attention. But I just let him lead.

GOT SO I just couldn't sleep. Least not long like when I had the tremor of the country and Granma'am's ancient breathin to dream by. In Detroit, machines pass in the night. Instead a layin in bed aimless, I took to gettin up soon as I woke up. Always plenty to do, since I am mostly in charge a the house.

One night, I have put up my cot around three-forty-five because I can see I won't get back to sleep. It will be Saturday when the sun hits, and so there is washin ahead. Course I cain't start to wash while everybody is still sleep, so I start dinner. I have potatoes peeled and soakin in water and back in the box, chicken legs seasoned and set to bake. I have just put the cabbage in the skillet when I hear Luke edward's hand turn the lock. He don't scare me no more like he use to. Maybe I have just surrendered to his clock, and so that's why I'm up. Maybe I felt him comin on home. I sure don't know what it is wakes me up like this, but he does not startle me when he comes in the kitchen.

He says quietly, "Neesey, I do not believe how crazy you are." His voice lilts up somewhere early in his sentence. He is beautiful and interesting and pronounced.

He does not startle me, but he does make me laugh. Now, here he is, comin *in* the house. Four o'clock in the mornin. God is busy makin dawn, and I am soon to start on my cornbread. And he is callin me crazy, laughin and lookin so sweetly tired, I know before I even look up at him. Of course, I could be crazy—why cain't I sleep?—but least I have had my bath and been to bed and got up to today's date. He is dressed in yesterday's clothes, leanin backwards into things that are rumpled and not fresh.

"Why am I crazy?" I whisper back to him. Smile is in my voice.

"You got the whole house smelling like cabbage," he says. I shrug my shoulders casual-like and he goes to his room to bed. I am lonely but still busy once he's gone.

My Two Mothers

I LEARNED HOW to cook and how to organize meals from Granma'am. When Margarete took me down home to stay, Granma'am had made a feast for us. Fried chicken, chopped turnip greens and turnips, corn pudding, spoon biscuits, and a few mashed potatoes to go under the gravy. The food waited until we came, and then waited while we took off all our wraps, and said hello and hello. It waited while Mama cried some, and while Granma'am wandered the house with me, telling me what was what. The food waited while Granma'am washed my face, and while Mama stood out in the backyard and breathed this good country air, she said. It waited while Granma'am hollered cross to Miss Macie that "Yes, Margarete has arrived safe," and we would step over later. Then the three of us sat down to the table. Granma'am blessed all she had cooked and blessed her two girls. Then we dipped our forks in and the food was comfort-warm.

We had lime pie for dessert, and we had a relaxing time down the country. After six days or maybe seven, Mama started getting ready to leave. She had to go back to Detroit and work, she said. And she said that since

Daddy was gone she had to be careful to make sure she got enough money to take care of everybody. She explained her intention to leave me with Granma'am. In Virginia without her. Without Luke edward, or David or Daddy.

I insisted she not leave me. I understood she had plans. But I argued. She could take me. She could take me back and keep me like before. But she wouldn't. She couldn't, she said.

MY TWO MOTHERS let me have my tantrums, so I knew I was losing the war. A child knows what it means when she is let to have a fit. *This is one a the hard knocks, honey.* Since I wasn't swaying Mama, I took a new tack: I stopped kicking and screaming, and started to plead.

And then after that, I publicly performed.

Granma'am has an oak in her front patch of yard. Small yard, big oak. It has aged like a sage as I have grown. Figuring to get between my mother and the rail stop, I made my first visit to Granma'am's front-inside-the-fence. Leaning on the oak, I testified. I wailed and I hollered. Thought about my mama leavin me, missed my brothers Luke and David in advance, glared at the country chillun glarin at me, willed my mama to the screen door to see. Feared bein alone with my ancient Granma'am and called my daddy's name.

Daddy. Da-a-a-dy. Daaaaaaddy. Hiccup.

Hiccup. I want my da-a-a-dy.

Mama took to bed behind all a that, and so she stayed a few extra days. I relaxed a minute but it was a temporary win. Much as we have discussed it, she declares she didn't sneak out on me. "You were sleep, Neesey," she says.

HAY DREAMS

MIZ EVELYN OWNES talked about her dead baby boy like he was a angel, while he was livin. He was really at the edge a bein a boy—seventeen when he passed— and nobody but his mama woulda said he was a angel.

Before Lonts was killed, he had gone bad. What it meant to go bad was the same as for fruit and vegetables. It meant there was hardly any use for you, except if the bruises and the mold was cut out. Salvage used in stew. No cook worth her salt would use the salvage a bad vegetables in separate spaces on the plate on account a the stringy moldy taste would expose you. Would give you a reputation of either not carin, or not havin.

Miz Evelyn caught mama-grief bad when they found her boy. He was all in pieces, cut up at the tracks. And so Miz Evelyn Ownes went to pieces herself—in his name. She got the fever and the sweats, and then, later, Lantene got the fever too, in imitation of the way her mama behaved.

Miz Evelyn Ownes was brought from the white- people's house where she worked. Her friends went and got her, two women and a man; they fanned around Miz Evelyn's head and face. The heave-ho of the procession disrupted me and Lantene. We was playin in her mama's room, experimentin with her mama's special things.

They come round two o'clock in the day. At first we had a pleasant shock that Miz Evelyn Ownes was too distracted to care about our wanderin hands, but then we bridled and subdued when through the heat and the visitors we understood about the pieces left of Lonts.

Lantene blew up into hysteria all at once. Miz Macie gripped her by her shoulders and talked straight into Lantene's desperate wild and searchin eyes. "Lantene, your brother Lonts done been kilt on the tracks." *The same tracks my daddy rode, makin a life?* Lantene, she raised her arms up quick, and knocked Miz Macie's grip away. She ran to her mama, she was flushed purple and she rocked back and forth. People attended to her in a tight circle that Lantene used all her strength, again, to break. "Mama, where Lonts? Mama, where Lonts?" Miz Evelyn Ownes did not answer Lantene. Miz Evelyn Ownes sat faint and gurgled, rubbed on her knees, called on the Lord.

I retreated to a corner and crouched, pinned by the heat and cut-up Lonts. No one noticed me. Then Granma'am came, large, and busy like groceries; she had heard about the tragedy and decided that where I was was there. Granma'am had put on a store-bought dress, but wore her house shoes still. She pulled me by the shoulder of my light blue summer shift; I was still small, about nine. We walked clear to the back where the drawn water was. Granma'am had the ice that the Kinseys had brung her, and in the closest container, she dropped the ice and poured just a drip of water over it. We went back up front—Granma'am was still draggin me by the shoulder of my shift. Granma'am set down the ice-cool water and melted a mound over Miz Evelyn. Especially over her sour sweaty face. I mimicked her: I stuck my hand in the bowl, and put a piece of ice on my friend Lantene, there on the left side of her neck that showed. On her right side, she leaned on the heave of her mother. Lantene did not notice my hand or the coolness, I guess. I held my hand there till the ice melted, which was quick. By then Granma'am had finished murmurin religion over Lantene's mama. She pulled me by my shift and we left; Lantene did not notice me leave. The house thumped a fitful rhythm behind us.

Granma'am forbade me to go there a while, even though she went every day. She took me to Lonts's funeral, which happened on the lot where they buried him, instead a at the church. We looked at the hole for his casket the whole time the preacher talked. Granma'am got me a new white dress from the Jenkinses in a hurry. It was hot hot that day, and I sweated in the dress. It pained me to run salt in my new clothes.

Lantene was slow to talk to me the rest a that summer, but then when I went back to school, she started to come round some at the end a the day after she finished helpin at the white house where her mama worked. When I finally got permission to go to her house again, Granma'am sent me with a nice flat cake, and me and Lantene enjoyed it, even before Miz Evelyn came home. That cake day, I remember, was the first I heard from Miz Evelyn of Lonts's makin brooms.

I looked at Lantene with question in my eyes and cake crumbs glued round my mouth. She repeated: "Lonts usedta make brooms when he was young."

"Brooms?" I looked from one to the other. And Miz

Evelyn Ownes explained with a light in her eyes that he made regular brooms for sweepin and spirit brooms to hang up over the back doors. "He collected hay from the west fields," she said, "and brought it back to this here yard. Piled it up till he had plenty, and till he had sawed enough handles. Then he soaked all the brush over two or three nights, and would spend the next few days cuttin and foldin and wrappin the straw. At the end of a week, he might have nine, ten brooms.

"And he sold them too. Kept a schedule in his mind of who bought what broom when, and then would go back and sell the same customers new ones. He brought me every dime he made," she said wistfully. "And he was just a sprout then. Seasonal work, you know," she trailed off.

All the time I knew Lonts was after he had gone bad. To tell the truth, I ain't never seen Lonts make a broom *or* a dollar. Fact, only thing I ever seen Lonts make was a escape, and he made plenty a those. I think I can say without speakin ill a the dead that Lonts was probably makin some kind a escape when he got caught by the train cars careenin on the tracks. Every body else down home said the same.

Lantene mistook my sugar-sleep and silence for doubt. I was actually thinkin that Miz Evelyn Ownes's mind had gone off to meet her angel boy, sad and sweet as she looked, tellin that story so wispy like she did. "Ask Miz Kinsey," Lantene said abruptly. "She bought Lonts's brooms. The Jenkinses too."

I did have chance to ask Valentine Kinsey one time. I sat for Miz Kinsey's kids while Miz Kinsey did other things—visited, went to Richmond with Mistah Kinsey, went round to show some a the new things they ordered from the mail. Miz Kinsey was one a the town's authorities, like Granma'am. "You remember Lonts Ownes?" I asked her. "Did you buy his brooms, Miz Kinsey?"

"Lawrence," Miz Kinsey corrected me. "The boy's name was Law-rence Ownes. Yes, I bought those nice brooms he made. Such a shame about that boy," she clucked. "They should have taught him to cane chairs."

GIRL BABY

GRANMA'AM TRIED TO involve me in church and school both, on account a she was a great believer in occupation. I did everything she said do, but it was the parade finally took my mind off my troubles. It happened late in the spring after the winter of my first year down home.

Members from all the churches were in the June parade. What few people in town who didn't belong to a church stood at spots on the sidelines or marched the rear. Granma'am's church, Calvary, led that year—what a great honor. The church prepared from February until Saturday, the fourteenth of June. That Saturday morning, we did our last rehearsal of the lineup and three marches at ten o'clock. At eleven the parade happened.

The months of preparation had specific stages. First, we planned the colors. The basis for everything was white. The girls wore white blouses, and purple skirts for redemption. The boys wore purple shirts and dark pants. The church mothers, who were the parade's core group, wore white dresses, white hats, white stockings, white gloves, white shoes. The youngest girls and all the babies wore their white Easter outfits.

Calvary women ordered tens of yards of purple fabric for the children from the Watkinses, months in advance of the need to start to sew. The Watkinses delivered the bolts of purple fabric in time, but the mothers whispered among themselves that the Watkinses probably went through the Jenkinses to get it. I heard them talkin about that at the church one Tuesday night.

Patuskie proper had two stores. One close by where we all lived: that was the Watkinses' store. And that's where we went for most everything we got. Most a what they had was exactly what you need: flour, lard, sugar, butter, barrels of dried things. Me and Granma'am mostly exchanged for fruit and vegetables we didn't grow; Granma'am made high, airy cakes, and so that's what we exchanged.

The other store was the Jenkinses'. They had more of the package things and had more relations with the stores that sent by mail. They had a bigger porch, and the walk to their store took nearly twenty minutes from where we all lived. But Granma'am did not allow me to go to the Jenkinses'.

I helped cut. Sleeves, cuffs, half-front and wide back panels. Collars, those were too hard for me. Four trian-glelike shapes, with flat tops and wide bottoms, for the skirts for the girls. Wide purple ribbon strips to sew into waistbands.

I did not want the girls' jobs. Rather than walk with the girls holdin banners that said CHRIST, THE OPEN DOOR, I wanted to be where my brothers belonged. I wanted to hit a big drum with sticks.

I knew Granma'am would never let me. Still, in secret, I begged Macie's son, Marcus Henry, to teach me. Granma'am was preoccupied with her church's leadership and with finishin all the many children's garments. My strategy was to stay quiet until the last possible moment, and seek the support of the Lord. If the two of us—me and the Lord—couldn't convince Granma'am, then wouldn't the limits of religion be shown?

I went to the church sewing days after school. According to God's intention, Granma'am came later. Usually, I had sixty whole minutes to practice: BOOM. BOOM, BOOM BA BOOM, BA BOOM, BOOM BA BOOM. Marcus Henry let me practice with his kit. Every day while all the shirts and skirts and plans were bein made, I hit the drum.

Miss Macie told Granma'am before my time was up. The parade was still weeks away. I had practiced with the girls and been fitted for a skirt. Thanks to Marcus Henry, I had worn the heavy strap that wound through wires on the drum. I knew I could carry it, and I knew I would carry it. I just didn't know how to get Granma'am to help me.

We were makin melon pie. Somethin I concocted a rainy day in the kitchen. Granma'am always applauded my inventions and helped me get my recipes scientific.

Granma'am said, "You want to play the drum in the parade?"

Lord have mercy, the surprise. "Yes'm," I said.

"Why didn't you mention it?" she asked me.

"I been prayin on it," I answered.

Granma'am went into her bedroom and brought out one of the purple shirts for boys with longer arms. It fit me. "Macie say you got the beat down good."

I grinned. Granma'am discussed necessary behavior, and lowered my skirt so my draws wouldn't show, what with the big drum and all. Granma'am paid the quarters to rent another heavy drum, and we tied purple ribbons around my cornrows at the ends. My head got plenty air.

BOOM. BOOM, BOOM BA BOOM, BA BOOM, BOOM BA BOOM. I played all day. I marched all day. In between rest calls, I fried. I thought I would die a heat. Granma'am walked in back with the missionaries and the Willing Workers Circle. We marched round and round. I pretended I was Luke edward, who could do anything there within the wide space of my memory. He would definitely outdistance Marcus Henry and the other tall parade leader, Junior Brown. Luke edward would walk taller and faster and stronger than anybody with that old heavy drum. Luke edward could drum march from Patuskie straight to China. Luke edward could drum march for months without a stumble or an ache. He would not quit or be pulled to the side by a Willing Worker, sayin Let your breathin steady, chile. I pushed onward and onward, at one with my tall, slim, tireless, handsome boy.

Granma'am said I did good, but she wouldn't let me march the last two rounds. She said I needed to steady my heart.

"You red in the face and all over, Baby Sister. You gettin exhaustion from the heat."

"No, ma'am, I'm not," I insisted, breathless. Anxiously, I persisted, as the parade group moved on. "Granma'am, I'm fine, can I go, can I go?" I said, "Marcus Henry and me practiced. I can finish, I can."

"You sit right here and wait," she ordered. "The rest a the chillun will be back and you can play some more."

She left me with the rented drum on the church green. Luke edward's image burnt away in the heat. So what if I was out a breath? I had been in this much heat before, all summer every year. Granma'am went inside the church to get the cool drinks ready, and she sent a baby boy out with some punch for me. He asked me if he could beat my drum, and I let him. Everything was over, anyway.

HAROLD GRAYSON'S FORD made tracks in the dirt outside our yard at six a.m. I was dressed and ready like I'd been taught.

I waited in our front room, which we called the parlor. Granma'am was in the kitchen. Once a week on Saturdays, I took a whisk broom to the two chairs and the couch, that Granma'am called a divan—by mistake, I found out. Margarete had come one time and said it was a couch, so even though Granma'am called it a divan, I took the whisk broom to the couch and chairs. Also on Saturdays, I wiped Granma'am's little coffee table so the top shined, and the wood pieces that crossed from leg to leg didn't show no dust in the corners. I took a wet rag to the curtains, and swiped the dust that collected in the folds. And the pencil that usually ended up on top a the little desk that sat by the front door, I took and put back inside the desk where me and Granma'am kept a few pencils and pens and the paper and envelopes for the letters she would have me write.

I had cleaned the parlor on Tuesday this week, since I was leavin on Thursday. While I sat there waitin for young Harold Grayson, I looked for somethin else to clean. Maybe there was somethin I had missed. I saw him drive up, get out, and push shut his car door. Dog, it was a heavy, final sound. He walked up the path in our little yard, his shoes squared carefully against the ground, so that mostly his soles made contact, and no dust rose.

Granma'am heard the car door close from way in the back of the house where she was. She got up from the table: her chair scraped back—not too hard, and not too far. I waited, but she didn't come up front, so I greeted Harold Grayson myself. Unwrapped the thin wire from its nail, pushed open the shut screen, cleared my throat and said, "Mornin, Harold, how you?" Then I turned sideways to let him by.

"Good morning, Neesey," he nearly sang. He waltzed into the clean parlor and put a little kiss on my right cheek. I am tall for my age, and he is a slight man, so he doesn't have to stoop too low. "How you feeling? You all ready to go?" He is cheerful with his questions. His voice, it was usual. You can tell he is unstampeded, not trampled like I am by the miles and years ahead.

I asked him: You want breakfast? You want coffee? You need to use the water? "No, no thank you, Neesey," he said, three times.

Granma'am's house shoes flap slow down the hall. Me and Harold Grayson both look in her direction. She stops before she gets into the room. The small grip we had packed was right where she stood. Both Granma'am and the grip solemn like caskets.

"Hello, Harold, hi is things?" There is fatigue in her voice. She made an effort to beat it back. Her housedress is weighed down by her hands in the pockets.

"We are all fine, Mother Dambridge." Harold Grayson intones, minister style, when he talks. He also speaks for many people at once. He walks over, places a kiss on Granma'am's cheek. Now Harold Grayson and Granma'am both stand with the grip. I am anchored by the screen and by apprehension of the highest order.

"Come on back here, Harold, lemme show you what I packed."

Granma'am has ordered the food on the table. Half the three chickens we fried last night, some biscuits she spoon-stirred this morning, a few apples and pears, two bananas. Three or four Mason jars with water, mint tea, and coffee. The hot coffee jars have pieces of wood spoon in the bottom to keep the glass from breaking.

They talk. I hear them through a fog of standing still. *Enough, how long, when? Margarete. Sad, Neesey, new pants, five dollars. Car, yes, brand new. You blessed.*

I hear a peace in what they say that I simply can't accept. Their quiet, measured words do not match my agitation. I know I'm not serene like them; I fold my lips together, determining what to do. Carefully, like religion, I wrap the thin wire back around the nail, fastening Granma'am's screen door.

Me and Granma'am had not slept, and so we could hardly stand up by this time in the day. What we had done was to try without saying to stretch those last days of my living there with her. As if we could stave off my future, canning pickles, baking pies. Granma'am rustles a paper bag in the kitchen, and I hear it. I know exactly what she does. A pain big as watermelon ruptures in my throat. Sprouts choking vines, that wring my neck of courage. I went right ahead: choking, I sobbed, standing by myself at the door.

HAROLD GRAYSON COMES back down the hall, talking about how he's looking forward to the pound cake, Mother Dambridge. Before I see his whole body again, I see his hand go round the handle of my grip, and then the grip leaves a shuddering white space where it had been on the floor.

Granma'am follows Harold, and I move abruptly away from the door. I move because Harold wants to go out. I move wanting to stay in. Granma'am and I look at each other across the room, around Harold's head, overtop of his citified industry. The sun had started to bake the chill off the air, and just as I was worried it might, Granma'am's bottom lip quivered some. I had stifled the noise of my floodgates opening, but so what? My face was swollen and running with emergency.

Harold Grayson says to the room and the morning, "I'll let you two say goodbye." He walks out with the pound cake and the chicken and my grip. Granma'am presses my face into her housedress. It is peach. I wipe my tears on her shoulder, and her fingers drum lightly on my scalp.

Granma'am asks me where is my pocketbook, and in her one hand she has something folded ticket-size. Abandoned in the corner of the chair where I had waited was a black pocket book, gold clasp. A grandmother's old bag, probably hadn't seen the light of day since the forties. A real combination with my traveling pants. I walk over to the chair, wipe my face on my sweater sleeve, and get the half-empty thing. I open its wide mouth to Granma'am, and look absent of mind down into the yawn it makes. Granma'am lifts my chin up with her finger and dictates: this is for your brother Luke, and this is for David. She unfolds one, then another, crisp ten-dollar bill. You tell Luke I said, and my mind half closes, I want him to get himself something clean. I won't say this to Luke, and maybe Granma'am knows I won't. It doesn't matter; she says something like it whenever she calls his name. Just like I know, Luke edward knows, that what Granma'am wants for him is clean.

There is a twenty-dollar bill for me, which is a fortune. And a small Ball jar of oil to help Margarete have the new baby. It has been steeped in rose petals for more years than I know and is wrapped in wax paper and some plastic, squeezed airless by rubber bands.

Granma'am involves herself closely, from a distance, in the birth of Margarete's children. Especially the girls. She sent the oil to help bring Clara, and as family story has it, she sent her oil to bring me on too. Both my father and Big Jim wanted girls. Once I heard the story told, controversy surrounded my making. What does this mean? Rub this on, and it will help you have the girl you want? It was the stuff of wonderment, like the wood bars on my crib.

Girl me, little me, late baby me, oil baby, me baby me in a jar. Sleep baby quiet, baby me in a cage. Did they carry me up from the country? Some old folk remembrance, some small and sapling seed, held carefully, wrapped in newspaper? Did I ride on the celebrated mortician's lap? Was there sheet cotton or was paper screwed down and puffed out like a skirt between my oil and my air? And when the oil lapped from jarring, did I wail that early, there in the back with the shoe boxes packed with fried chicken, napkins, and chocolate cake? What did Mr. Harold Grayson Senior do with me? When he emptied his shoe box, did he sit me down on the floor, covet me, corner me, anchor me between his two new wingtips, black, special, hard-earned for mortician school? Did he drop the crispy greasy crumbs of disappearing chicken legs onto my Mason lid? Small, neat plinks. Did I hear this noise of feeding? Was I sad to leave the warm and making hands of my Granma'am, to be let loose from the compost heap, her store of power? Was I sad to leave the country? Is that where I was born? Am I my grand-mother's child? Am I a child of potion? Am I a child of folklore, or family crisis, some need for gender bal-ancing? Maybe some need to keep my father? And who is my father too, is he Buddy my daddy, or is he some country man whose lasting seed my Grandma'am could pickle till it got to Detroit? Maybe a man prone to girls, maybe Mr. Howell Jones or Mr. Harold Grayson Senior or maybe his brother who looks nothing like him. Are my brothers really brothers to me, or am I sister to bay leaf and scorched root of cayenne?

CAREFUL WITH GRANMA'AM'S treasures, I clasp the bag and hang it in the corner my elbow makes. I look straight into Granma'am's face, which I hardly ever do. Her mouth is a little open; time has caught her in surprise. I am shocked too now that this morning and the car and the end of us is here. Her hair and eyebrows are blond gray and sienna brown, and she has two strands of long hair in her chin. Her nose is respectable, a round-point survivor of pinching in her youth. She has instructed me to rub the baby's nose, firm between my fingers, at least until she's three. This baby will be a girl, Granma'am has decided. I should rub the nose, though, Granma'am has directed, boy or girl, either. I will remember to do this, because if the child's nose is wide or flat, I will be blamed.

Granma'am's skin flirts with her age; she is deft with plants and oils, and so her cheeks and neck and eyelids droop but are not cracked. She has an old woman's moustache.

I am bold enough today, this morning, to look dead into her eyes. She is wracked by this rip in the fabric. Her eyes, the whites of them, are reduced to burlap. The seeing parts of them are dark with experience and gloom. Only a minute can pass with me glaring this way, but Granma'am allows me, knowing. I etch a picture for my memory with this stare; I have to get the edges right. I try to draw her thinning eyebrows and her medium-brown skin. The lines of her nose are close together, since she has that nice nose, pointed up. And then the gray-flecked moustache hair on her lip, and how her cheeks hang just so slightly. All this I try to draw on the plates at the back of my eyes. A place where I can turn in and look at the picture I have drawn of Granma'am to take with me.

But when I get to the backs of my eyes to record my memory while I am still in it, I find that the well of all feeling is there. The drawing pad is not firm, but water. And water that is rising from the well. The water rising is warm, not cool, the color is gray-clear and holds nothing. Nothing that I try to draw, and nothing that I try to hold, either. Finally, when I am almost desperate enough to run from this, not run forward, but back somewhere, Granma'am tries to grin away a sob. It wins; I hold her choking, me choking; we cry.

I lay my forehead on her shoulder, and breathe in through what little space is left in my nose. My last inhale of Granma'am's smell: Oxydol, and the hair pomade, and her snuff from all the many uses of her tin and her handkerchief, in the years I had known her, and before that. Newly free in my travelling pants, and held into obedience by Granma'am's straight back, I lift my right leg, like I might double over, which I felt like I might do. This relieves the pressure, but still I feel like howling. Quiet, I hold on. Lift the one leg, again and again, in the rhythm, I presume, of my fear.

"We done said everything, Baby Girl. Now you go on." Granma'am pushes me on to my next. It felt like the forward press of a plow, me in the harness, and the ground looking nothing but bald and flat in front of me, the harvest far away. I balanced myself. From her pocket she pulled out a small Bible; more money stuck out from its leaves. For if you have a emergency, she told me, and she pressed the Testament inside my palm.

"Iss cool," she said abruptly, and turned back toward

the room that for six years had been mine and, for torrid, hopeful years before that, had belonged to my mother Margarete. "I think you better take your coat, just in case. You can give it away when you get to Detroit." And back she came with my too-small blue coat; she had it stretched out from her body cause her arm wasn't bent. The flap of her feet against her house shoes made me think about this movement: Granma'am walking back and forth to give me things. She is not the person who should bear the gifts. But of course what did I have right then but my leaving, and all the years of taking that I'd spent. I wished, like David, that I had built trellises, then at least a piece of wood would be left. Or, I wished that I was going, to come back summers; then there'd be the promise of the growing months. As it was, here was Granma'am carrying things to me, and all the things I'd made were cooked, eaten, disappeared, and by Sunday, new dust would lay on all the furniture.

Polite Harold Grayson had not started the car.

I hugged Granma'am again, snapped her arm to bending, pressed the coat between us. Whispered to the folds in her neck that I didn't want to go. Laid my head down on her shoulder again. She let me rest it a last minute or two, then again:

"We done said everything, Baby Sister." She patted the back of my head, then she swiveled me on my own feet, and pushed me by my shoulder blades toward the front door.

I made my way to the car, and got in. Harold Grayson started his brand new engine. He didn't move for a moment, but I held my head down. My tears fell in dollops from my eyes to my lap and stained my pants with fury about this leaving again. The car moved a teeny bit, but I did not. Harold Grayson said, "Neesey, you should wave bye-bye." I looked up through the window, my last look at our house. Granma'am was standing on the warm side of the screen. Her face was muddied by the black net between us, and when she saw me look up, she came clear out. Everything above my shoulder blades threatened. My tears betrayed me.

Harold Grayson had steadied the car. I fumbled for the window handle, looking to meet her eyes, and I rolled the window down. I could see her deciding whether to come to the car.

"Iss cool, Granma'am," I said. "Go in."

HE LET ME cry undisturbed till he ate his banana. He offered me mine, but I didn't want it. What I wanted was more air through my nose.

We were going first to Washington, D.C., to pick up his cousin. "Soon we'll be crossing the Potomac," he said. "Have you ever seen it?" He took quick glances at me. My arms were folded hard across my chest, and knowing I had about three words to say, I wanted to save them and so shook my head no.

"No you don't want the banana, or no you haven't seen the Potomac?" He was trying to entertain me or maybe trying to distract me, but I had to keep a deluge dammed. I waited some time, swallowing. I was thinking, neither one, but I didn't answer. I looked out the big clean car window at the ground: the road was divided, painted hard down the middle, cut in two like me.

I looked inside my head at Granma'am: she would be sitting in the parlor in the big chair where she and the good Lord met to wait for her burdens to lift. She wouldn't be doing much else but that, we had cooked all the food she'd need for some days. At just the last moment before you give up on someone, decide they're rude or lost or just won't talk, I pressed a voice and answered Harold Grayson, "Neither one," about the banana and the Potomac.

In a few years, Granma'am will send a letter to me, thinking it is probably time that I'm looking at boys for boyfriends. Among other things she says in the letter is this: *I want you to consider Harold Grayson, he's a good, steady boy, ain't he?* I am not surprised, reading it, at what Granma'am has to say, but I do think it's funny, and out of the question. By the time I get this letter of hers, I am only interested in teaching or nursing, and nothing in between. But Granma'am and I are so far away by then that she wouldn't know how my interests got squeezed into form.

We did cross the Potomac, took barely thirty minutes. Harold Grayson talked about the rivers he'd seen. He hadn't been these places to do his mortician work: their family worked mostly in Michigan and Virginia. But because the dead increase, he had money to drive and cross rivers.

By ten, we were at the home of Harold Grayson's aunt Ruth. Harold Grayson's cousin had changed his mind about going, and Harold was for a moment disappointed like a pet. But Harold Grayson's aunt Ruth had fixed us a big breakfast. In honor of Harold's visit, which she knew would be short. We all sat to the table, Harold at the foot and his uncle Elvan at the head; Harold's cousin, Elvan Jr., blessed the food and asked the Lord's protection for our trip. As my verse I said, "Blessed are the meek, for they shall inherit the earth."

Harold and I both ate like travellers. I surprised myself. His very kind family ate well too, and didn't contain their delight at seeing Harold. We ate all the grits and slab bacon, scrapple and eggs, plenty hot bread and preserves. For them, it was a noisy, happy breakfast. I didn't talk really, but didn't cry either; I considered that my best. The breakfast took as long as it needed to, and not any time more. Industrious Harold Grayson invited me to wash up, and told his family we'd be going. It was eleven-thirty, and we were driving straight through, he said. Behind the latched door, the family's laughing was low-voiced and mixed with food. An easy goodbye. They had had their meal in the name of joy, and full as I was, the food had been a shovel, its weight thrown like dirt into the hole of me. I didn't know how Harold would drive after all this; I would either sleep, or suffocate.

WE GOT BACK in the car, and got back on the road. I could not settle down. Too full, too anxious. Too, too.

Harold had everything we brought with us lined up neat on the back floor. Nothing spilt. The Mason jars all had pieces of plastic stretched over the mouths and the lids screwed on over top, which made plastic skirts for the peoplelike jars. The brown paper bag housed chicken, fruit, and pound cake. In the midst of my misery I had thought the pound cake was spoon biscuits. But everything stood upright and immobile, ready to be reached in. I couldn't think of eating, not today, not tomorrow. I wanted to vomit, to break all the car windows, break all tradition, break Harold's neck. I sat still and quiet, deferential, well trained.

The car was big, and warm inside due to the engine running. I didn't feel too much of the road underneath. Soon as we got going from the Washington, D.C., stop, Harold told me in conversation that as the one passenger, my job would be to keep him up.

"You git sleepy when you drive, Harold Grayson?"

"Actually, I don't, but it's every passenger's job to keep the driver company."

"Oh," I said.

"Do you like this car?" he asked me.

"Yeah," I answer. It is a nice car. It moves. And the engine sounds quiet like a hum. It eats up the road, and that part makes me angry, but I just concentrate and swallow, and the bile goes back down.

"Do you like the brown, Neesey?" Now that made me chuckle a little. So like Harold Grayson to get a brown car. Middle brown, like dirt, like flatland, like the country where I had lived.

"I like the brown," I answer, and it is not a lie. The whole car, though, is brown and white. Brown on top and around the bottom and the sides, and white in between and around the tires. Like spats.

"And what else?"

"What else what?" I say.

"What else do you like?" he asks, and then goes on, "It's brand new."

"I can tell," I say.

"So, Neesey, what do you think of my new car?" he insists. He might as well grab onto the steering wheel and shake himself.

"Iss like ridin in new spats," I tell him.

He laughs out loud but quietly, more a mutter than a ring. He has a dimple in his right cheek, off center and down. He glances at me sideways, I look back at him. He drives.

I enjoyed that one moment, and then was sad again. I had good reason to be sad. The world did not look like Virginia anymore. Didn't look like the country anymore. I could see stone buildings off to the sides, and more cars than would come near Patuskie in three years. The lines in the road were yellow and white, painted hard and straight. Harold had said we were driving west northwest now. There was moisture in the air. I thought it was the oceans, but Harold Grayson said no, we were driving away from the ocean. I kept quiet but I knew I felt wetness, and sure enough, just before Pennsylvania, we hit rain.

Once he got going good, he talked and talked, all in my business. Glad you stopped crying. Must be real hard. How long you been with your grandma now? And how are Luke and David? You'll like Detroit. Won't you be glad to see your mother? She's expecting another baby, right? Oh, what a blessing! What are you praying for, boy or girl?

Had one conversation with him—trying to keep him company—and another one with myself. At his praying-for question, I broke off. I wasn't praying for either, or neither. Hadn't prayed for my mother's new baby yet. Well, once or twice, before I left, I had prayed for no bitterness at being called back. Don't know what I had thought really, had tried not to think too much.

Harold's talk crowded me, took me out of my own mind. Guess he was trying to distract me from my misery, had me half-pouting, half-lost, full of the vex of expectation. When he took a breather, I asked him a question. "How will I know if you fall to sleep, Harold?"

He chuckled, "If I fall asleep, we'll have an accident, Neesey."

"Well, what happens before that?"

"What?" he says.

"What happens when you fall to sleep," I repeated, "before we have a accident?"

"Well," he said, "it all happens very fast."

I waited.

"Maybe I swerve off the road," he says. "Or maybe the car slows down to stopping and moves around the lane. I'll nod," he said, "it's very dangerous."

He is so earnest, so grave. Scrapple thick in my throat, I said, "Well, if you nod or swerve off the road, I'll call your name."

"Loud," I added after a minute, and smiled at how I raised my voice some, just then.

"OK," he said quietly, and commenced to being quiet. Good for Harold Grayson, to let me have some time. I knew I could touch his funereal training if I tried. Very glad for the quiet—and hoping it would last until we got there—I settled into my peace and pouting, and I watched the punishing road.

HAROLD GRAYSON PULLED up in front of a two-family in Detroit's cool night at eleven-thirty p.m. on the same day we'd left. The streets were paved and run over by cars, so there was no crunch of dirt, announcin us. All the houses had electric lights and the streets had electric too. The houses looked all to be large and they had more than one floor each. Once we got off the highway, we drove down big wide streets, where plenty other people were drivin too, many a them Negroes. Harold used his blinker signals when we turned corners; all the corners we turned reminded me just how much I didn't know where I was, just how lost I would be, if I wasn't sittin up in the car with Harold. I had to admit to myself I was glad the trip was over. We had drunk all the coffee: warm and then cool and then cold, and I was taut and awake like I'd been slapped.

BIG JIM WANTS a girl baby. Margarete sent word of this to Granma'am, and ever helpful, Granma'am has sent me with a jar full of oil. There are petals three inches thick sunk through to the bottom. The oil is clear and viscous, thick. Its color has been shaped by the dried flower petals—whichever is the strongest—yellow, fuchsia, gray. Some of the medley I recognize as roses and hyssop, but I can't tell what else. Other kinds of sopping leaves. I ask Granma'am. She tells me never mind. I am so drained what with the leaving and all. I can't continue to try to impress on Granma'am about what things I need to know. Granma'am knows a little bit how I can't stand not learning. She also thinks it's up to her to decide what will help me or hinder me, in terms of knowledge. What news I'm ready for and what not. What if I later need to do the same thing for myself? Or somebody else? Doesn't she think I should know? Why can't she just tell me what flowers she soaked?

But she doesn't. And so again there is knowledge I have lost. I resolve to myself to ask again sometime. In the meantime I take the jar to Detroit with me like I'm told and I worry when the crust of fried chicken I am eating falls plink plink on its top. I am eating in the car as Harold Grayson and I ride through Ohio. I hurry to clean off the jar lid. I put my chicken down on the seat between us, and Harold scoots in the driver's seat toward his door so that no grease gets on his pants. I wipe off the top of the Mason jar with a clean napkin, and Harold Grayson watches me with quick, sidewise glances. He tells me to set the jar in the back on the floor where the rest of the food is. He knows even less than I do. This is not food.

Granma'am has sealed it securely. I study the skirt that the piece of plastic makes under the tight-screwed lid. I wonder very briefly if the skirt has to do with the girl baby this oil is supposed to help bring, and I decide to be more careful with the chicken. I hold the jar steady between my legs—I am wearing pants after all—despite Harold Grayson's mildly disapproving sigh.

I keep the jar of oil up front with me. I get the jar of oil safe to Margarete.

Margarete's Hugs Again

"IT'S THE BEIGE one," he said.

I strained my eyes to see beige. A woman at a second-floor window stood up. "Neesey, Harold?" the silhouette said.

"It's us, Margarete," Harold answered, out of the car almost before it stopped, seem like.

MY MOTHER CAME down and opened up the door for us. She stood at the well-lit foot of the stairs while we walked the concrete path to the door. I had left my grip in the car.

Margarete, coming toward us, threw her arms out wide.

"I lef my grip in the car," I said, too soon and too loud.

I turned to go back, but Harold caught me by the arm. "I'll get it for you in a minute, Neesey." That's what he said, so I turned back around.

My mother Margarete's face had sunk. "Neesey?" she said. She looked hungry.

I grinned, just to put some expression on my face. She liked that and held out her arms again. "I fo'got my grip in the car," I said again more quietly as I walked into her embrace. I stretched very slightly over the baby in her belly.

The little entryway was crowded with all three of us. Harold stayed behind me, in case I made a dash for my grip, I guess.

"You so grown up, Neesey!" My mother held me slightly back to look. "How you like y'new pants? How was the drive, Harold? Neesey!" She hugged me again. "You so grown up!"

"COME ON UPSTAIRS, you two," my mother continued, as she turned to take her belly back up the stairs.

"You goin to git my grip, Harold?" I turned to challenge him.

"I'm going to get your grip," he said. He went back out the door.

My mother took my hand. So as she walked up the steps and asked me about our drive again, she pulled my arm along with her.

"Come on upstairs, Neesey. What's the matter?"

"I'm waitin for my grip."

"Lord chile, will you let Harold bring that grip on upstairs? Come on," she said and dropped my hand. "Everybody's waiting."

Right away, I feel stronger with my limbs to myself. I follow her long skirt and low shoes, and I think again that I don't really know who she is. I plan to keep my heart to myself because of it. Granma'am said that I'll feel at home again soon. "You and Margarete will be a good team. You just wait and see," Granma'am had said.

Upstairs was my brother Luke edward with his sleepy eyes and ready smile and long legs stuck out in the floor like poles. And David. Steady Eddy. Mr. Regular. Still serious, and stocky, and just on the safe side of round.

"Hey, See-David. Hey, you ole crazy Luke edward." I couldn't help but grin. I was glad to see them two.

"Hey, Neesey, how you?" Their voices shock me, low like bears'.

"Lemme look at y'all!" I say to them. The smile blazes in my voice. Dog, I think to myself, they men now!

David is taller than Margarete; he wasn't the last time I saw him. The both of them, David and Margarete, paper-bag brown. David looks so serious; is he sad? His face does not exactly agree with the *Hey, Baby Sister* he says.

Granma'am say David was a focused boy, a child who wasn't scared by study. David have good sense, she said. *You better off like David, to be acceptin of the surprises of life and the Lord. When you handle the world that way, you grow joyful and watchful, instead a gettin full a frustration like so many.* That's what Granma'am always said, especially with respect to David. *He such a watchful child.* Down the country we called him See-David sometimes. It was affection made us call him that, and respect for the traits Granma'am named in him.

Granma'am's opinion about David caused me to watch him: first he would study, and then he would decide. I watched him watch Granma'am go outside every morning. Early in the day, she would go stand outdoors with her regular armor of busyness, with her litany of things to do. David said what she really went outside for was to feel the weather on her skin, to check on the flowers and the vegetable plants, and to stay familiar with the progress of the seasons.

Granma'am was old all the time I really knew her, but David had seen her age. David told me that when he used to come to visit, when Daddy would sit him and Luke edward on the trains, that Granma'am would come to meet them with a big basket a sweets for Daddy and other things for Daddy to bring back to Margarete. He said Granma'am could walk fast then. He said Granma'am's hands were straighter and smoother, and that she used a shaved stick to whiten her fingernails. He said Granma'am has not always complained about her knees; that sometimes she bent down and taught him and Luke edward how to play games she drew in the dirt. He knew Granma'am's history and her habits late in life. So when he visited one a the last summers he was there, he said he wanted to build a front porch. So that she would have a place to sit and watch spring grow green and hardy round the hills.

Granma'am saved all the heavy work she could until summer, for David to do when he came. David always looked to help. When he got down home, he did all her heavy work first. Before the summer took over his life. He cleaned the shed. Painted the pickets and the screen doors their annual white. Washed all the venetian blinds that Margarete had sent for Granma'am's windows from Detroit.

He built some rickety trellises for Granma'am's grapes one year. And afterwards, he thought he was a carpenter. Granma'am helped him believe it. They both talked about the grape braces, like it was Joseph the carpenter who built them. She was as proud as the mother of the child. Those braces had crumbled and Mr. Howell Jones had rebuilt them, sturdily, by the time Granma'am's backyard was mine alone. Granma'am was so sad to see David's trellises go. She saved one a his little strips a wood. For years after that, David intended to become a carpenter. To spend his days with aplenty electric power, and the floor a sawdust record of his work. He did end up working with furniture for a time, even though he wasn't making none. And then he went to work at the plant in River Rouge, where there was a world of electricity and not much wood.

Tonight, he wears a messy dark blue turtleneck with old gray workpants. He gave me a sweet kiss. I can still feel the brush of his parched lips at the far corner of my right eye. He only has to bend a little to kiss me because I have grown a lot. I have closed the gap that used to make me little to their big. His clothes smell like they've been packed away. I wonder if it's so.

Luke edward is thin, lanky, and on the red side of brown. His nubby hair, close cut and rubbed to shining, has much of the same red as his skin. On the street he looks different than us in his family. More akin to clay. Luke grins quickly, shows teeth standing square, as ordered and short as wash cloths hung on a line to dry. Our two mouths are the same. Luke's eyes—I notice them again as we lean back in a V; we hug, we laugh, we inspect each other—his eyes are as full of good humor as they are light brown. He lets me go suddenly, then catches me as I get off balance. He laughs at it all.

He is the kind that makes women want to follow. To talk among themselves about his long legs, fine fingers, good teeth, speaking eyes. They said *Girl, hush* to each other about him. I have heard women talk among themselves about Lucky Luke, even when he was much too young for the things they said. (Lucky Luke edward got the eyes he got; they beautiful, and talkative, but they also obviously sly. Anybody look at him close can see how jokin is the pigment in his stare.) Luke can get what he want from most any woman. Mostly because they will give it to him. But ain't hardly a woman can attach to him don't know from his eyes how quick he might change. Any woman says she doesn't know how Luke edward is, is either telling a tale, or she totally backwoods, or she blind.

When they were young boys, David's thing was color, and Luke edward's, runnin round. David used to study all the red and orange, blond, and light brown things that were different than the dirt brown and grass green of the country. Many times he would come into the house with a fat caterpillar, tomato worm, or other wrigglin creature that had had no chance to hide, the head of it squeezed between his stubby fingers. *Granma'am*, he could say, *look at this*. He would find out what Granma'am knew about the critters, and he tried to let them go before they died.

Luke edward ran from fence to post, from the tracks to town, and anywhere else he could get to. His runnin amok like he did made him late a lot. This did not please Granma'am. He made a lot of discoveries of his own, though. Not havin to do with worms, but more with who's arrivin or leavin or who looks like they in trouble. Luke edward could balance on his feet on top of a fence in a minute; he would stand up there and look at everybody travel. When grown folks wanted to make Luke edward mad, they would say he gossiped like a woman. Luke edward knew more, and different, than most gossipy women, who only looked from their front and back doors. He was a citadel; he looked all around the town. Lantene was in love with him and so was I.

MARGARETE'S NEW HUSBAND, Big Jim, is sitting in the one big chair in the living room. Some dining room or kitchen chairs have been brought in. I forgot while I was coming up the stairs that to me he would be the stranger in the house. We looked at each other then as strangers to each other, not just me to him. Now I check into my store of getting ready, to see what I carried up for him from down home. Granma'am and I had talked about Margarete's new husband, although he is not a very new husband anymore. Granma'am has told me he'll be glad that I have come to help, and that all I need to do is be nice to him and make sure I don't walk around the house half-naked. She told me to give him the jar of peach preserves.

Big Jim watches my two brothers greet me, and he has seen how glad I am to see them. Margarete and I have said hello in the landing under the light bulb, and so he can't observe how that was done. I am happy and involved with my brothers and at the same time I look at him out the side of my eye; he sits way down in the big chair, staring on. Harold Grayson comes back in with my grip and my pocketbook. I had forgotten to remember it too. Both Big Jim and I are distracted by Harold, mostly because you cain't help but think that isn't he neat as a pin. It is after eleven o'clock at night, and he still wears a tie and white shirt. Big Jim watches the same things I watch, because as I think about how store-bought and clean Harold looks, Big Jim says out loud, "Well, Harold, you are a meticulous young man." He says me-ti!-cu-lous, like so. A big word, maybe something he learned from *Reader's Digest* and has just now seen in Harold Grayson. Harold takes it as a compliment. He smiles, puts my things down, adjusts his tie.

Big Jim's hand is enormous as he leans in the chair to take the jar of preserves I teeter trying to offer.

My mother Margarete has brought herself over and perches on the side a Big Jim's chair. To watch him accept his gift, I guess. The chair is beautiful—brown brocade and sturdy—holding them both. Margarete's back is straight, and she smiles at what her husband says about neat, meticulous Harold Grayson. They look like a family, the three of them there: Big Jim, Margarete, and her baby in the belly.

Is Margarete going to say anything? Is she going to tell me *This is Big Jim who you know so much about?* Is she going to say to him *This is Baby Sister, this is Neesey, who we brought back just now to help with our baby in the belly?* From the drive, and from the talks with Granma'am, and from the time since she wrote that I should come back now—these are some of the things I am ready for her to say. At least: *Neesey, this is my new husband Jim. And Jim, this is my other child, Neesey.* Big Jim continues to observe the outsiders, not himself. He moves his eyes deliberately from slight Harold to new me and says in a voice proportioned to his size, "And where did you get that pocket bag, Miss Deneese?"

Everybody thinks his question is funny. Luke's laugh jumps stallionlike out of his throat, and Margarete's giggle strides on top like a jockey. David chuckles, humbly—or distracted one. Harold Grayson even joins in with his titter. I reach inside to display the trinkets I have carried, before I give myself a chance to think that I don't have to answer when people make jokes on me. I open the flappin bag in a rush, and the first thing my hand grabs I pull out. "Luke edward, Granma'am said to give you this," I say. I hold up the small New Testament big as day. I am sorry at once. Luke's history with Bibles does not deserve to be waved like a flag in this room, but at least the money in it shows.

"Yeah, yeah, I'll get it later," he says. "Harold, let's go see your car," he says.

I determine to remember about Big Jim's piercing eyes.

Chatter. Big Jim: *So, Harold, the drive was fine?* Harold: *We didn't have any problems. Mother Dambridge made a fine* lunch, *we ate most everything.* Margarete: *Well, let's have the dinner we got now.* Luke edward: *Hey, Neesey, how much taller you plannin to get? You think tall as me?* David: *We glad you back, Pooda. We ain't had no lil sister to mess with.* Margarete: *Don't she look good?* Me: *Turn me loose, Luke edward!* David: *Aw, you love it, Baby Sis.* Luke: *Harold, what's the horsepower in y'new engine?* Luke edward: *Let's go see the car.* Big Jim: *Those the pants your mama sent?* Me: *Yes, these the pants Mar — Mama sent.* Big Jim: *Neesey, you a young woman, these folks here had me expectin a little girl.* Margarete: *Ji-im, she is my little girl, even if she grown.* Luke: *She ain't grown.* Margarete: *You want roast beef, Neesey?*

In this way, the subject is changed and changed.

Harold replays conversations we had on the long drive up, when it was my job to make sure he stayed awake. He said once he told me what my job was I performed it well. He told them about the rivers we talked about. In that way he gets to talk again about rivers he has crossed. My mother gleams about Harold's travels and my responsibility. Big Jim reaches up to the edge of the couch where I have perched across the arm of the sofa, me in my new pants. He shakes my shoulder without much effort and in this way he tells me something, like maybe he approves of me being responsible, or maybe they need me to be responsible, or maybe he is glad that Harold Grayson approves of me, or maybe he approves of me. Or maybe he is happy that my mama Margarete gleams and is happy and maybe he is looking forward to me carin for this baby that will come out of her, or maybe he's relieved I have arrived. I guess about what Big Jim may be thinkin because I don't know him (either), and so I don't know what his hearty shake of my one shoulder means. My mother Margarete gets up and goes to the front window; Harold and his authorities continue to run on high. Margarete comments on all the many activities, and she breaks into her own conversation to ask me again if I'm ready to eat. At near midnight on any night, I am not hungry, and tonight I am only dazed. I tell her that I would like to drink something, in order to be polite in someone else's house.

Margarete has bent over to plant a kiss on Big Jim's forehead, and I try not to look. She asks whether he is hungry. He says he is always hungry. I wonder who he is talkin to, since if he is always hungry, Margarete must know that. He gets up and leaves the room. "Excuse me, folks," he says. Then his voice booms from the kitchen, "Margie, you want me to mix you a taste?"

Must be tough for him, I think. Never seen me at all, and here I am comin back into the family. I am surprised at how big he is.

I am left with the flap of the bag hangin open and nothin to do but put the Bible back in it. While everyone talks, I secret Luke's Bible away. Luke edward and David get up, say across the room to Margarete that *they* are hungry, they hug me again, then tap me — then commence to push me like sport. Like no time had passed or no change had come since the last time they saw me, when my little made me cower to their big. "Quit it!" I giggle. They both laugh. The boys all rush downstairs, Harold Grayson behind, and Margarete's belly is the only person left to look at.

Margarete gets up and goes into the kitchen. I do not follow her immediately. Then, thinkin that I would have followed Granma'am, I get up and go behind her.

THE KITCHEN IS big with appliances soldiered all around. A big electric Frigidaire. A nice white gas stove backed right up to the wall. No griddle. Plenty cabinets up and down, pine, stained brown. Nice, big table, flecked linoleum top, six chairs to go with. Look like Margarete and her new husband doin good; you can tell by the ease a the kitchen.

Margarete leans not too close to the counter, due to the baby in her belly, I suppose. She cuts pot roast with a knife so dull that she only tears the meat. This reminds me of another time. On the counter near the pot roast is a loaf of sliced white bread in store plastic. To her left is the sink, which is modern; it has two bowls.

Margarete, it turned out, cooked her food the easiest way possible. The kitchen's nice setup fooled me into expectin somethin else. Well, somethin skipped a generation, I guess. I had been raised to adopt Granma'am's attitude toward food. I bent over the food I cooked and would spend all day on a meal in a heartbeat. Would cry easy tears if it didn't turn out, would retrace my steps in my mind, and would intend to get it right the next time, say, I cooked turkey wings.

In any case, I wouldn't put a knife so dull it tears to no meat I had cooked.

MARGARETE AND BIG Jim and me are left upstairs in the apartment where I now live with them. My grip is beside the long couch. Big Jim goes back to his chair across the room and asks me if I'm tired from the trip.

"Lord knows I must be," I answer, but I am wide awake.

"Yeah?" he says. He is pulling pot roast off the plate onto some white bread, and into his hand, like his hand is a saucer. He has a look of sweet interest on his face; his face is turned toward the pot roast platter that Margarete holds. After Margarete moves away with the tray of cut meat and bread, he gets up saying he's going to the kitchen to get mayonnaise. (Margarete forgot the mayonnaise.)

I have a glass of punch in my hand and the ice tinkles so sophisticated against the glass. I don't put the glass on the coffee table because I am worried about the sweat of the glass wet-etching a permanent circle in Margarete's thin wood, although any eye can see that plenty circles have already been accidentally made. Margarete sits the tray of meat and bread on the coffee table and asks me if I want to see the rest of the house. I answer, "Uh-huh," and I take my glass with me.

There only two bedrooms even though the flat is spacious how it's laid out. The house is settled, full of everyone's things. I scour my mind trying to see if I know how long they have lived there. Margarete and Big Jim sleep in one room; they have a large bed, and Margarete has a vanity. They also have a chifforobe, dark brown outside, cedar in. Beautiful piece a work.

Luke edward and David sleep in the other room. They have small beds. David's has clear space in the middle only. In case he wants to fall down and sleep, I guess. His bed does not pretend to be made up. Luke edward's covers are pulled to the top. His bed is clear but not neatly made. Two weeks' worth a socks make mounds on the floor, and things spill out the closet like somethin is throwin it out from inside. They got one bureau, with six drawers. Not one a the drawers is closed, and on top a the bureau is all kind a pomades, hair brushes, and two, three stockin caps apiece. Course all the stocking caps could be Luke edward's, since David hasn't cared about how he looks since he wore short pants. Luke edward, on the other hand, never lost interest in himself.

David and Harold Grayson have come back into the

front room. Big Jim has finished his sandwich, but the last bites still show through his cheeks as he chews. "Neesey, your brother had to go out," David remarks. Margarete immediately says, "Wha-a-at?"

David holds the paper bags from the car's back seat, and Harold Grayson has my grip in his hand again. "Should I put this somewhere?" he asks. It's clear. He is ready to leave.

I walk over and take the grip from him, and I thank him kindly for the ride. He tells me he is sure he'll see me, and he tells me to have fun with all the new things I'm going to learn. We all say goodbye to Harold.

ALL LINED UP AND SMILING

MARGARETE AND BIG Jim have friends come over on Saturday nights. Some a their friends is also friends with Luke edward, especially this lady name Miss Tip.

Miss Tip got legs like in magazines, and she wears high heels like Margarete did before this baby. Miss Tip thinks Luke edward is handsome and that he don't need to answer the door when it rings. Miss Tip is one a them ladies with too young ways. She chases after men—like my brother—who are the same age as her ways.

One Saturday, shortly after I arrive, Margarete decides she should invite some kids over and have a little comin back to-do for me. She ask Luke edward what he think of that idea, and Luke edward say he think I *should* have kids over, so I can be popular in school. While they talk back and forth to each other, I wonder will Margarete ask me.

Margarete looks at my face and says, "Neesey, you look disappointed."

"I ain't," I answered.

"Well, good," she said. "I bet a little party will erase your long face."

Margarete invited kids my age, and they all come to

the house at three. This was maybe my third or fourth Saturday back. Margarete and I had got up early and straightened up, and Big Jim went out and got the things on the list. While Big Jim was gone, Margarete and I tussled bout what I should wear. I won. I wore my white dress I had had my picture taken in. Margarete insisted it was out a season. I said it was party style. And it was. My best dress. Margarete wanted me to wear a sweater a hers with the pants she had sent, but when I tried that outfit on and looked in the mirror, I looked like the legend — the Margarete who run off. I could still hear the country folk comment on my mama, so I adopted some stubbornness and wore my white dress.

By four o'clock Margarete and Big Jim's friends started to come too. Margarete told them she was givin me a party, and so they came by early cause they want to see the kids.

Was six kids among all the grown folks. Margarete was the first one to comment on how many grown folks was there. She said she got good friends, they so nice to come over and help her give me a party.

Margarete introduced me to her friends one by one. She met her friends when they came to the door, and then she called my name. I would get up and walk over and then she would say, "This is my daughter Neesey. Ain't she grown?" Every one a Margarete's friends agreed that I was grown. All a them except Miss Tip bent down and looked me in my face to discuss with Margarete that I did look like her. I don't really look like Margarete, though. I don't think any a those people seen my daddy. How old was I, they asked her. She told them I was almost thirteen; "Right, Denise?" she said. I nodded. Right.

Miss Tip tugged one a my plaits in the back since she

already met me before. She walked away from the cluster a the grown people to fix herself a fresh taste. She said somethin to Margarete and them about my legs. They all laughed, somethin bout me being lanky. I perked up my ears to try to hear more a what they said. Miss Tip was still doin all the talkin, and they weren't talkin bout me anymore. Her words hit the wall over top a my head.

During the party, Margarete stayed mostly in one spot, like me. She stayed in the kitchen with the grownups and they tastes. All us kids stayed in the front with Luke edward and the records. I try to pay attention to what songs Luke edward likes, thinkin I will learn his favorites later, while I am straightenin and when I can play the records by myself.

Far as I could tell, I was dressed nice as the other kids. I could tell they clothes had probably been new when they got them, but I was clean and my dress was long as any of theirs. The skirts I had brought to wear to school was the right length too so I didn't know what Margarete was talkin bout, my clothes too short.

I sat on the arm a Margarete's couch in the front room, not too far from the hi-fi. It was two or three girls sittin down on the couch and the boys was on the other side, on the chair and on the floor. Luke was in charge a the records and the dancin. He would put on songs he liked and say, "Dance, y'all," and then go talk to the grown folks till he heard the needle lean against the paper label in the center. Then he'd come back out and change the record again.

Everybody seem to like different music. Luke edward played mostly Jackie Wilson, and Margarete's friends like Ray Charles and Sam. Miss Tip's favorite is Sam. Luke edward also played some groups, and that's what I like the best. All the nice boys, lined up, smilin. Dressed up in suits and ties. Little Anthony and the Imperials and Nolan Strong and the Diablos.

Big Jim like King Pleasure.

"NEESEY, WHAT GRADE you gonna be in?" The girl talkin to me is named Dana, and I had already seen she would say somethin when nobody else would.

"Grade seven," I told her.

One a the boys got in, "You supposed to say seventh grade."

I just look at him. Even if I am supposed to say it, don't mean I have to say it after him.

"You gonna be in seventh grade, you gonna be in Missus James's class. That's the class I'm in." Her name is Brenda, and she so polite. Chubby, she has glasses, and long hair in three plaits. She has sat still in one place almost the whole party and her dress of all is the newest. She say she live with her grandmother and I think I like her the best.

I smile at her and her cheeks push her glasses up when she smile back. Her eyebrows disappear behind the heavy glasses frames. Her hair is not pressed, but brushed hard and plaited down. She has Glover's Mange on her scalp; it reeks and glistens, but everybody has been nice and not said anything. Hers is the only hair longer than mine.

"You been kept back?" It is Dana again.

"Naw," I answer.

"You have so," this a girl named Karen Lynn, hollerin. "I'm thirteen and in the seventh grade and I been kept back, so so have you."

I open my mouth to answer, and Morris the chubby boy cross the room licks his lips and says, "Karen Lynn, you always tryina make somebody dumb as you. Schools down the country is different, and she don't have to be kept back just cause you have." Morris is loud back at Karen Lynn and the record needle leans on the paper label, and Margarete and her friends hoop and holler in the kitchen; Luke comes in.

"Why ain't y'all dancin?" Luke wants to know. He puts on some music by the Marvellettes. (Lantene would have loved it—the music, Luke edward, the party, the North—the whole thing.) Luke grabs my hand before I realize embarrassment is comin. He gets me into the middle of the floor and pulls lick-your-lips Morris to dance with me. (Gettin me up, and then he won't even dance with me.) Morris is happy, and they both—Luke and Morris—start to do some steps. It is clear Morris is my dance partner and Luke edward is grown up.

Now, I don't know how to dance. Not then anyway. This is a problem.

Lantene has spent many afternoons tryina teach me, but I usually had my mind on some story told at school or some dinner I was plannin to cook with Granma'am. Payback at Margarete's party.

I tried to remember to turn my feet right or left—to bend my arms both in the same direction and slide them back and forth like a pump. That's what Lantene said I should do. I didn't much look up at Morris; I watched Luke pull other kids to the floor. Somebody in the kitchen said, "Luke got em dancin," and in a minute all the grownups circled round. Everybody knew the songs. Everybody clapped. The room bounced on the beats of the records. I heard Miss Tip talkin bout what we children did: "It's a suprise Morris can dance, ain't it, Margreet? Neesey know a few steps too. She learned a little bit down South."

The dancin and stompin raised the heat in the house.

Miss Tip watched me till I nearly gave up, and then she came and joined us kids, so then I couldn't sit down. She took one a my hands into her sweaty left palm. Dog. There I was in the center a the dance party. I started hoping I was doin somethin close to right. The hope caused a crease in my forehead. To hide the crease, I looked down at the floor.

Miss Tip had started another rowdy, thumpin circle. "Go head, Dana," was the first thing she said. And then she went on to comment on everybody. Thank goodness she didn't say nothin loud about me.

I liked dancin, or I liked music one. Lantene's mama Evelyn say of course I like music cause my mama know more bout music than anybody ever lived in Patuskie. One time Margarete come down home, and she left a 45 record of Fingertips. Me and Lantene near played the grooves off that record.

Lantene was practicin to go north round then. (She had always been fixed on that migrant dream.) Margarete had brought us the Fingertips record and showed us some new steps. The steps got sloppy from down-home silences, wild limbs, and our forgetfulness. But we still practiced what we could remember from what Margarete showed.

Lantene said I cain't dance. "I can too dance!" I hollered back, but I was lyin and we both knew it.

Lantene studied dance steps hard. She was almost mathematic about it, which was funny. Lantene could hardly count three dollars in the sun. But she could and did tell me: *Put your arms down some, don't bend em so hard! You makin corners with y'elbows, you puttin y'feet out too far, Neesey, don't let your head fall back. You sposed to keep y'head and neck straight, Neesey, pretend you lookin in y'boyfriend's chest.*

I know Lantene practiced when I was home doin lessons or when I was at school in the afternoons. But Lantene say she didn't practice, only when it was the two of us together. But I knew better than that cause she was such a sight better dancer than me.

Lantene would roll up the mat in her mama's room, and we would take the top a the record player box clean off. That way we wouldn't have to keep liftin up the top to put the needle back down on the record edge. I figured that out. When the record player was first brought, the handle went back to the front by itself. That don't work no more. We had got a little system together: whoever was closest to the record player when Little Stevie Wonder stopped blowin the harmonica, that's who moved the needle. So we just kept dancin; my arms was swingin, my hair half comin loose, us pretendin we know all the steps the city girls know, and nobody there to see how country we was. You couldn't tell Lantene she wasn't Margarete, and you couldn't tell me I wasn't Lantene. Every turn or two or three, Lantene and I would bump each other somewhere, elbow or ankle flyin. We didn't stop or say it hurt or even notice it always. We was keepin up with each other and the time. We was havin a party like in the city where we wasn't.

Got so close to night, I had to run out with the record still playin. Me and Lantene ain't say one word a partin. Grabbed up my shoes from by her mama's bedroom door, left Lantene just a-twirlin, her head hitched up the way she kept tellin me not to do. We had had us a good time, I thought, gettin back to Granma'am quick on my bare feet. When I sat down out back to wash my feet off, my teeth still lit up my new memory, and Granma'am was callin my name.

Brenda, with the glasses, involved herself in the dancin demonstration. I lined up next to her. Miss Tip has on a light green sweater top with a turtle neck; her sweater shows all her bosom shape. Miss Tip's blue skirt has neat little specks of green and orange and red in the material, brushed up like. It is a beautiful skirt, straight cut and short, and I ain't seen no material like that before. The neat nylons she wears stay right on her skin like they lickin something sweet. She has on green shoes to top off the whole outfit.

These are what I try to follow, the feet. I will never be able to shake my hips like she does, and I never get, in all my life, a full brassiere to turn and twist above my waist. I don't want to do exactly what she does, anyhow, because she is fast. So I try to mock her feet, that's all, and she says, "Good, Neesey, good."

After I get my feet to repeat her steps without stumblin, she pulls Morris again from behind, and me and Morris do the steps over and over together. By then, it is very very hot in the room, and Mama's other friends have stopped makin a circus of us kids. The grown folks are talkin again about all kinds a things and drinkin again from their tastes in the cups. Luke keeps playin records and keeps playin records, and in between the changin, he dances with Miss Tip. I can tell by their feet on the floor, they know each other pretty well. I don't look at them directly, but Luke's creased pants so near Miss Tip's nylon-naked leg make a full picture by themselves. You don't even need to see above the knee to hear the story told. He has on roach-killer shoes, so hard to come by down home. Curious, I try to do this twirl-around they showed me, so I can peek at Luke edward's top and face. His brown button-down sweater is loose on his chest and though it is striped, it matches exactly the brown of his slacks. I got a good look at my brother, but my twirl was messed up. His clothes are not remade or handed down like mine; his clothes are not gray and navy blue like David's. He does not wear plant shoes like Big Jim, and the grown women watch him dance.

Luke edward and Miss Tip dance together and talk together all afternoon. Miss Tip has accepted responsibility for keepin Luke edward's cup fresh with what's in it, she said, and Luke edward ask Miss Tip what she want to hear, or what she want to hear next. I watch them as best I can. She too old for my brother.

BOUT FORTY MINUTES before it got dark, in between records, Luke said, "Y'all better get goin." He was talkin to all us kids; he faced the hi-fi, and we were in the room behind him. Little Anthony and the Imperials start to sing, *Love is not a gadget, Love is not a toy.* Luke is slowin the music down.

Brenda walks over with her empty glass and a folded-up napkin. "Thank you for inviting me," she says while I take her glass. "I'm so glad we're in the same grade. You'll like Missus James, our teacher. She's nice." I am glad she talks to me.

Luke has opened the front closet and the kids are takin their coats. I go in the kitchen, where Margarete is, to tell her everyone is leavin, in case she has to do something.

After all the kids have left, Margarete and her friends and Luke edward and Big Jim spread out over the flat. The space that was taken up by Brenda Greenfield, her glasses, and her Glover's Mange now has ashtrays with cigarettes. The front room full a smoke.

So much goes on all evenin long. I finally found myself a corner chair sometime after all the children left.

Down, way down, I went into it. Had to be the lowest chair in Michigan. I imagined I was a lace curtain, hung quiet and still. The breeze of people's comments made me swing, but just a little. I could see, and was see-through, but mostly I was fixed in my window. Josephus come over and wanted to talk and talk to me. I'm shamed to say I fell out, dead sleep, in that chair, and I'm sure I snored through years a the stories Josephus told. Margarete woke me up when everybody was gone. I don't know what time all the grown folks left. "Luke, put up Neesey's cot, honey. Poor chile," she said, standin over my crumpled dress, "she tired as me."

After I laid down on the cot, in the middle of the house, and it was finally no people around me, there was quiet to frame me like a window, and I was still the curtain. I remember thinkin there were children from school and Josephus from the country and grown folks—Luke edward's and Margarete's and Big Jim's friends. David disappeared early on, gone to Serena, I guess. *This is as big as it gets*, I told myself. I turned over, knocked out.

In the middle of the night, I wake up thirsty. I go to the kitchen, where every dish, cup, pot, and pan in the house was dirty and on its side. They all called my name. As I recall, I took off the dress I still wore and washed up all the dishes in my slip. Also, I remember washin every ashtray ever made. Me and Granma'am ain't have no ash-trays; she used handkerchiefs for snuff.

Only a sliver of window showed through the curtain, and my head, at that time, reached the line of the lowest pane. In the glass was my reflection, and behind that the dark; I talked to myself that middle of the night: *Well, Neesey, now you here.*

THE DAYS WERE so short when I moved to Detroit that by the time it was time to cook dinner, the panes in the window were dark. So most of the time when I looked there, my face stared back from the glass. Over time I began to witness to this window, and to imagine that the window witnessed me. I watched myself grow in the black night reflections. I tried to ease the sadness I had noticed from my face. I saw the inches of maturity gain on me, as I grew up over the bottom panes, and up toward the top ones. I mouthed words to Granma'am as I faced the window that faced south.

It was the window over the kitchen sink, where I spent all my meal-cooking, dish-washing, and later, diaper-soaking time. I came to know everything that could be seen from that window, and in all the seasons too. Got to the point, of course, that my daily watching happened fast, so my eyes turned inward then.

That was my window. I was twelve and standing at the sink when we met.

I ONLY HAD that one party at Margarete's. Most of the rest of the time I lived there, I was alone. I cleaned and studied and learned to play the hi-fi.

In the back of Margarete's closet I had found something that wasn't hers. It was too big, and it was too old for anything she would like to wear. The first time I stumbled on it, I was scared Margarete might come in and catch me there so I didn't pull it out. But once I got her schedule down good, and once I knew the schedules of the rest of the house, I could go in there and take my time.

The porter's smock had SOUTHERN machine-stitched on the sleeve. It was white, but dulled to maize by time. From the size of it, you would think my daddy was almost as big as Big Jim. Course, I don't know how it fit. The sleeves were long and seven large buttons proceeded down the front. From the way it smelled, you would think my daddy wore Margarete's perfume.

I usually went to look at the smock when Margarete first left the house. Because then I could know that she wouldn't come in on me. I was scared to take it off the hanger for a while. One day, I was playin Little Anthony. I had decided they were my favorites. I went to Margarete's closet and took the smock hanger off the rod. I took the smock off the hanger and put the hanger on the doorknob. I stood in front of Margarete's vanity and held the smock up in front of me. It had SOUTHERN RAILROAD stitched on the chest pocket too. Little Anthony sang, and in the mirror, I danced behind the smock. Then I turned the smock with its procession of buttons to face me. I threw the right arm over my shoulder, and rubbed my hand up and down the back; eight buttons there were. I held the left arm out. We danced. *If we could start anew, I wouldn't hesitate. I'd gladly take you back. And tempt the hands of fate. Tears on my pillow, Pain in my heart, Caused by you. Ooh, ooh, ooh, ooh.*

GIBRALTAR JONES

WHEN I WENT to ask Missus James how come I couldn't find the Carolinas she told me that it's a plural name for the two Carolinas in the United States; she asked me do I know about North and South Carolina. I tries not to get situated in my disappointment that I didn't figure that out, and I answers her Yes, I seen the Carolinas—lease I can say it and picture it in my head now that I know what is bein discussed. To prove myself, I tell her that North Carolina is long and South Carolina is short. Best that way, I keep talkin, cause my mama and my Granma'am say it's a lot a problems in the South, so it make sense that the South is short like it is.

"Where is your grandmother, Deneese?" Missus James ask me.

I sure do like the way she talk. She so crisp and proper and even like a drum. All this rumination and I done forgot the question.

"Scuse me, what you ax me?" I have to ask again.

She wince. I realize I seen her do that before. I think, dog, after I done answered smart, now I'm askin stupid. I feel like runnin out, but I just picked up one foot and start to rub it on my other sock.

Missus James looked down at my feet, me standin next to her desk and all. "Stop scratching, Deneese," she say.

I put my foot back down.

First, she sighs. "Neesey, do you know your language is atrocious?"

This halts my thinkin altogether. She returns to our conversation then as if I don't look blank or smacked down, as if she has not expected me to answer after all. Atrocious, I decide to wonder exactly what is that. "I as-k-eduh where your grandmother lives," she say.

She might as well say Cakka Lakky at the end. She leave a space between her words, like I don't know where they start and finish. She makin me nervous.

"Down home in Fuhginia," I answer. "Down Souf," I add, quietlike. I try to leave some space between my words.

"South," Missus James say back to me, and she aims her head at mine and holds her tongue between her teeth like beef in bread.

"Say it, Deneese," she say to me; "say South." Tongue sandwich again.

"Say ask, Deneese," she say to me, "ask." She still looks at me straight on, close like I'm a newspaper.

I run out the room. Then I start to hope that my socks is soakin up the pee, cause before I got through the school-house door, it's just a-runnin. I hear Josephus callin t'me, and I imagine he will catch up, but finally he doesn't come along. I decide he has left me alone to my shame, and so I forget all about him.

I didn't run all the way home cause it's a long way, but I ran four corners away from the school, had my coat in my hand and my geography book pressed close to my chest. Missus James sure did get my shame to racin that day. I am a country gal, and I don't know top or bottom a them city sounds she be makin. I keep hearin her say that word ask, could hear it only in my head on account a I don't have no ability to make no sound like that, not with the mouth I got, at least. Sound to me like somebody in a hurry to leave the table, rushin, got the chair cocked on the back legs, and they mind already in the next room.

The walk home was all the way one wet step on ask, the next wet step on south, big tongue a beef sandwich between my teeth. My socks just squished, gettin clammy in the cole. My freezin cole feet in my wet socks is what reminded me to put my coat on. I had it on my arm while I was lookin inside my head at Missus James movin her tongue round. I wished I could make the right pronunciations. Exchange for the nice coat she give me. I wished I hadn't a peed and run off like I did. I wants to stand forward like somebody with sense.

Our geography books is the newest books we got, and they nice. We only have geography lessons two days out the week, but I carries mine home most every day. I has looked ahead at all the maps. At the front and at the back is pictures a the whole world. The maps in between what has all the names a states and towns and cities and counties on it, well they is just as interesting. Every place inside a every other place got a name of its own. Sometime I would like to understand all these things about continents and countries and bodies a water automatic, instead of havin to read about it over and over every time. I would like to rememorize all the cities in one state, but I cain't yet decide which state. Missus James say it's a good idea I have, it will do me good to work on recitin from memory, it will help my pronunciation.

I looked close at Georgia when Missus James say she

leavin, see is Georgia the one. I looked close at Virginia too. Patuskie is not on the map, and Missus James say small places are not on the maps because not enough people live in each place. Virginia is so far away from Detroit it just makes my heart ache, so I looked again at Georgia. Georgia could be far away as the moon, and it wouldn't unsettle my heart.

Georgia is next to Alabama on one side and South Carolina on the other. Underneath Georgia is Florida, and that is where the United States end. It pushes out into the ocean. Missus James say she live near Valdusta, and when I looked on the map I had to change how I spelled it, to Valdosta, even though if you sound it out it sound like Valdusta. Missus James could live in Florida, on account a the map show state lines, and Valdosta is near the state line between Florida and Georgia.

Margarete say they got a boy, a son, so I guess it's three a them movin to Georgia. Georgia is more south than Virginia, I noticed from the map. But it's all south. I'm learnin plenty about this line between the South and the North for the whole country. Missus James say this line is named after two men named Mason and Dixon. Used to be a line about Pennsylvania—that's another state— and then it became a line about South and the slaves.

I tell Missus James that I wished I could understand this better. She say don't worry about understandin it cause knowin that there is something peculiar, something to understand, is enough. And that later on, I can go back to this thing that I will most certainly remember because it puzzled me, and learn to understand it then. I say OK, but I kind of drag that agreement out a my mouth: she is leavin and I have the fear that this won't be discussed anymore. I ain't never heard nothin about it before now. She looks my disappointment dead in the face and she say the important thing to learn from this is that history complicates things.

History complicates things, I think. Ain't no way I'm going to forget that. I don't even write it down. And now, here it is, all these years later, and when I think of history, I think of all this, and the way it complicates.

I WROTE TO Lantene bout what I'm learnin—the letters got thick while Harold Grayson worked so hard. Lantene used to always be talkin bout what different places and things she wants to see, and in my geography book, there is a name for every place. Except places small as Patuskie. Lantene don't want to go no small places nohow, and I wished she had a book to look in like me.

I wished I had known about state lines when I was ridin with Harold Grayson, see what they look like on the road.

There is plenty more to this geography than I know bout yet. I cain't really tell if I'm behind or not cause when the teacher ask them geography questions hardly nobody can answer, so I guess it's new for all us.

Now that I have the maps to look up all bout this country, I occupy myself sometimes lookin at the rivers. I imagine where Patuskie would be, what the geography book calls inland. I look for place names to practice my pronunciation.

Luke edward had tried to tell me bout the country way I talk when I first come, same as Missus James. I had just shut my mouth there round the house. Wasn't nobody home most a the time but me no way, so it was easier to just keep quiet than to give Luke edward somethin to be makin a mockery about. Plus I thought he was teasin, or pickin, like about my headrag and cleanin clothes. But he was tellin—or foretellin—the stone gospel truth.

Missus James, she wasn't makin no mockery. I knew that. She was talkin to me bout the same things the other people laughed at, but she wasn't laughin. She was just waggin that tongue round tryina demonstrate how my way a talkin got to change.

Granma'am said I ain't no ways ignorant. She said God give me enough in the head for several. *You kin read and you kin reason and that is good. Valentine and Fitzwilly both say you could improve y'writin and I trust in time you will.* I remember this that Granma'am said when I got sad bout my talkin, and I practiced movin my thick tongue round.

I also remember that Granma'am was a little shy discussin education. Her experience of it was shallow, she said. She told me to do everything Mr. Fitzwilly said, to the letter. And she asked Miz Valentine Kinsey to look over my homework; they arranged that that would be my payment for sittin for Miz Kinsey's kids. Miz Kinsey said that wasn't enough, though; she said you have to give children, me included, some reward, and she always gave me a few quarters in addition.

I THOUGHT I had seen the ocean closest to Richmond one time, when Granma'am took me and the boys. But Margarete say that she remember that time and it was the wide part a the New River we went to.

Well, it was the one time we went to the water. Luke and David used to come down and we would remember it all together, seem like then I could remember it better. I know that means I hardly remember it at all, but also I know I was a little mad bout it cause Granma'am always say that the water was too cold, and I was much too little a girl. Not like I knew how to swim. Figures, I thought then, the one time in my life I gets to see real ocean and they don't let me get in the water. From what they told, my brothers swam they behinds straight across and now that I got my geography book and have learned about rivers and oceans, I know that what they said ain't so at all.

OUR NEW TEACHER wrote her name, *G. Pearson, Teacher*. And she wrote *A. James, Former Teacher*. Put both names on the chalkboard and on the tackboard, written in her teacher-drawn hand. The new teacher was in the class-room, and the board covered with marks, on the Monday after the Friday when Missus James left. No seam in that cloth.

One a the first few days after the new teacher come, she asked us to write down what we like or what we miss about Missus James. She say Missus James had told her about each student, and now she wanted us students to tell her about Missus James. She say we could tell what Missus James taught us that we liked. Or some things she did that we will miss, or some songs she taught us to sing that we want to sing again.

She say we got to write at least five sentences, and if they real good, she will mail them to Missus James in Georgia. I was very excited about the mail to Georgia. She say that's our assignment for the rest a the afternoon, and when we finished we could give it to her and come back tomorrow.

I finished fast on account a I been writin so many let-ters to both Granma'am and Lantene. But I was careful on account a I secretly would like my letter to get in the mail. I wrote: *It was cole when I first come to Detroit and Missus James tole me I could ask her any thang I want to know. And so I ask her how come it was so cole in Detroit, and she explain to me bout the farther north you git the more cole it git and how plus in Detroit the wind off Lake St. Clair pick up water and that make the air wet stead a dry. And any body kin figure that the cole water in the wet air is worser on the skin than cole dry air, and thas how I learnt bout the weather and geography at the same time. And then Missus James ask me if I had any sisters, and I said naw I got two big brothers and so the next Monday she brought me a hand me down coat from a girl at her church and Lord that coat was so much warmer than the one Margarete give me it have a big button right up at the neck.*

And then after I looked over my work, I tried to correct my spellin. Missus James had said I had big problems with communicatin in English, and that my problems with spellin was part. Missus James had made me cry several times, but I didn't write that down. Josephus say his uncle Jump say ain't no problem can be solved till what the problem is is clear. So Josephus say I should be glad Missus James say what my problems are so I can get to solvin them. Missus James don't say much a nothin to Josephus far as I can tell, and since Josephus is havin somethin to say right then I want to ask him what do he think about that. But Josephus is wantin to race me down the boulevard and that takes my mind off things.

Missus James paid a lot a attention to Morris in our class. Seem like she give him the attention for all the boys put together. She call Morris to the board to do math problems. She have him read out loud in the front a the class by her desk. Once, I seen her give him a bow tie to wear. Like she give me the coat. She send notes home to his mama, and talk to him bout how was church when he stop by her desk at recess on Mondays.

Morris is a very smart boy. And once, later, Josephus did say that he thinks teachers prefer the smartest kids. He don't think they can help it. Well, Morris is very smart. He told me he has encyclopedias at home that his mother bought, and none a the books are missing. When I found that out, I wished he was a girl so he could invite me over to his house so I could look and see. Brenda Greenfield had more a things than anybody I visited: gloves, a piano, hair ribbons, hats, more than ten dresses. No encyclopedias, though.

While I was chewin on my pencil, still concentratin on my spellin, my distraction bout Morris reminded me bout a poem he had read front the class one time. I liked the poem very much and Missus James gave me a sheet a paper with the poem written down. I rememorized it on account a it reminded me a my daddy. And Missus James had said good. Poems were good for me to study and recite cause it would get my ear used to hearin good English. Thinkin bout it, I wrote the poem down at the bottom a my letter.

"Epilogue" by Countee Cullen

The lily, being white not red,
Contemns the vivid flower,
And men alive believe the dead
Have lost their vital power.

Yet some prefer the brilliant shade,
And pass the livid by;
And no man knows if dead men fade
Or bloom, save those that die.

My letter did get mailed.

MISSUS PEARSON ASK me where I am from.
    I answer her, "Patuskie."
    "Where is that?" she asks me.
    "By Richmon," I answer her.

Missus Pearson say for me to repeat, "Rich-monD."

"Rich-monD," I repeat.

Missus Pearson say, "Near Rich-monD."

"Near Rich-monD."

Missus Pearson say that when the kids talk bad bout me and call me Cakky-lakky they makin jokes bout me bein from the Carolinas. Missus James had told me that. Missus Pearson say the kids sayin southern Negroes don't know how to talk. I don't know why they say southern Negroes don't know how to talk. They may not talk North-like but they—we—talk. I kept my head down in the books much as I could, on account a Missus Pearson like to stop me in my sentences, not like Missus James who least would wait. And I kept my mouth shut much as I could. While I was studyin the maps lookin for places for my pronunciation, that's when I found Gibraltar. This was Granma'am's mama's name, Gibraltar. It's in a country called Spain, which I ain't never heard tell of before. I didn't know Granma'am's mama was named after geography. Granma'am ain't said nothin to me bout Spain. Wonder why Granma'am ain't never discussed this with me, what with her mother havin that name and all.

I remember what Granma'am said bout Gibraltar: *Gibraltar was my mama like Margarete is yours. Jones was her plantation name. Gibraltar Jones. The people what owned the land was origined from Wales. They talked amongst themselves about Wales and England too. They had things stitched in their linens havin to do with Wales. Every mornin when all us chillen got up, my mama Gibraltar had us to take turns tellin what we had seent in our sleepwalks. This was what we talked amongst ourselves about. Mama said at night is when the secrets show. If we didn't wake up wid our night dreams clear, Mama had us to talk about what we remembered from what had happent durin the day before. I never did learn how to make my mind make good records like my mama intended us to. My mama's mind was like a broad high stone. She had it full wid pictures a all she had seen and heard tell of, etched in and kept turnt from the masters. All a coloreds would come ask Gibraltar somethin they got confused about, or check wid Gibraltar when some'm seem to be gettin falsified in time. Other coloreds come to ask her what she thought might happen, too. When I was near grown, bout twelve or thirteen, my mama said that somethin was bout to bust inside her and she thought h'it would take her on Home. She callt each one a us to her side at the washin pail; she ask me if I had learnt how to watch and remember, how to witness. I told her that I had. She made me promise to look after my brother. He was a year older than me, and he refused to hear talk a Mama goin, po' thing. I promised Mama I would take care a him, and I did. I don't know the timin, after she told me she thought she was goin, and when she actually went. But she did go on. She never looked sick or peaked, and she kept up insistin that we should watch and study our own inside. She beat our clothes clean to the very end. She cooked cornbread and hog maws till the very end. She gave us her mornin instruction till the end. Was many a grievin nigra once Gibraltar went on.*

Folks didn't understand my calm, thought I was stopped up. The women took me and gave me a hard river bath tryina git me to loose my sadness. Finally, I told them that my mama had warned me. They made me tell them all that she had said, and then after I did that, then they let me be.

We was two motherless children. I took care a my brother like I had promised, and the other womens took care a me.

I asked Granma'am about her brother. "Oh, he done passed on now too, long ago."

"What was his name, Granma'am?"

"Joe. Joe and Martha Jones was us, children of Gibraltar."

A LOT A these names a places is really nice. Florida, Indiana, Montana, Missouri. There a place way up in Canada called Alberta. What a nice name, Alberta, sound like down home. For a minute, I wished my name was Alberta. Like a woman's name, and a man's name, and a place in a foreign country at the same time. But then Canada started to rise for me, like steam from the cleanin pail. Spain too. Canada is big and wide and north, and I ain't never heard nothin bout it, not until my geography book. And Spain is the country surroundin my great Granma'am's name. That made it even sweeter. So then I start to wish my name was Canada. And then Spain. Canada Deneese. Or just plain Spain. Seem strong to be named after land.

ONE DAY WE was coming down the boulevard and I was thinking about the cold. So to distract myself I went back to my last night's dream, where Margarete's stomach blazed like a lion's hair. That's when I thought to ask Josephus about Margarete's belly, which had been worrying me.

"You know about the stomach shape when you pregnant, J?"

"What you talkin bout, Denise?"

Maybe I could shake something up in him, maybe he knew and didn't know he knew. Josephus usually knew the common-sense practical things. But usually he knew he knew, too.

"My mother Margarete's havin a baby, you know." I sighed and explained. "And I cain't remember which shape a the stomach means girl or boy."

"Oh," Josephus says.

"It's if it's high it's one thing, boy or girl, and if it's low, it's the other."

He laughs and says, "Yeah."

He knows what I'm talking about. "Did you forget too?" I ask him.

"Never paid much attention, didn't know in the first place. Mostly ladies' things to know, Deneesey. You better hope the baby's strong, and not be worried about what kind it is."

I want to go back to the subject to try to encourage him to get behind his "ladies'" and "not ladies'" things to know. But then I decide to forget about it. Either it will come back to me, or it is just part of the country I have had to leave behind. I expect and hope it will come back to me. My memory does come back sometimes, bold and unannounced, intact.

My forgetting the stomach part was curious and huge. How was it that something I knew, really knew, had simply left my mind? (I had forgot that gravy can only be made with hot, hot water, but this was more basic than gravy.) I tried to call my knowledge in, to rake it up, to sweep it to the middle of the road. Nothing worked. All the time I stared into my dark mind, searching for this memory I couldn't find, I had the sense that somewhere in my head it looked at me dead on, legs crossed, and the top one swinging.

As quietly as it kept its distance, it reappeared later on. All at once, there she was, alert, invigorated, and not apologetic. From this my first remembered struggle to recall a forgotten thing, I learned how memory does its circle dance—steadily, deviously, protectively—in the head.

ONE A MY early days in her classroom, Missus Pearson said we will now have a lesson on grammar. We gone talk about nouns, pronouns, and adjectives in this lesson. She said out loud: They called the young man a cad. She say cad is a noun because people called the man that name. She want us to give her a different noun. She writes on the board: They called the young man a _____. The chalk sails over the black slate making lovely curving letters; not screeching or scraping like noise us kids make who don't know how to write with chalk. "All right, class, what might people call him?" Karen calls out a knucklehead. Missus Pearson smiles and says, "Another example." Dana calls out a hard worker. And Missus Pearson says good, and writes the two words, hard worker, neat across the blank.

I have never heard of that word cad before, and so I stop at her desk at the end of school and say, "Missus Pearson, what do cad mean?"

"You mean, what does cad mean?"

"Yes," I say, "what does cad mean?"

"Look it up," she says.

"OK," I say, opening up my book again. "How you spell it?" I didn't write it down before.

"How do you spell it?"

"Oh," I say, "how do you spell it?" Now I'm concentrating on remembering what we talking about. Then she said, "Look it up." She handed me a old school dictionary. She said I could have it for my own. I was very excited. There wasn't much wrong with it, only the back cover was missing, and page 144 was half torn out.

She had me use the dictionary to learn to spell. To sound out words so I could find them, and then to seek their meanings. I realize from trying to look up words that I don't know how to spell most of what I say out loud. When I finally get it found in the dictionary, I usually am right about what I mean. This confuses me some, that I don't know how to spell what I know how to say. Another plain thing; not forgotten, but never learned.

Missus Pearson say I should match every word I say out loud with a word I can find in the dictionary. She say because I'm speaking English, any word I cain't find in the dictionary is either not a word, or I don't know how to write what I'm saying.

Missus Pearson say this looking up will not help me with the rules, however. Mostly because the rules explain how to use words in combination. But, she say, the individual words I can work on learning by myself. And I should concentrate on learning the rules from her, since the rules are best explained, then practiced.

I had known how to use a dictionary before, even though I didn't have one of my own. Mister Fitzwilly had taught me. One time he was reading us a poem from a book and he used the word loam. I asked him what do loam mean, except in my mind I was spelling it like lome. He pointed to the dictionary on his desk and said to look it up. I picked up the dictionary and looked in it for lome. It was a big rich book what with all the pages, with all the different words. I wished I could stop and read the other words I passed going down the alphabet to l-o and then to l-o-m and then to l-o-m-e. "Mister Fitzwilly, it ain't in here," I said. "The next word after where it should be is loment," I said, some kind a fruit.

"It is spelled l-o-a-m," he told me, using his one good arm to stack together the papers he had graded. I had finished straightening up the classroom and taking out the readers for his Tuesday night group. Tuesday nights the older kids who had to work but still wanted to read came, like my friend Lantene. "Oh," I said, and before I turned the pages back, I snuck and read the meaning for lofty.

Well, the all-in-all is that loam means dirt. A richer mix a dirt than regular, but it still means dirt. And I had thought that I only was able to find it because Mister Fitzwilly had spelled it out for me.

"How can I look it up when I don't know how to spell it?" I asked Missus Pearson about that word cad. She told me I knew enough about the English language to figure out how to spell things. "If you look up the word and it isn't there, you know that you have misspelled it, and you need to try another way. There are only a few possibilities for any given word. And besides, spelling from the sound of words will help you with your speech problems."

When I got home with my new dictionary, I started with k-a-d, and of course that was wrong. I almost tried k-e-d next, but after I listened in my mind to what she said again, I knew it sounded like add, so I decided to try "c-a." There it was, plain as day, a lowbreed of a man. Only one *d*.

She promised me that if I did what she said I would learn to speak English and to make a life for myself. For Gloria Pearson, one was the same as the other.

Missus Pearson say, "Learning to speak proper English is absolutely necessary for all Americans." She say, "People come to America thousands at a time, and they would give an arm to have the opportunity to learn rules of English grammar and pronunciation, to learn to speak proper English."

She stop. "Say that," she say to me. I'm good at repeating by now and I'm ready whenever she stop.

"Larnin to speak propah," I try.

"Learning to speak proper English," she stop me. She

leans to me, I'm in the front desk. She fixes her mouth like a duck bill, coaxin me to say learn.

"Larning to speak prop-per English," I try.

"Learning," she prompt me.

"Learning," I say.

"Learning is ab-so-lute-ly essential," she prompt me.

I take a deep breath. "Ab-soe-loo-tuh-ly essential."

Missus Pearson is smilin.

Missus Pearson tell me to practice closin my throat on all the i-n-g words. I been practicin, that's how come I can finally say learning. Close off my throat to make a endin, she say. She also teach me about pushin out my lips to improve my vowel sounds, and pushin my tongue off my teeth to make clean *ts*. "Remember that words have beginnings and endings, and if you don't say the beginnings and endings clearly, then you haven't said the word," she said.

The hardest words I have left to get are the *here*s and other ear words. You see a short word, but you got to move your mouth around a lot to get it right. She had me promise not to say mouf or souf anymore too. She say very few words in English end in *f* or *f* sounds. She say *of* and *staff* and the rough-tough family are just about it. I promised, and now I practice harder on words like *mouth south birthday*; I put my tongue between my teeth.

MISSUS GLORIA PEARSON say the only thing she want me to think about is learnin to speak the king's English. I told Missus Pearson I wants to learn, and she say, "Say I want."

Missus Gloria Pearson say she used the sentences we wrote about Missus James, and the things Missus James told her about us to decide how to work with each one. She start up the after-school work right away.

Missus Pearson say me and Josephus Johnson is the two worst in the class on account a we'se both straight up from down South. She say we got to stay late in school until we understand more about English and can speak the language so we is understood by other people. Josephus, he ask her what's so wrong with the way we talk and Missus Pearson say she gone show us one mistake at a time. She say Josephus can walk me home since it be gettin dark early, before we finished. Josephus was already walkin me home, but neither one a us said. She tell us, "You both tell your mothers you'll be getting extra help." Josephus's mama is in Arkansas. I told Margarete I have to stay late at school to learn the rules a English, and she say I have to learn them by the new moon in March cause after that I have to be home, help with the baby.

One day Josephus and me is the only ones in the classroom; it is clear by then that we are the two to stay the course. I intend to learn while I can before I have to spend all my extra time with Margarete's baby. Missus Pearson has been talkin bout verbs. It's time for us to go home, and I am plannin to try to understand this that I have learned today, later on tonight, after I wash the dishes. Missus Pearson go back to the board and write D-E-N-I-S-E.

"Deneese," she call me, "are you aware that this is the usual spelling of your name?"

Usual, I think. I shake my head. Naw. "Don't shake your head, Denise. Say no."

I say, "Naw."

"Say no." She has no impatience in her voice, but there's something else in it that makes me want to tip my head to the side. She pushes her lips out saying no, and holds them tubelike.

"Noe," I say, with tubelike lips.

"Well, this is the correct spelling of your name. It is the American spelling. I will record your name this way in our school records." She keeps on: "The two of you are excused for the day. I will see both of you again tomorrow. Josephus, walk Denise all the way to her block."

We get up, and put on our coats, and leave Missus Pearson in the classroom.

Josephus take me down the boulevard way like usual. There is shrubs and trees without leaves. Would be kind a like a park in the spring and summer. Josephus is talkin a little. I'm not really payin attention to him or the boulevard cause I'm thinkin I'm dumb I have spelled my own name wrong.

What if Margarete's baby had already been born? Then I would not have been round after school to learn this. I would have grown old and older spellin my own name wrong! And why don't I know how to spell my own name? My blood starts to rush; what else have I missed? Josephus is talkin, but I do not listen. I hear him callin my name, and in his voice, my name is spelled wrong. "J," I say, "you think I'm ig'nant?"

He stops what he talks about. "Naw, you ain't ig'nant," he assures me and he laughs a little. "We jes country, an we gotta change cause we ain't in the backwoods no more."

"You think I kin learn all these things she talkin bout, J?"

"You learnin bettah than all these ole city kids," he say. "You probly the smartest in the classroom."

My worry narrows my face. I have worked hard just to come to find I cain't spell my own name. Josephus continues to talk to me, and I can hardly hear. "You mind that I call you J?" I ask abruptly.

He stops what he mutters. "Naw," he says to me, smilin again, "I like jes one letter by itself."

So when she wrote them letters up there like that and look at me bout how to spell my name, well, I didn't rightly know what to say behind that, and I thought I cain't say much a nothin on account a I don't know nothin bout the rules. I remember to this day walking out that room with them DENISE letters I ain't never thought of before written in the neat schoolteacher block cross the front board.

Next time somebody as-su-kuh me my name, I'm a say Gibraltar. Gibraltar Jones.

MISSUS PEARSON TOOK a likin to me after I spelled my name right. She asked me to stay in recess one day, and she sit me down in one a the front seats. I liked that too. She asked me if I knowed I'm a smart young lady. I left the air for her, and she went on to tell me that I could be a teacher one day if I kept goin to school and if I studied most all a my spare time. She start to tell me about the college she went to and how important it was for Negroes to be both teachers and pupils. I was distracted early in the sentence: thinkin bout keepin in school and how Missus Pearson say I have to do the after-school work exactly from three to five-thirty, and how the baby comin soon and I will probably not have no spare time. Plus, Margarete done already told me I have to leave right when school end, come spring.

Missus Pearson see my eyes walk away. Then she ask me do I know what my problem is. I leave all the air for her again. She tell me that I ain't ig'nant, that I shouldn't let nobody make me think I'm ig'nant, that my problem is my language. That I live in a country where English is spoke and I don't know how to speak it. Missus Pearson say I have good things to say, ideas and observations, and if I could learn to speak English, I could become more important. Nobody who sounds dumb will ever be important, she say, no matter how much potential they have. Nobody will ever understand you, nobody who can help you rise, unless you can speak the language of the nation. That's what she said. Missus Pearson tell me that first I need to learn how to use my mouth, that English is a hard language and that it requires that the mouth do its share a work.

I like the way she talk. And I know she right about hard work on account a she been tryina teach me to make sounds I ain't never made, and to say words I thought I was already sayin all the time. When Missus Pearson talk, sound to me like some other language, musical. And when she talk specific to me like she do sometimes, I be tryina to keep my eyes from dancin all in her face.

WHEN I DO good in the after-school class, Josephus will reach up and shake my shoulder with his big, country hand. He be sittin behind me, and glad I can improve. I don't have to look back to know what his grin look like. Josephus think he ain't no good at this talkin, or practicin English. He think he ain't good at school, period. But he say Missus Pearson really like me cause I learn so good and so fast. I done seen Josephus grin about this many times. We be walkin home and he tell me how smart I am. He tell me I'm smarter than most a these old dumb kids from Detroit and that Missus Pearson act like she think I'm real smart. I ask him is that last part true.

MISSUS PEARSON ON another day is having me repeat things about the weather. "Col-duh," she make me say.

"Cold-uh," I say, concentrating on the "duh" sound at the end.

Josephus say that when I repeat after Missus Pearson I sound more like her all the time. I listen to what Josephus is saying to me, and in my head I repeat after him the way I repeat after Missus Pearson, and I make the words have beginnings and endings in my head on account a Josephus don't say them. So then I realize that I'm not really paying attention to what Josephus say. All his thoughts is stopped and tumbling in my head.

Missus Pearson don't stay on J about how dumb he sound, not like she do me. He talk almost the same as when we started the after-school work. J said he don't care; he is just waiting after school to walk with me. My forehead creases: why ain't she making a improvement out a him? Why don't she care about his English like mine?

Right use of the English language. That's what Missus Pearson say she want us to learn. No, appropriate use is what she call it. No, proper English, that's it.

J and I are leaving Missus Pearson's classroom. She wants to know why we fly out the door like we do. "Fly out the door?" I ask her. I might of said already that I left her classroom longingly.

"Yes," she says. "I watch you two through this window." And she points to the first window in the classroom; it's directly across from the teacher's desk. I follow her finger, and look through the glass, and there is the road we go down before we make our first turn. The road stretches out, concrete gray-yellow in these days before spring. I wonder how we look, me with my brown legs and white socks, racing J down the block, trying to keep my books from falling out the strap.

"Josephus, do you have anything to say?" she asks

him, while I stand there dreaming, watching that special kind of future, the road.

"Naw," he answers.

"Noe," she says.

"Noe, ma'am," he repeats.

"Denise, why do the two of you run away every day?" She turns back to me cause she knows if she presses me, I will make the struggle and answer.

"We ain't runnin *away*, Missus Pearson," I say. "We jes runnin."

She doesn't correct me, but I hear in my English where I'm wrong. Not only that but I ain't said much a nothing. Her authority and corrections a my English all the time make me tend not to say what I might say from my head, since I know she probly won't let me finish my thought. She dismisses us, and I think to myself that her question ain't answered. *Children just run, where there's space to*, is how I answer her question in my head. Me and J, we are careful not to run that day. But this and her later noise about Clara let me know that children are not what she knows about or really cares enough about to understand.

HOG DREAMS

DAVID IS UP and bathed, and he tells me Serena is coming over and that she will have dinner with us. Then he and Serena are going to go around and see all her family, he says. I say OK and take out another plate to add to the stack I have set on the counter.

Margarete is reading in bed. It is Easter. I am a mess. Margarete is so pregnant her voice has lowered, so every time she speaks, the baby's in it, even if she's just asking me to bring her nail polish from the coffee table. And Big Jim has asked me to cook a ham for Easter Sunday. Margarete knew he asked, and nobody was saying anything. So I went to the market and got his ham; my hands shook and I felt sappy sad, like crying. At home, I absently smeared a paste of honey, orange rind, and powdered cloves over the store-bought ham skin.

It was when I was smearing the ham I decided to go on to church by myself. I went to the notebook I kept and found the bus directions to Hartford, Brenda Greenfield's church. Saturday night I washed and ironed the best skirt and blouse I had. I went into Margarete's room and told her that I thought I'd go on to church and was she sure she didn't want to come with me. "No, Neesey.

I'm too tired," she told me, so I got up Easter Sunday and went to early service.

I saw the raised arms of the church from the bus. Reminded me a how the trees broke the fields down home, providing a direction for you to point yourself. You just angle for that break in the trees. Each arm of the church had a bell in it, and the bells were already ringing when the bus let me out.

I half concentrate on the service. Sitting in the sanctuary, I just think about Puckett and my daddy. Missus Pearson say I dream a lot. I don't think I dream as much as I remember. Thinking about the two a them, I wonder if Puckett is dead or alive. Regardless, Puckett and my daddy are both long gone now—my daddy to heaven and Puckett to somewhere. The church seem like it's healthy, and I'm glad to see it. May be in a little of a downward cycle, but the program say that Hartford church been there more than seventy years already. So if they go down, they probably will come up again in time. When service ends, I go to the missionary bench to shake hands with the church mothers. I am reaching for Granma'am, of course. And also for my father, and for when I was little, when Easter was easy and ham didn't shake me.

SOMETHING BOTHERED MY vision, like a fly buzzing round, after I got to be friends with Brenda Greenfield. At first I thought it was just how much her house and the cars on the block reminded me of the well-off Kinseys down home. Took me months to see clear, took me that long to feel recognition come down. But finally, one evening after we had ice tea in Brenda's room, I knew hers was the same neighborhood we had lived in before my daddy died. It just came right to me in her bedroom, that secret I didn't know I had, and that buzzing fly finally dropped dead.

The houses were sprawling and all the lawns neat cut. Negroes had new cars. They shopped at Hudson's, and some of them, like Brenda, had vacuum canisters to use on their rugs.

Margarete had moved and moved. I guess you can't keep no nice house when you don't have a husband to help you with it or some granddaddy money like Brenda Greenfield got. I looked up at the houses, see would I recognize anything else. Most every one had new paint, and I wasn't about to wander around looking for the blue house with the changed-every-year shutter colors that we had lived in with my daddy. The blue would probably be long gone, and plus, I might get lost.

"David, Brenda Greenfield lives over on Dexter, off Grand River. Is that where we usedta live?"

"Yep."

"Where exactly?

"Two blocks over from Dexter, on Tireman."

"Yeah, you seen our old house lately?"

"Nope."

WHEN I GET back to the house from church, I go straight back to the kitchen. Margarete has moved from her bedroom to the couch. Big Jim is happy as usual about the food the house smells like. I have already snapped the green beans and put them on. I watch this morning's church, and Puckett, I look at the old missionaries in my head; how they leaned back in the benches and asked me *Where is your family?*, peering up through thick experience and weak eyes.

After Serena comes and after David and Big Jim and Margarete start to hover round the food, I set the table.

Can't wait for Luke edward any longer. When she hears the plates clattering, Serena comes in from David's side and starts to pour fresh glasses of the punch I made. She puts one at the right of each setting because she loves a nicely set table. Serena loves my punch too, and she brought me the colored tumblers we use after I fixed punch at a dinner that she came to one time before. She calls it my country punch. (We made it for parades and such.) The tumblers are bright, and each one different, and they are cool when you touch them. Aluminum. Every time I use them I wish we had other nice things to set places with, like matching silverware.

Big Jim sets his little ham dead center, and is standing up choosing the knife he wants to use. Serena and I are talking about what she is sewing, and Margarete is telling David how starving she is. I know she is trying not to say she wonders where is Luke edward, it is quarter to three. Luke edward knows that we eat around three—that's when I always set dinner on the table, every Sunday the Lord send. He will come sidling in, at just the last minute, looking like he's had a long Saturday night. Big Jim will set his jaw and glare at Margarete, and Margarete will not look back at Big Jim until the subject is changed, and Margarete will be calmer and less exhausted now that she can see Luke edward is all right.

But *I* am not all right. I am tired and nervous, too much of both for somebody my age. I want to serve Granma'am's dinner—a nice roast chicken with light gravy, rolls. We could still have snap beans. The cast iron is too heavy now for Granma'am to lift. Maybe Macie's daughter is there, taking my place, lifting the cast iron, serving the dinner. Maybe not. Maybe Granma'am has put on her beetlebug wig and gone to serve church dinner with the other church widows. The plate I have left on the counter for Luke edward makes me nervous and pulls my eye to the right.

Luke comes in the door as Big Jim is cutting. I am sprinkling paprika over the serving bowl of potato salad. We all hear the door open and shut, and each one of us looks at who we know the most about, although I notice that Big Jim looks more steadily at the meat. That's all right; my eye sweeps past Margarete to check on her relief, and goes right back to the mound of potato salad. Big Jim and I both choose closeness to the food.

Luke edward comes in, taking off his nice raincoat, and goes right to kiss his expectant mama.

"It smells good in *here*," Luke says, leaning down to Margarete.

"I know, child, your sister is a-cookin somethin," Margarete answers him, kisses him back, smiles.

I take Luke's place setting and squeeze it between Margarete's and mine, so that he is not at Big Jim's end of the table. Course, ain't no names at the table, but I move my chair over, and say, "Go git yo'self a chair, Luke edward," and that way he is clear what I mean. I mean, you would think Luke edward would stay out of Big Jim's way on his own, but he hasn't up to this point, so I do what I can.

Everybody has set down when Luke edward comes back, so everybody has to scoot so he can get his chair in. I'm coming to the table with the steaming bowl of string beans, concentrating hard on the heat. Luke edward catches me off-guard, tips me with the chair he carries, and I drop the whole bowl of cooked-all-day string beans. They go crashing and flying to the floor.

Serena squats down with me immediately. We are mice with intensity. We both pick pieces of glass out of the mess. I quickly check under the table to see that nobody is in their sock feet, and I picture in my mind the few loose string beans that still float forlornly in the pot liquor.

Everybody talks at once: Luke edward knows I am very upset and he is sorry and he didn't mean to get in my way. He is still holding the chair, for Pete's sake. David, in his quiet, is saying, "Neesey coulda handled it, it's just that it was so hot." Margarete says from her chair not to worry, it's OK and she's sure there are more in the pot, and Big Jim has sucked his teeth in spite of himself, but he does come to help; he brings the dishrag to brush the mess all together so it can be gotten up. Me, Big Jim, and Serena are all three down on the floor. Margarete, Luke edward, and David sit at the table, all wearing shoes, thank Jesus. Everybody is breathing over the spill.

Luke edward puts down his chair next to Margarete by lifting it over the head of the commotion. He takes the slotted spoon I have left angled in the pot and scoops the pitiful rest of the string beans out into the ugliest remaining bowl in the house. Big Jim has taken the two ham hocks off the floor and rinsed them, and he drops them in the bowl Luke edward has made, mumbling, "Ain't nothing wrong with that meat." And we all sit down to the table at once, and David thanks God for the food and for the family and says if we can ask a favor, please don't let there be any glass swallowed, or stepped on, in this house, this day.

We all say Amen, and everybody tells me what a mean cook I am. Big Jim says I put my feet in the food and Margarete says she's so glad I'm here to help her out. I have time to calm down, and I think that somewhere in me I knew this dinner would be messed up, even with its teeny tiny ham.

I DID HAVE the mind to ask Big Jim whether he wouldn't like to have chicken for Easter. "Naw, I rather ham and potato salad," he said. I had waited until he was on his way out the door, had kept wishing Margarete would say something, instead of me. Hadn't she told him? Maybe I was the only one reeling. Nobody else seemed to be bothered. Wasn't nobody else cooking, though, either.

I do not eat ham. It is not because it doesn't taste good, because it does. Nothing better than a thick slab of smoked ham, quick fried to brown, between hot buttered fresh baked bread. Not a thing. But if ham kills your father, then common sense will tell you not to eat no ham.

Nobody else in my family seems to feel this way. I am surprised and at the same time not surprised about this. I have a baked chicken breast tucked in the oven for my Easter meal. I will eat it after the set-down dinner is through.

After dinner, David and Serena put a exclamation point on everything. They announce they are getting a place to themselves. Two weeks later David takes all his things from around his bed, and he leaves Margarete's house. Margarete tells him she is proud of him and tells Serena that she don't feel old enough for a daughter-in-law, but Serena is a good daughter-in-law to be coming in the family. In two months, David and Serena get married. We all get dressed up and go down to the court-house. I bring Serena's hand arrangement as a gift. Luke edward is dressed far snazzier than my sweet brother David, the groom. Serena kept a lovely house.

MAMA DRAPES ME in a apron so I can butter toast. She tells me to do the whole loaf cause the boys will be hungry. I feel the heat from the oven door I stand next to, where our Virginia ham is baking. Mama sends my sleepy daddy into the bathroom, and he gives me a big hug and kiss on his way through the kitchen. Then Mama goes into Luke and David's room; their heads are heavy globes. Of course, they don't want to get up, but thanks to our daddy, they took their baths last night. Mama totes the big jar of petroleum jelly.

David and Luke edward are both old enough now to grease their own legs. They just refuse. Mama tells them all the time they shouldn't walk around with ashy knees, and they say OK, in a drone. Every time she leaves them alone to get dressed up, they come out ashy, expecting to go to church or go visiting, looking like that. You wouldn't catch me with no ashy elbows. They just don't care, I think. Funny what boys don't care about. It makes me laugh; can't be they don't know what Mama is talking about, after all these many times. And so Mama goes after them with the Eboline.

Of course, Daddy and Luke edward and David want to start the ham for breakfast, but Mama is firm. She says it isn't ready, and we don't have time. She tells all of them—she is kissing and coddling my daddy, brushing and smoothing his hair—that they should eat the toast I buttered, and they'll be good and hungry for dinner.

Daddy wants to know who's coming over, and Mama names some people who are coming after dinner. All the people coming are friends of my daddy's, and I haven't seen these people in a long time. I am marvelling at how wonderful my mother has been at organizing everything, and I like the way she is smoothing and pomading his hair. I notice how much harder he smells than we do, and I have a piece of buttered toast. My mother has a piece of buttered toast. The boys are well greased, and I go for my dress, and the boys and my daddy eat the whole loaf of bread.

We walk to church. Zion is not far from where we live: two long blocks down and one block to the left. Mama usually sends David and Luke edward and me to church by ourselves. We usually race and ruckus all the way down the blocks, and I holler to my brothers that they better not tear my dress. This morning, it is Easter, and our daddy is home. We are walking not running; we are passing our neighbors. We cause comment, us all in white and yellow, five.

My daddy is handsome, and he is a man who's been places. He has shirts from Ohio and shoes from New York! My mother lusts for these things just like my daddy; she is wearing white shoes with scalloped edges that he brought her from somewhere the train stops. I asked my father how he knew what shoes to buy Mama. He said he knows her size. That wasn't what I meant, what I meant was what she likes. Whenever he came in with a shoe box, she would rush to open it, and would squeal, delighted. She would find an outfit to wear with them right away. The spike heels and pointed toes are what she likes.

Everybody looks at us on our way to church. My mother is beaming; it is not usual that my daddy's on her arm. Daddy and Mama both grin, giddy. She leans into his side. I skip. David and Luke edward stay just on the good edge of bad. Mama and Daddy wave at people, say we can't stop, but maybe on our way back we will.

Everybody in the neighborhood is better dressed than all year. Like a pageant: a flag of happy colored people, wearing whites and pinks and yellows for the spring. I have Daddy to skip beside, my brothers dash around in their short pants—they are punching each other—and everything is wonderful.

Daddy says it's time for David to have long pants. And

Mama says Luke will be too upset. They decide that next year both Luke and David will wear long pants together. Daddy promises that next year we'll have a car to drive to church. I don't understand this since we walk to church easy as pie, but Mama reminds me that I should stay out of grown folks' conversations, and since Daddy gives me a swing, I don't pout. Daddy promises to take us sometime to Montreal on the train. I ask from the air his arms give me, "When we going to Montreal, Daddy?"

"Sometime soon, Baby Sister, I promise."

Church is long and exuberant. All humanity is there. By the time service starts, the benches shift and shudder while latecomers squeeze their hips into places where the ushers have seen a sliver of brown and have held up a finger, One. The late man or woman will rush toward the one finger and wriggle themselves into the sliver on the bench; everybody in the row will have to squeeze themselves narrower, rehang their spring coat over the back of the church bench, move their pocketbook off the seat and put it down on the floor in front, frown frustratedly if you're a child like Luke edward or me, smile apologetically if yours are the squirming hips. Turn around and blaze—Good morning, Happy Easter—to the last arrival.

We are not late, and so all five of us line up on a bench together. We sit on the right, where Mama likes to sit, so she can have a full view of Reverend Puckett and the choir, which she sings in off and on. Reverend Puckett's first name is Niles, but he never uses it because he says it isn't Christian, so he refers to himself as Reverend N. John Puckett, which Daddy thinks is hilarious. Us kids call him Reverend John, and Daddy just calls him Puckett, at home and to his face.

"Blessed assurance, Jesus is mine, Oh what a foretaste

of glory divine, Heir of salvation, purchase of God, born of His spirit, washed in His blood. Perfect submission, perfect delight, Visions of rapture now burst on my sight; Angels descending, bring from above, Echoes of mercy, whispers of love. This is my story, this is my song, Praising my Saviour all the day long; This is my story, this is my song, Praising my Saviour all the day long. Perfect submission, all is at rest, I in my Saviour am happy and blest, Watching and waiting, looking above, Filled with His goodness, lost in His love. This is my story, this is my song, Praising my Saviour all the day long; This is my story, this is my song, Praising my Saviour all the day long."

My mother got me used to good singing early in life. She did not have a high voice, and she didn't try to stretch it to make it high either. Her voice sounded reedy, and she sang like she was lost in thought.

The lady in the white dress who had slivered next to us was more like regular ladies who sang in church but never in the choir. Her voice sounded tinny and uncomfortable; she strained to sing on top of the music, and my mother says you have to find a place *in* the music for your voice. The music is full of notes, my mother says, and there are always some notes you can match or mate with, don't strain. This lady had never talked to my mother about singing and so she choked her voice and stretched her neck and strained and finally cried. She waved a fan she had in her hand that had a picture of sweet Jesus on one side and the funeral home record on the other. It was one of the fans with the curvy sticks. When she sat down tired, I leaned back too so I could save my little space to sit. Later in the service, I change seats next to my daddy, and it saves my ears.

We sing "Up from the Grave" before the sermon. It is

the snappiest of hymns. Everybody loves the story of the Risen Son and Saviour, and so the church is a blanket of tilted heads and moving mouths. Even Luke edward and David sing—we learned the words in Sunday school. When the verses are over, and we sing all four, the congregation sits down, and the organ keeps playing. The organ is a man and he continues to sing, once everyone else has sat down. The man does not sing as fast as we all did, and we can all hear his voice roll from low note to lower, telling us a story about the mercy of God. The voice deepens and seeps into the floorboards of the church. The floorboards make a tremor underneath the hard shoes of the men, the high heels of the women and the banging legs of children. My feet want to feel the shaking floor but don't reach, so I slide off the bench to lean on the singing man. The blanket of heads sways in the benches, like the voice has been a wind. One by irregular one, ladies get up, clap their hands, praise the Lord. Women drop their hats accidentally behind them. They holler out loud, or faint. The men just stand if they want to, in straight-backed testimony, while the women continue to rise and to fall.

The nurses are mobilized and the organ man still sings. All space is activity, tears cut through pressed powder and make lines on the face. Eventually the organ man, who shepherds the church, leads the flock back to quiet from the heat of the interlude. *Hush, now hush. (This is my story, this is my song.)* Then N. John Puckett seizes what the wailing man has left. Reverend John reads a roll of Bible verses, and speaks with his finger pointed up in the air; he holds his open Bible toward the dark ribs in the ceiling of the church.

What I have left in me of what Puckett had to say that day is this:

Sit yourself down when you enter Your Father's House. Notice, children: I did not say kneel. Kneeling encourages hurry, children. And when you enter Your Father's House, you must not hurry, but tarry instead. I say (clap) tarry, instead.

Sit down and linger with Your Lord and Savior. He (clap) gave everything for you. Rest your feet, and talk (clap) with Jesus. Give Him your heart while you give Him your time. Tell Jesus what you're thinking that you need. If you do that (clap) then you *will* take time. And while you are waiting and while you are praying, what you need will (clap) come, white clouds on a Monday. Sit down with Your Father, *sit down*, with Your Father. Sit (clap), down (clap, clap) in Your Father's House.

Some people sat down, but most people stood up. Puckett is a good preacher with a big booming voice. He grabbed his big Bible and took it open, walking up and down the church aisles. "The doors of the church are open," he chants. His voice always sways in the rhythm of learned religion.

Collection. People rummage into their pockets, into their pocketbooks. Either you need an envelope or a dollar bill. Just try to put a quarter in a Bible.

The organ music blares "Thank you, Lord" at a fast and lifting speed; the congregation passes money down to the left of each row. The lady next to me hands me a stack of dollar bills, and before I can look good, Mama snatches them from me. Luke and David hardly got their hands on the money either. Daddy adds his envelope and waits at the end for Puckett to come by with the Bible. Puckett puts his hand over the money in the Bible and the ushers come up behind him with a straw bucket.

He pours all our offerings in, and on to the next row he goes.

At the end of the service, "What a Fellowship" leaps from the organ. Everybody shakes hands with everybody. The sliver-wigglers smile apologetically and either explain what detained them or comment on how full the church is this lovely morning. The sliver-wigglers are forgiven. The aisles are packed, the doorway is packed, and the getting out of church requires that twelve thousand hands touch my head.

THE HAM I had put the cloves in rose like a big tinfoil rock from the center of the table me and Mama had set. We had green beans that I had helped to snap and a big bowl of potato salad Mama had made. We stopped down in the church basement and got some bread—so the rolls had been made by somebody other than Mama and me. Mama had got pie and ice cream for dessert; she had bought more than enough because we planned to have dessert with Daddy's friends.

ME AND MAMA gave the Easter dinner very much discussion. Even then I was learning the kitchen, while David and Luke edward were outside playing ball. Easter dinner got hovering, stooping care—mostly since Daddy was home.

"How's dinner, Buddy?" Mama asked, and I wanted to know too since I helped.

"A clean plate tells everything," he said, and proceeded to clean his plate. Twice. Everything got eaten up, except there was some of that big ham left. Mama said, "We can pinch off it all week," satisfaction in her voice.

Luke and David had huge appetites too. Was it the boy in them that made them eat and eat? And then, too, is it the boy in them that makes them play so hard, no matter who's been calling, and no matter for how long? Did they stay out playing because my father was out working? Was that the boy-child equivalent of the man-child's life?

I pulled off my dress and put my apron back on, to help Mama with the dishes. The boys changed and went outside, since we weren't going visiting for once; people were coming to see us. Daddy said he was tired, said he was going to take a nap. He lifted me off the stool I used to reach the dishes good, and said, "You look Easter pretty, even in your apron! Thank you for dinner, Little Miss." Then he and Mama went in to their bedroom and closed the door.

After I finished all the dishes, I wondered if I should try the pans and pots. Mama had told me that I should never touch them, they were too big for me to handle yet. I thought it would be a nice surprise. But before I could get my maturity going, there were hard knocks at the door.

The noise was instant, so many voices at once. I waited. "What y'all doin in here, Margarete? We was about to go make another party somewhere else! Where's your travelling husband? Y'all go to church today?"

"Come on in here," Mama was saying, and pulling this hand and that one. Everybody kissed everybody else. My daddy came out of the bedroom, and picked me up from where I stood. He carried me right to the door with him, and I had one foot behind the other one, prim and shy. "Well, isn't she growing into a doll baby?" My cheeks got pinched. "Ain't she a little old for you to be carrying, Buddy?"

"She's my baby, I don't get to carry her much," my daddy said. One man pinched my leg, and my daddy smacked his hand. Everybody laughed (me too). "Where those boys a yours?"

"Out runnin amok," my daddy said.

"They be in here before too long," Mama adds, "hungry again."

The ham we brought from Virginia was a hit. The people who visited put slices of it between the rolls from the church. "This is good ham, Margarete!" And Margarete told the story of Mr. Howell Jones, and I listened to get the pieces of the story I wouldn't know, so that if I told the story myself, it would be as full as thick soup.

Them Washington Pigs

AFTER DADDY ASKED for Virginia ham for Easter, we went to visit Mr. Howell Jones, who smoked meat. Mama was happy to arrange a spring trip to see Granma'am. Mama took me with her, and after our visit with Granma'am, we carried our sweet Virginia ham from Patuskie back to Detroit. Mr. Howell Jones smoked the best of everything east of Arkansas, which is where he had come to Patuskie from.

Mr. Howell Jones looked like he had smoked himself along with all his meat. Near purple-red and with skin ridged like hide, his sausage fingers were thick to bursting. He was gleeful near to drooling when people came to choose from his smoked and hanging parts of pig or whole smoked chickens. I liked to look at the chickens, and I wished we would have bought a smoked bird sometimes.

Some of the chickens had heads still on. All the pigs had been axed into parts. You could get any piece or part of meat from Mr. Howell Jones. What you didn't see you asked for; the stranger it was what you wanted, the slower Mr. Howell Jones would grin, and usually he said, "Hold on, I got a piece a that."

Walking under his hanging slabs of meat made me curious. He never looked bloody. Blood splatters, don't it? I wished I could catch him one time or another with the blood of a pig on his face or in his hair. How come I couldn't see him dressed in redwash from the pigs? When did he kill them? And how did they yowl, dying?

He used a great long stick for unhanging. As he lowered the meat, he told you the age, season, and source of pig, whether or not you asked.

Other animals smoked a different color than the pigs. They were larger or greener or redder or blacker than the pork pieces hung down the center of his smokeshack. Those were the pigs. "Any piece a meat hung up and roasted by smoke take on its own look and taste," Mr. Howell Jones was apt to tell you. "That's why it's good to come and see and pick yo' pieces a meat yo'self." He had the habit of rubbing his thick fingers together; the rubbing made a soft, mild noise. He is quiet, near invisible, while you inspect the meat and then point at whatever hang you want to buy.

"This is one a the last pieces a them Washington pigs." He is aiming his unhooking stick at Margarete's ham. The Washingtons, a clan a stringy peckerwoods belonged to central Virginia, had been run off they rented farm. "You remember the Washingtons, don'cha, Margaret?" The hook had caught the heavy smoked-brown rope that ran through a hole in the meat. As the past had it, the Washingtons were evil, ornery white tenant farmers who worked one more parcel of land every season. (We call those kind peckerwoods.) Worked as much land as they could run niggers off of, with they niggardly spirits and snaggle-tooth heads. Mr. Howell Jones kept muttering, "Marryin each other like that. Yeah, you know they got run off? That land overtook them—child marryin child like that, brother marryin sister, tryin to stay that pitiful white they was. Cain't weaken yo blood and strengthen the land all at the same time." (Heh, heh.) "They eyes got glassy and nervous as marbles, and they teeth start to comin in fewer and farther back in they heads. Been here seventy years, bout time for em to go. And I seen em go through all they changes, weakenin and dyin off like that."

Mr. Howell Jones lowered our ham with confidence. He was a legendary smoker and would not let his meat hit ground, especially not in front of the customers. "Guess you come all the way from Dee-troit, Missy Margaret, to get this here ham." He laughed at his own celebrity, and asked Missy Margaret how was things, though, seriously. And where were them handsome boys a hers? And how old was she now?

Mama told him that Luke and David are fine, at home. And she is old enough now not to say how old she is.

Mr. Howell Jones chuckled and tendered one ham. Mama ran her hand over the ham skin, and since she was accepting, Mr. Howell Jones got the paper. He wrapped the ham in a couple of layers, knowing we were taking it far away. He was saying how he remembered the week they left (he's back to discussing the Washington pigs), all the animals they couldn't tie to the dray got scattered. "All them sunken chileless women huddled on the flatbed. Was bout five men for each one a the women they had. They was workin them women too young. I knew they was gone either lose the stock or the women one, but they dragged the women on and we split up they wanderin stock."

He went on and said some more about how he had fattened up the scrawny stock the Washingtons left.

"I know you did, Mr. Howell," Margarete said, relish in her voice.

"Well, little Margaret"—he handed her the ham like it was already on the serving platter—"this here is a sweet Virginia ham." And she took it.

I started begging my mother to let me carry it soon as we were out of Mr. Howell Jones's hearing. "It's too heavy, Neesey," she said but I begged. She handed it to me, and it was like a boulder. I couldn't even manage holding it by its neat cross lace of twine. Mama either had to watch me drop it or take it back, so she took it back.

Me and Mama carried the ham back to Granma'am's. "It's one a the Washington hams!" I burst out, up-to-datin Granma'am soon as we walked through the door. Mama slipped the black hog's hair that Granma'am had asked for into a pocket of Granma'am's housedress; I saw. Later, we carted the ham back to Detroit. My daddy's Easter dinner, and he would be home a whole week! I was seven.

Riding back I had some rough moments, giving up my mother's lap to that big white anchor of a lump. It took up the most comfortable space there was. From time to time, Mama moved it to under my feet on the seat, so I could lay down and sleep.

Daddy came home for Easter with presents, as usual. He will be home all week, not usual. David and Luke edward both got new shoes. He brought me a yellow Easter coat.

"Daddy!" I squealed. "How'd you know to bring yellow?" Somehow I thought my mother and father never talked.

The coat was the new material for spring. And it was honeysuckle yellow, not pale. It had a white collar and white cuffs on the sleeves and a little stream of yellow lace sewn round the collar and cuffs. It had half a belt, with two buttons, in the back. And out from under the belt, the skirt was pleated. So the top was like a suit jacket and the bottom like a skirt. It was the most special of all the coats the world held.

"No ice cream today," my daddy said.

I looked at him to make sure it wasn't nothing I had done.

Mama leaned down to me and took my chin in her hands. "That coat cost your daddy a pretty penny. No ice cream on the new coat."

MY DADDY'S EXHAUSTION is carved into his face like a mask, and shows too through his hands, their stiffness. His hands are hooked as if somebody's suitcase he is carrying is still lodging its weight into his fingers. He is as close to boisterous as Buddy Palms gets, and he would have to be. We are all so glad to see him. I run to him and leap, fully expecting that he will catch me, throw me up into the air, look closely at my face, tell me I'm his darling, take my weight. David and Luke edward come running, grab him and hang like he's a boxing bag. Margarete hangs back and waits for all his attention after we run to get all the curled paper things and other nothings we've done while he's been gone. When we get back into the living room with what we have to show Daddy, they are standing in the same place, hugging with their eyes closed.

Fatigue lists his mouth to one side and nips its corners. He chisels a smile over it, but it is recognizably a routine smile, maybe the same one he uses on the trains. The same one that earned coins for him through the many family-absent nights. It was not a smile that warmed me, it made me think that he should rest.

THE PEOPLE WHO visited Daddy wanted to play cards. "Cards!" my mother said. "It's Easter!" They did not use the kitchen table—my mother had set it for dessert. Daddy set up a card table in the front room where they played Bid Whist all afternoon. I had a nap, and woke up again. David and Luke edward came in and gorged the dessert. The grownups had tastes and played cards and more people came, and my daddy laughed and got to looking more tired. All his friends were there; he was happy and falling to sleep at the same time. He held my mother's hand through the card games and the evening.

I got put to bed before everybody had gone. And late in the night, in my turns I noticed that the house finally did get quiet.

I WOKE UP Easter Monday as chipper as a blue jay. My daddy never did get up.

People get selfish around the dying. They want whatever will help the dying live, they say; no matter how impossible those things have been before. All of a sudden, the dying person could have done all the things the dying person ever wanted to do. We have no shame promising the impossible, trying to call a person back to life. And, all at once, there are no limits to what we can or will give, to make sure the dying person has all that he needs. We fall resolutely from realism, we can't be honest in the world, not at this time, anyway. People can think of nothing but the dying person's grace, needs, longevity. The dying face floats a helium balloon in our air, all smiles and strength and ease; we dream. There is nothing but drama and romance around a deathbed. My daddy was the perfect man.

First my mama shook him, but then she relaxed since he was breathing. She thought he was fooling, but I knew better. I was standing in the doorway to their room, and Margarete was leaning over him, teasing. He had nothing to say. She thought his sprawling was just to slow down the rush of morning, so the day would be longer too. I knew he would greet me, whatever kind of joke he was playing. He did not open his eyes to wink at me, he did not twist his fingers together so I would know the fun. He did not wiggle his toes, even though his feet stuck out from under the covers, callused, and reddish like his skin.

Mama shook and shook him—"Buddy, Buddy," she was calling. He was limp and heavy like a drunk.

Nervousness dropped over my mama like a net. Very quickly she stopped making sense. "Please, please," she begged. David and Luke edward flanked me in the doorway; I started to cry. There was a patch of blood, like a dime, at the end of his nose.

David dashed out the house and came back with Miss Lena, who came in the house and slapped Margarete. I wanted to slap Miss Lena, but I wasn't big enough. She hurried us dressed and shuttled us outside. A doctor came. A siren came. Neighbors came. I sat outside pouting at the corner of our grass. The ants were celebrating their low-world spring. I wondered do ant-fathers die.

It wasn't until Friday that my daddy died from a stroke. He stayed home almost the full week he intended, but he never did get up. Never said another word. My mother held his head. And rocked. They said he ate salt and bacon. Mama called his name. They said he was not healthy, red. Mama didn't answer. They said who knew about his diet, what with him being gone all the time.

I wanted him to get up and be lively with me. Mama wanted him to wake up too, she tried to talk him into it. But he did not talk, did not wink, did not twist his fingers, did not wiggle his red, red feet. He stayed until Friday, and died.

Mama cried and cried and cried. She made hardly any noise but her face shined with tears. She lost weight, which I noticed cause her eyes seemed to grow bigger in her head.

David and Luke edward moped, and Margarete and Aunt Lena joined mama-forces. Not that this meant any greater strength, because Margarete needed a woman's care, and until Granma'am came, Aunt Lena gave it.

People kept coming with business to take care of. Margarete was unresponsive, and so Granma'am rode the train through the night between us, came to Detroit and stepped in. People brought food from all corners of Detroit. One night, late, we were all in the kitchen trying to eat some hot fruit Granma'am had made. Mama threw out twelve pork chops, two pounds of bacon, and some pig feet. Granma'am said she was in a fit of loss. Was some other covered up trays that people had brought got thrown away too. Big elaborate cuts of meat somebody had slaved over, in the trash and to the alley where dogs left bones and died themselves.

Granma'am's knowing hands, so soon again. She tucked me into my bed, while the door to the house kept opening and closing, what with people coming through. Margarete was not who I expected her to be, and although Granma'am did not wear one housedress while she was there, she still smelled like her usual snuff and detergent. Her walk was a rhythm I could rest on.

Granma'am and Mama were at angles, even though Mama was kind of sick. Granma'am did not think Mama should have Daddy's suits on the bed. Miss Lena told Granma'am it would be OK, and Granma'am mumbled about not having good Christian sense. Miss Lena and

Granma'am settled that Granma'am would watch out for us kids, and Miss Lena would keep Margarete. Granma'am and Miss Lena planned the funeral together.

Granma'am came to rub my forehead when she heard me crying. "Y'daddy's gone on to Paradise, darlin,'" was what Granma'am said, stroking. It may me cry even more. Paradise was where he had been on the trains. Even if he had gone there again, he wouldn't be coming back this time.

"It was the Washington pigs," I whimpered.

"What you sayin, Baby Sister?" Granma'am charged.

"It was Virginia, the ham," I whined. The only time in my life it got said aloud.

"Oh. Yes, baby," she said. "Y'daddy shoulda been eatin mo' diffrunt kindsa things."

MISS LENA DRESSED the three of us for our daddy's funeral. She went out and got Mama a distinguished suit and veil in black. We all stood at the graveside where my daddy's coffin lay. Oh, the postures of children at the graves of their father! They make small hooklike outlines—thin bodies, bent heads. They think they are like soldiers because they give so superhumanly to stand there, but anyone can see their hearts and shoulders flutter, their little wills shake. And further, I can tell you, they don't know what it is, what it means, that the life and the voice are gone. Only a hole remains where a heart and loving eyes had lived, had bounded in with trinkets, had bent with joy and wonder. No matter how much dirt is poured on it, or how much time passes by, that hole is not filled. And guilt—it settles and settles.

Like a puzzle put together from shards of recollection, I held and loved my hazy broken dreams of him. As I grew and changed, the haze stayed steady. There was nothing to do but hold our romance close. At any point in time, he was perfect, just perfect, and he became more so as time went on.

My daddy was forty-two when he died. He never got any different in his crawlspace in my head. Never did get mean, or blind, or bitter, or brittle, or sick, or dispossessed, or old. I watched as many men as I could, as I grew, looking for the man my daddy was. Eventually, my life caught up with his. As he stared back at me from his frozen age of dying, the loss in me would chant: he was a young man, he was a young man.

Days of Disbelief

A MAN CAME who worked with Daddy on the trains. He put a big hard hand on my hair, which had been ruffled by all this business; he smoothed it down and told me that my daddy talked all the time about his princess little girl. Mama had us all sitting in the front room. She said for us to listen to what the man from the trains had to say. Luke was curled up under Mama like he was still in the belly. The man from the trains gave Mama some papers and said, "These Are Very Important," and she should call him if she needed help. He also handed David—for his family, he said—a fat envelope. Inside there was money, curling, having been through many hands. It had been collected, pressed flat, stacked up, and brought to us.

AFTER DADDY WAS finally gone for good, Miss Lena made sure we three got back to school. She started talking to Mama about going back to work. Mama finally did go back to work after the envelope was empty and the papers were turned in. I think Miss Lena had to walk her there like we got walked to school.

Mama finally started to come around and make decisions. She spoke authority again; we kids depended less on what Aunt Lena said do. In the evenings, when Aunt Lena came by, Margarete reported on each of us: Luke edward needs, David needs, Neesey's school shoes ain't gone last. She developed new plans about what she would do; each one less grandiose than the one the day before.

Margarete had laid out Daddy's suits in neat layers on the bed, and she slept on them. Nobody went into their bedroom but her for a while. The memory of the blood dime kept me away. She came into our bedrooms to check us: she rubbed Luke and David on their heads, and told them how sorry she was that they were boys without a daddy. I understood what she was saying, because at least I had her.

MOST OF MY daddy's good friends were men on the trains. They did different things: cook, clean the cars and the toilets, attend to the people who had money for the sleeping cars, lift luggage, pass out pillows, fetch things for the passengers. My father did these last three things, mostly being in charge of the luggage.

Daddy had said all he and his men friends talked about on the trains was their kids and wives. He said that people who would never see us, probably, knew all about us. Daddy said he had told his friend Warren Blanchard about my skinned elbows from when I tripped on the scooter, and Warren Blanchard made his home in Cleveland!

I had imagined Daddy and his friends plenty of times, lonesome men on the tracked motor cars. I believed that my daddy must never stop feeling the buzz of a moving thing all the time, and I was proud that he never did complain about that. I could see these men, telling stories of their kids and wives, and planning hungrily for the off-week coming up this month or next. I saw them, shining their teeth into the late night, a semicircle of work and joking and much sadness. Travelling men, working men, men with chiselled grins.

My daddy Buddy was never as loud as his wife Margarete can be. And Margarete is not very loud. My daddy Buddy could turn the latch, come into a room, put down his grip, and still surprise you when he threw you up in the air. He was known for sneaking up behind Margarete in the kitchen, socks on his feet; he would interrupt what she was doing at the stove (whatever it was), and put his arms around her. She loved it, and she would put her head down and get quiet, stop midsentence if she had been talking. I don't know how it was for her, she and I hardly talked about him, and definitely didn't talk about how he made her feel, but if I can imagine it from this romantic distance: she steadied herself in the width of his arms, which were gone most of the time; she revelled that he was there, and that she was cooking what he'd eat; she smelled the soap and traces of motor oil and hints of the other cities he'd seen; she told God she loved him and blessed the floor under his feet. Then she turned around laughing, gave him a kiss, and said, "Get on out a here while I finish."

BEFORE SUMMER ENDED Mama had decided that she had to make some changes, and she had to make them now. We had kind of a family meeting, and she said she wanted us to be cooperative while she tried to work this out. We were all three confounded, knowing, I think, that she had to do something about Luke edward. She said that maybe we wouldn't have to move, but maybe we would have to change schools. She said that the train company had given us some money but not much and she was going to have to work more and spend less time with us.

She decided to go down to Patuskie, like Granma'am had said, to rest. She told me she would take me with her. I was ecstatic.

Luke edward and David went to stay with Aunt Lena.

They still let us ride the trains even though my daddy was dead. When Daddy was still on the trains, some-where on the tracks, we got on in Detroit and the men took care of us till Virginia. But when Margarete took me down home with her, the men recognized and were kind to Margarete. Being alone like that was new as spring onion for me and my mama, surrounded as we had been by boys and men. In our flat in Detroit, Mama had been sleeping in the day while we went to school. And then when we was home, she was doing hair in the evenings in Miss Sally's basement hairdresser shop. She hollered and pleaded at Luke edward and David: do this thing one way and at this time, and another thing that way and at that time. And Luke and David—near buck-eyed, sad about Daddy, wild as two puppies out yelping in the grass—trying to attend to their mama and to me. All Daddy's things right where he left them, and he gone. This train ride was calm and pale green, in comparison. Me and Mama played clap games. And we looked out the window.

Mama reminded me about how good I could read. She had packed four books for me, two I had had, and two new. She told me Granma'am didn't read so good, and so Granma'am looked forward to my reading to her. Mama told me stories about Patuskie on the ride, how she grew up, what she was doing when she was little like me. Mama packed plenty food, and we ate it all. We had cakes from the mothers at the church, and I had a whole box of clothes that the mothers had collected and also packed for me.

"Why we takin all these clothes with us?" I did ask.

"It ain't that many, honey, and besides they all new. You can have them to wear down home." My mother's suitcase was big as the bag I had, and so I let that go. It was so nice to see my mother distracted, to see her looking out a window, instead of down into her hands. I treasured that train ride, all our time together. I laid across Mama's lap and slept sprawled all over her, since my brothers weren't there.

And when we got there, Granma'am was gladder to see us than Mama had been glad, at all, since Daddy got sick and died. On my schedule at that age, Daddy's getting sick and dying lasted a long time. Really, his dying still continued. We all stumbled over the permanence of his departure, where before we had danced toward his returns. None of us did much of anything right those days. But the trip me and my mama took was lovely and fresh, compared to the gray ash of evening our home had become.

Irene Jenkins and Valentine Kinsey and May Belle Watkins all come by Granma'am's to visit with Mama at once. Margarete Palms had been widowed since they last saw her, so their throaty condolences flowed like song. Mama had a second funeral dinner on the Wednesday afternoon, with her old-time women friends from Patuskie. They wanted to know if she needed any kind of help, anything. We ate fried fish and green peas. They discussed The Boys, and How They Took It, and then they said I was sure up under Mama. They gave me cake and said I could go out front. I was glad cause the cake was chocolate, and I had not had to finish my peas. My daddy's dying was enough to cause all the ladies Margarete had been friends with to put on tie-up Sunday shoes and put a handkerchief in they pocketbooks and come round to sit with Margarete. I listened to their talking from inside the screen door, but their voices were drowned by my chewing.

Evelyn Ownes came late in the evening. She and Margarete talked half the night. Miz Evelyn worked past dinner for the whitefolks, usually. But she was stepping sprightly when she come. My head was heavy, wanting sleep. She was cheerful and declared how she missed Margarete. Miz Evelyn always was one for telling jokes from her memory. Not made-up jokes, but the funny things that life had let happen, or as she said, life let her live to tell. Turns out, Miz Evelyn and Margarete both had had eyes on my daddy. They were teenagers, both wanting to catch him. He was brownskin with teeth like clean sheets on a line, Miz Evelyn said. He had finer clothes than could be bought in Richmond center. Margarete had been outside of Richmond, and Evelyn Ownes had not. (So that meant he had finer clothes than Miz Evelyn had ever seen.) Miz Evelyn thought that was probably why he had finally gone for Margarete because she had seen more of the world. Miz Evelyn talked to me through my sleep and drooling. She said I should wake up, cause Lantene be by soon to say hello to me. I tried to perk up, but I was pooped and full. I don't even know if Lantene got there, but while Margarete and Miz Evelyn laughed themselves to tears, I sunk through the couch pillows into the way of life of dreams.

"NEESEY, YOU WANNA put the cloves in this ham?" I went dashing into the kitchen, travelling high speed in my sneakers with the rubber tips. My favorite things to do were the things I could do myself. That ham would sit half-eaten on the table, and I could still point and say, "I put in the cloves."

We had a lovely Easter dinner. We all sat down to one table; that was the first thing. Maybe in some families it is regular to have the boys and the daughter and the mother and the father sit down with knives and forks and plates and glasses of fruit punch for each one. But, like I said, my daddy took his meals on the train. Plus, holidays are famous for the feasts, and are only peppered by whatever other activities happen. This dinner, that Easter, began with a delicate routine, designed to let my tired father sleep as long as possible. Mama woke me up first. I remember her leaning over my bed, shaking me, "Wake up, Baby Sister, honey, wake up."

The Window in My Mother's House

MISSUS PEARSON HAD a visit with Margarete when I said that I couldn't stay after school no more. I had stopped to the store with Josephus, he bought Chesterfields. J get on my nerves the way he act so grown sometimes. Something told me I should of gone home anyway. As I got near the front door to our flat, I heard her voice. I barreled in and almost dropped my things. I didn't notice how I was throwing myself till I looked in the faces of my teacher Missus Pearson and my mother Margarete. Faces like brown pies, open *o*s for mouths, they looked at me careen through the door. Margarete was in the chair she usually be in, and Missus Pearson was in the low brown chair don't nobody like.

Missus Pearson looked different outside the classroom. She looked like somebody I'd never get chance to talk to. Somebody who ain't have no reason to talk to me. Like Valentine Kinsey, but richer and more educated. But she my teacher, and she probably here to see about me.

"Hello, Margarete, Mama," I stumbled. "Hello, Missus Pearson," I said. I was trying to pull together some grace.

Missus Pearson smile at me, and Margarete say, "Miss Pearson is a Miss, Deneese."

"Yes, Denise"—Missus Pearson cleared her throat—"I just said to your mother that many of the students coming up from down South use Missus as a statement of respect, like ma'am. You see what I mean when I tell you how difficult it is to understand your separate speech. Anyway, your mother was under the impression that I had moved to Detroit with my husband. I have explained to your mother that I have no husband; I don't know if that's what you thought."

Lord Jesus. Here is Margarete, tired and full of today's baby, picking in my teacher's business, trying to stir up some mess. It was just like Margarete to get that unmarried fact spelled out first off. Missus Pearson kept on talking. "I came to discuss your continued study with your mother. We have had a good chat. But your mother desperately needs you here, as she tells me." She held her head down at the end of this like she planned to clean her fingernails.

Now, who was Missus Pearson talking to? Not to me directly, but not to Margarete directly, either. Her words clunked around, heavy like nickels in a old tin can. She did not sound like my teacher of the fluid language and lovely life. I looked and Margarete was looking mad at me. Missus Pearson had looked up, kind of absent, but at me too. I blushed, embarrassed. I don't know what this situation is exactly.

Margarete had told me nine times if once that she needed me to help round the house and with the baby, and that I was gone need that know-how in my life for sure. And Margarete said I already know how to read and write and spell. "You even know already how to make fractions," Margarete had said one night when she come into the kitchen and I did my fractions while the short ribs stewed. Only on account of Missus Pearson had helped me learn, I remember thinking, but I didn't say that to Margarete. Margarete stays in the kitchen checking into the pots and refolding dishcloths. I guess she want me to say something in reply.

"She ain't talkin bout fractions and them things. She say I cain't talk English," I say.

"She say you can't what?" Margarete asks me.

"I cain't talk English," I mumble.

"Who is this teacher?" Margarete turns around and asks me. "Have I seen her?"

BUT MISSUS PEARSON had a righteous nerve coming up in Margarete's house like that. She sat straight up in that old low brown chair like her back ain't never been bent; coming in to tell a lady what she just ought to do with her own daughter. Needn't worry, if Margarete was considering letting me keep staying to school, her mind is changed now. Margarete was like Granma'am in that way. Neither one cottoned to interference from people.

Missus Pearson looked the schoolteacher and the uppity woman, but she didn't actually look no better than Margarete used to look. The baby done changed how Margarete face the days now. But she still look good. Margarete's skin had been humid since at least December, and her hair growing out thick, always bushing like fresh-washed. She full in the face, and her ankles is puffy. But she will be small and pretty again like she was.

Margarete had said to me in her bedroom one day that she too old to be havin babies, but she just thirty-six. I think she means she tired, what with the three of us grown or near grown, and now one more. I hoped she didn't have nothing to say about being too old or too tired to Missus—Miss Pearson.

Margarete had her feet stretched out in the floor

between where she and Missus Pearson sat. Missus Pearson had turned toward me when I came in, and she hadn't turned back toward Margarete at all. Seem like she didn't intend to.

Missus Pearson think it's downright dumb of me and Margarete not to be sure I get all the education possible. And for free. Missus Pearson had already told me that the education I was getting for getting up and walking to school could not be bought for a girl like me in the place I had just come from. She meant Patuskie.

MISTAH FITZWILLY TAUGHT us mostly from what happened where we lived. He only had one good arm. Fact, in the outside Richmond Negro school down home, school with Mistah Fitzwilly wasn't like this at all. We was all in one schoolroom, seem like all in one grade. And I was one of the smartest. In Patuskie, I went to school to help the younger children learn how to read sentences and tell colors. Like what colors the soil change in answer to time: when it either grows food or swallows up the spoils of it. And who it is you live round: what kinds of things they probably need and what kind of schedule they life is on. He told everybody, including Granma'am, how he depended on me to help him teach. Everybody expected Mistah Fitzwilly would need help since he only had one good arm. As my reward for coming every day and keeping up the work with the younguns, Mistah Fitzwilly let me carry home the few new things come for the school so I could learn before the other children use up all the wear.

Mistah Fitzwilly say Luke edward was another excellent student. He told the story every Christmas about the nativity cradle Luke edward made from mud and flour-water paste mixed together. He said that the cradle was the perfect shape and architecture, that it rocked on the ridges Luke edward had shaped. He tried to talk to Luke edward about drawing blueprints or making furniture and instructed Luke edward to find out more about it when he went to school in Detroit. Mistah Fitzwilly said a lot of wonderful occupational things could be done in the big northern cities; he waved his shrunken arm to help with the points he made.

Mistah Fitzwilly was a sad little man when he heard Luke edward wasn't coming back south. He asked me and Granma'am how was Luke edward doing. He came to visit Granma'am to ask more detail. When Granma'am handed him his books when he left, he said he hoped Luke edward would continue to grow smart. Too much opportunity can be a sea of temptation, Mistah Fitzwilly had said. Granma'am just pursed her lips.

Mistah Fitzwilly taught from what people said and did. Margarete and Mistah Parsons' sons, and, of course, Harold Grayson—they were Mistah Fitzwilly's examples a lot of times. They brought Patuskie almost all the news we got of outside Negroes. When they came and said colored men's getting factory jobs, Mistah Fitzwilly explained to the children my size the difference between industry and farms. When Margarete told the whole town about taking the boys to Belle Isle, Mistah Fitzwilly passed around a picture card with a motorized boat on it, and he talked about the power machines have these days. When I first came to the school, Mistah Fitzwilly had me talk about how it was to come back down South. I pretended I was Margarete, and waved at the country people with my remarks. I mentioned Detroit's great size, Negro men with jobs, and traffic lights, and paved streets all cross town.

Luke edward's nativity cradle was good for almost all

the Christmas lessons: mud and how to make mud hold shape; cradles and how long children sleep in them; Jesus not having fancy things to sleep in; furniture, furniture height; how important it is to learn how to make things, to occupy your hands constructively; giving, and giving to others from what you have made.

We had our own news too that we talked about in the schoolhouse. When Casiah Greenfield brought back her first baby, Chessie, it got raised as a subject. I told the schoolroom that I had visited Casiah and Chessie and took some mashed fruit. I said, "Casiah's baby Chessie is healthy and round." People know this day that Chessie Greenfield liked bananas and mashed peaches when she was a little girl. And James Jr. Lawes, well, when he run up against that rusty rod and cut his arm so bad, we was all standing out in the yard looking. Victory Simmons ran all the way to the edge of town to the whitelady's house where his mama was taking the piano lesson to get her. People said James Jr. Lawes's mama was crazy, taking piano lessons at her age. But Granma'am say people just mad about the Missus Lawes being so light. She had come from Poughkeepsie, New York, to Patuskie. Married her cousin. Handsome family. Time she got to James Jr., me and Mistah Fitzwilly had held down the skin and tied his arm with a piece of clean window curtain. Well, she took and carried him all the way to Richmond center to get some shot she called a noculation. Said it was the only thing she was sure would keep his arm from falling off. Then, Mistah Fitzwilly discussed noculations in the class.

And always, when Mistah Fitzwilly made the class learn about the outside Richmond things, he talked about them all as if they was one and the same. Harold Grayson, who went to school and travelled round, and

Jerry Parsons who lived in Cleveland, and Margarete Starks who was my mother, all got discussed as if they was living in one neighborhood called North. Everything outside of where we were was one and the same thing. Only reason I knew any different was cause I had been to Detroit, I had walked the paved streets.

MISSUS—MISS PEARSON was saying, "I was just telling your mother what a credit you will be as a teacher one day, Denise." She stood up, talking, and Margarete stayed where she was. Miss Pearson kept going on, saying things about teaching and learning and effort and credit. It was all bursting sweet on my head, like soap bubbles; I couldn't help myself. Margarete was perturbed as any old thing, mouth turned down at the corners.

Miss Pearson walked over to me and asked me to get her wrap. I put down my books—I was still holding them—and got Missus Pearson's coat off one a the hall nails. I brought it back and held it up, wide, for Missus Pearson to get in it, like Mrs. James had done when she gave me the church coat. Missus Pearson's coat was heavy.

I was feeling flushed and nervous. I wanted Missus Pearson to get in her coat and be on her way. I could see Margarete staring the both of us down. I walked ahead in my mind. Margarete was gone have plenty to say about Missus Teacher being so bodacious, coming into her house like that. I knew Margarete was gone say I had asked her to come. But I didn't. I sure appreciate Miss Pearson wanting me to keep learning so much, but I didn't ask her to come.

Miss Pearson stood in front of Margarete and me and gave a silent sermon, putting finger by finger in her gloves. Margarete's mouth was holding shut with not much patience. I could see Margarete without looking—she watching me watch the teacher. I'm looking down at Missus Pearson's gloves.

Dog, Margarete is mad at me. My mind shouts.

Once her gloves was on, I opened the door for Missus Pearson to leave. She put her firm covered hand under my chin. "Well, Denise, I'll see you tomorrow, and we'll figure how to keep you studying once your mother's baby comes."

"Yes," I answered her, pushing my teeth together at the end. She winks at me. I grin.

MARGARETE WASN'T SO nice to me that night. She was hot as white coal.

When I come back in from letting Missus Pearson out, I expected Margarete to want to holler at me. I was gone let her, but first I wanted to use the bathroom. I had had to pee since me and J left the schoolhouse. "Margarete, I jes hafta go to the bathroom," I said.

"Come here, Neesey," she said to me.

I stopped in my spot and repeated myself.

"I said come here," she repeated herself too.

I stood in front of her, not too close. "Did you ask that teacher to come to this house, Deneese?"

"Noe, I didn'tuh," I answered her. I didn't say 'Margarete,' on purpose; I was thinking it might make her worse mad.

Margarete lifted up her head off the chair back, slow. She looked me in my face. I looked back, but not too bold. The situation was dangerous, close to impudence. Margarete had me stand there a long time. I thought I would pee on the floor.

NOW, WHEN I was down home, children stopped school all the time. I didn't. I was a continuous student, thanks to my Granma'am. It was my job to do the catch-up work with the kids who stopped all the time. The ones who'd be lucky to get education enough to read the Book of Psalms by wick light. My friend Lantene was one of those kids, except she wanted to read newspapers, not Psalms.

AFTER I DON'T know how long, Margarete said, "It's a chicken in there need to be fried for dinner. Jim'll be home in forty-five minutes."

"OK, Margarete," I answered and turned toward the bathroom.

Margarete raised her voice, "GO IN THAT KITCHEN AND FRY THAT CHICKEN I SAID." I turned around and stood still again, trying to check on her face.

"Go in that kitchen and fry that chicken, Deneese. I'm not gone tell you again."

There were two chickens, not one. There needed to be two. Big Jim and David and Luke edward all ate three or four pieces of chicken apiece. One chicken don't hit it. While I cut up, put seasoning and flour on the chickens, I tried hard to keep my fury up over my drawers. I looked out the window, and evening hadn't come. I peered close to see my face in the pale white glass. Nothing showed. Of course it wouldn't. Decisions belong to the feet, and only come much later to the face.

Now, here I stand: in Detroit, frying chicken, looking out the window trying to decide what I hate. I like to cook, still. I like the changing of food from one state to another. So it's not the cooking I hate. It's the bawling threat of the baby I don't like. It follows me everywhere. It is responsible for my having to leave Granma'am. Now that I have moved, and I know there are other worlds, the baby is forcing me to lose again. I've started to see how much I have to learn, and Margarete's baby is going to keep me from doing much of anything but frying chicken, and later on, pulling the chicken off the bone for the child. And right now, when I could be looking at the diagrams I'm studying, it's Big Jim's dinner I'm fixing. Both my brothers will come in, hungry and expecting too. I wonder about all this. Somehow it seems like I fail myself.

I HAD THE chicken browned on the second side and was peeling the potatoes when Margarete called in that I should go to the bathroom and get out of my school dress. My need to pee had turned into an angry burn. Hold it, I kept telling myself. I did what she said: I went to pee and changed my clothes, but I did not look at her when I walked back through the front.

SAILING THE BLACK SLATE

"NEESEY, STAY WAY from that hot water now!" Margarete had a warning way of teaching. When I was a little girl, I used to try to run baths for Margarete. The water would always be scalding hot. Can't tell you how many times I had to jerk my hand away from under a spigot, hot water just a-running. I jumped around yelping, skin singed.

In the kitchen, I would get up on a chair and just turn the hot water on. I liked to let it run until it steamed, and then I liked to watch the smoke, how it made the air white and then disappeared. The hot water would whiten up the air above the sink, and I liked to feel my face change temperature. Hot water has power. It can sear your fingers and make you run the dickens away. It has strength enough to burn away dirt, and filth, and dark spots of things. At the time, I didn't know many more potent liquids, and none that could be turned on and off with my own hands. Mama said she didn't know where in the world I got that fascination, but she said I better stay way from that hot water. She said I was gone learn something ugly, the hard way.

See what I mean, warning.

TODAY IS MARCH 2nd.

Dear Granma'am,

The baby is gone come real soon. You probly know. I wonder how the moon will be when the new baby come. I look at the boys and girls in my class see who got birthdays round now. I wish I was with you so you could tell me about the stomach shape. I jes cain't remember. Her stomach low. Even if it ain't real low, it is all round not pointed and hi up. Don't that mean a girl? It is a girl in my class with a birthday next week. I been watchin her about this new baby comin. This girl she nice but she seem spoilt. But that is her rearin right? Not like she was born like that. It is a boy in my class, he been my best friend. Did I all ready write to you about Josephus Johnson? He ain't much fun as Lantene. I ain't known him as long. Plus he ain't a girl best friend. But he still fun. He from Arkansaw. He stay after school with me while our teacher try to make us speak english better. He say the teacher think I do good. Our teacher she say may be I can go to normal school after I finish grade 11 or 12. Isnt this excitin Granma'am? It is exackly how we said may be I could come up here and do good. Josephus remined me today how I stayed in my grade. Most of the kids come up from down south have to be put back some in school. I might get behind when the new baby come. I think she will have a girl. May be it is your oil I believe in that make me think that. The teacher visit here to find out if I can keep up english study after school and not take care of the baby all the time. Mama said no. May be we could find somebody else to keep the baby once she can crawl and have milk from the store. I want to stay to school. I want to tell you bout what I am learnin but I am sleepy now and I am scared to think bout when I will not have the english study. My teacher she say no body can understand my bad english. She say I got to learn. What do you say bout all this? I am prayin you miss me but not much as I miss you.

Love, Denise.

Earlier, in the daylight, I had decided I want to spell my name like it was in English.

I EXPECTED HAROLD Grayson to be through round the fifth. He came like a timepiece. Lord, I wished I was going back with him. I miss Granma'am. I miss standing by her in the kitchen, hands on the food. Not much would be growing full yet, but the yard would hint of green. And me and Granma'am would be making our way through the last put-up pole beans and tomatoes. I miss eating what I planted, picked, and put up in Ball jars. I miss running out in the yard to get pickings for dinner.

MARGARETE IS THE cause of all this I miss and all I worry about, I decide. She is having the baby. She had had Luke edward and has let him run wild. She had had David too and seems to have let him stoop so under and under that he didn't learn the difference between building and hauling. She running Big Jim out, and so now she has to make up to his anger with good treatment. And her need to give him good treatment has plenty to do with this chicken I'm frying. I have always had a thousand things to do, and loneliness to do it in, here and there.

Miss Pearson says that there are only a few things in life that really need remembering. She says most everything important can be found. She says I should read and write as much as I can. She says I should parse many sentences to teach me the parts of speech.

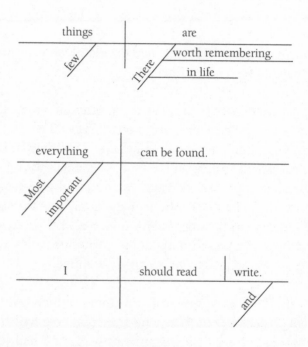

Knowing which things she taught me that needed to be remembered would be easy. Certain times, her eyes would get bright and more latching than ever. She would put down her chalk and pause her lovely writing on the board. Maybe sit down. She would ask, *Do you understand?* I got to the place where I drew a box in my book by whatever it was she was talking about that lifted her eyes so high. I would stop writing in my book, and I would look at her lifted-up eyes and listen to what she was explaining. When I got home I would write what I remembered about it and put a checkmark in the box. It was something I had seen her do, and I liked it: the boxes and the checkmarks in my notebook. Doctor Dew Boys—I wrote down his name without knowing how to spell it—was somebody she introduced me to with lifted-up eyes. He had a box in my notebook for weeks since she talked about him and about a lot of other things at once, and so it was some time before I caught it really who he was and what he did.

First I got to put a check in Doctor Carver's box. And before Doctor Carver, I got to study Scarlet Sister Mary. All the time Miss Pearson was mentioning her, I thought she was a real person, but when Miss Pearson brought the book, she told me Scarlet Sister Mary was made up. "It's called a novel," Miss Pearson said, "a very long made-up story." I read all of *Scarlet Sister Mary*, by Mrs. Julia Peterkin. I loved it. Miss Pearson said Mrs. Julia Peterkin got a prize for writing the book.

When Miss Pearson asks me to pick a hero, I was too shy to say her although that's exactly who I should of said. She says, that's why I've been teaching you about all these different people, so you could choose a hero. Now, there has to be at least one person you admire, for the time being.

So I mentioned Scarlet Sister Mary, and Miss Pearson says, shocked, that she was a servant, a slave. That she didn't give me the book for me to admire the servant.

Confused, I said, "Well, I liked the book."

"If you liked the book, then that has to do with the author," she said.

"The author. The lady who wrote the book?" I ask, to get this thing straight.

"Yes."

"Can I pick Mrs. Julia Peterkin, then?" Now, how did I get sense enough to ask?

"Denise, Mrs. Peterkin is a whitewoman."

I didn't know that.

"You choose a hero to help you color in the outlines of your dreams. Can't you think of a bright Negro who has accomplished some of the dreams you have?" Confounded again, and deeply respectful of all she knew, I said nothing. Miss Pearson finally chose Doctor Carver for my hero, just so I could get on with the learning. "He was a farmer," she said. "You can understand about that."

Now I understand exactly what book learning is. And I'm practicing how to get it out the books into my head. Miss Pearson say that only books can lead the way beyond my station. Miss Pearson say that books can teach about everything. Even about down-home things. Miss Pearson brought in a book on canning one day: *The Bell's Home Guide to Preserving Food*. Miss Pearson say preserving is another way to call canning, and that I should look up the verb *preserve*.

A nice book, jewelry-box size. Talked about putting up food different than we put it up down home. Said you need to get the temperature for the water with a cooking thermometer, and use a special pot what got a particular rack for jars. Well, Granma'am and I, we used the same heavy gray pot all the time, and we just arranged spoons to keep the jars off the bottom and separate from each other. Had to save bent-up spoons but that's all right. I didn't say too much to Miss Pearson about that book. I told her I liked it and told her I probably write to my

Granma'am about what the northern cookbook say about putting up food.

"Will probably," she answered me.

"Will probably," I repeated, not having the first idea about where it went in what I had said. But I had learned from repeating after Miss Pearson that there is proper English, and then separate, there is your train of thought. As long as I repeated what she said, she was satisfied, and then I could follow my own train of thought.

I guessed it was a whitepeople's book Miss Pearson had. Granma'am had already told me that whitepeople got special equipment to do all the same things we did with our homemade glue. Miss Pearson is very particular bout whitepeople and they ways.

Miss Pearson smile at me about the writing to my Granma'am. She always want me to feel encouraged to write, since it will be so helpful to my learning, she said. (It is during this time, I think, that I decide I have to write myself to a future. One that leads to eleventh grade, twelfth grade, normal school. Way out beyond Margarete's little baby.) I look back at her and smile too. Miss Pearson's hair, it has the nice waves put in it like Margarete say take so long to do at the shop.

BOB

IN SEVENTH GRADE, I started to pin the ends of my plaits down with the bob pins Margarete had. None of the girls in Detroit let their ends stick out. Shortly after I start the eighth grade, in September, Margarete tells me I need to wear my hair a new way. I am not surprised because Margarete has been complaining about my plaits. That's part of why I pinned them down. One Saturday when Big Jim say he'll watch Baby Clara, Margarete has me go down to the shop with her at seven-thirty. Her first Saturday appointment is at eight-thirty, so she has me wash my hair the night before.

It is the first time I sit in Margarete's hairdresser chair. Clara is out and gurgling, and Margarete has lost all the weight she gained. I still feel Margarete's stomach press into my neck where she leans on the chair.

First, she uses the hot comb. In the mirror, I see her fingers—long and knobby and shining with grease. Miss Sally has already come in. They are talking to each other over my head. Every once in a while, Margarete will say something to me directly. Or, Margarete and Miss Sally will say something about me, and Margarete's stomach will jiggle near my neck while she laughs. When Margarete wants me to hold my head down, she pushes it forward.

Miss Sally thinks I've grown so much! Miss Sally remembers when I was talking so clear and so early. Miss Sally used to get so tickled at the poems I used to recite at Zion church. Miss Sally thinks my hair ain't so bad. Miss Sally thinks maybe my ends could use clipping. Margarete thinks so too. Miss Sally wants to know do I have a boyfriend. Margarete wants me to hold my head still. Miss Sally thinks I would look cute with a little bob. Margarete wants to know do I want a little bob.

"Noe," I say.

Margarete says she keeps telling me I better sit still before I get burnt. Margarete wants to know don't I even want to see some pictures and Miss Sally thinks I should at least look at some pictures. Miss Sally wants me to let her show me the pictures before Audrey Chatters comes in at eight. Margarete wants me to look at the one Miss Sally is pointing to, and she holds the hot comb in the air so I can look. I turn my head sideways. Miss Sally's almond nail points to a pretty girl, no hair. I shake my head and say "Noe" at the same time. Margarete catches my ear with three fingers of her other hand and holds my head. She pulls on my hair with the hot comb again. I stretch my eyes to raise them to the mirror and I see that there is still half a head left to be straightened.

Miss Sally recognizes refusal in me. She takes the book of hair pictures away. She smells sullen, but she is wearing her be-nice-to-the-customers posture, so you can't really see what she smells like. She goes to the bathroom. Margarete keeps a silence of sucked teeth, or maybe not quite that bad. Maybe she thinks I'll always be country, what with the bob I don't want. Audrey Chatters knocks at the locked front door. Margarete puts the hot comb in the orange-glowing steel oven with the black leg base so it can heat up. She goes to open the door. Her feet shuffle in the flat shoes she has changed into, and Miss Sally flushes the toilet. I stretch my neck.

Miss Sally says, "Audrey, this is Margarete's daughter." I stand up to say hello. Miss Chatters smiles at me and says I'm pretty. I still have a nappy quarter head. Miss Chatters says, "Who knew Margarete had such a grown-up daughter?" Margarete urges me back down in the chair by pushing my shoulder with her hand. Then she has the hot comb again. Margarete says she will be running late if she don't get finished. Margarete mumbles that she cain't be running late first thing Saturday morning. Miss Sally takes off Miss Audrey's hat and dives into her hair.

Margarete tells Miss Audrey she can't get me to let her give me a bob. Miss Audrey talks about something from way down in the hair wash bowl. I can't hear because the voices and the press of hair and the sink water and the radio on and then the click of scissors jumble all the sounds. Margarete keeps repeating that she's trimming my ends, not even taking off an inch. She pulls my straight hair with a comb, catches a section and holds it flat between two fingers of her other hand. She snips below her fingers. She does the back, the sides, and the top. She says this will help it grow. She says she will give me a flip. All the girls wear flips, she says. She finishes cutting; she has given me bangs. She curls what long hair I have left with a heated roller iron. She mumbles while she finishes that she ain't curling it too hard, it'll be nice and loose. She shows me myself with a hand mirror. Miss Sally and Miss Audrey—whose head is wrapped in a towel—say, "Ooh, that's sweet. You like it?" while Margarete sweeps up a lot of straight hair off the floor around the chair. I have a flip. It looks all right. (From that day forward, I have to sleep in curlers in order to look right the next day. Until I take control of my hair again.) I don't like the bangs. Margarete says you have to have bangs to have a flip. Margarete says to Miss Sally, "She doesn't like it." She sounds disappointed. Miss Sally says I will like it eventually. Miss Audrey is sitting under a dryer bubble, looking on and smiling. Margarete's eight-thirty comes in while Miss Audrey is saying, loud because she can't hear, "It just takes some getting used to." She is saying that to somebody. While Margarete is saying hello to her eight-thirty, I put on my coat. I say, "Thank you, Margarete." Then I say, "Bye-bye, bye-bye," one bye for each one.

I RUN TO the school, where I sit on the steps. I have on my coat Mrs. James gave me. I can smell the sheen on my hair. I am still there when the buoyant gray evening light comes, recasting the yellow day. My hair and the morning had been yanked away from me but look what I got for just sitting still. I have never met any movement more startling than the sun. That sun! Time, heat, weather, light, safety, view, vista, mood, date. I had watched the sun's many moods this day. This yellow day I have watched go by, sitting on the schoolhouse steps. In the first moments of darkness, I get up to go home. I can still smell the sheen on my hair.

THERE WAS A big window at the end of the school hallway. It was tall and wide. It was big enough for me to stand in.

I ran down the hall toward the pale gray of that window light, my feet clap clapping on the dark and polished wood. I thought it was school that had made me, but it wasn't. It wasn't Miss Gloria Pearson either. It wasn't Margarete what with all of her controls. I was made by the insistence that I cut the teetering pumpkin. Just by that sliver of window in the wide building of the days.

I wash the diapers and the blackboards. It is also that specific. That direct.

THE LANGUAGE OF MASTERY

MISS GLORIA PEARSON tried to help me bury my backwater bad habits. She'd be there in the mornings: sweatered, straight-skirted, and wearing perfect stockings. Unmarred by any hurry, or anyone's baby, or a struggle to get a stroller out of doors. She wore gloves every day, cotton in the spring and fall, and some other smooth material in winter, no heavy, scratchy wool.

She would fill up all three blackboards, writing with chalk. She started at the left, and progressed to the right. She erased one board at the time, starting with the left. If you daydreamed—and I did—then when you got your mind back in place, you wouldn't know the sequence of the boards. So, what I copied would occasionally be jumbles of things. When the first blackboard I copied was the center, but she was actually at the center having started on the right, so right was first and center was last and the left was the middle of the lesson, I would have center first, right second, and left last, hurrying to catch up. So what I got, early on, was in segments not in sequence. This was before I learned to turn my mind to a subject like a flashlight. Miss Pearson had me practice doing that. "Concentrate," she'd say.

Doctor Dew Boys. Now he was her hero. I knew I spelled his name wrong and got none of the zillion initials in front. But Gloria Pearson could talk days about him and did, in the five years I did everything I could to learn from her. She got elated when she talked about him, her eyes shining like Margarete's when Margarete and Big Jim were having their parties, and they had beer after beer after beer.

I didn't quite understand all she said about him, but then when did I ever understand all she said? Miss Pearson said it was very important for me to understand about heroes, and to always have one chosen for my own. It's like having a star to follow, she said. I wish that then I could have made my way through my stumbling, faltering English to tell her I already had a hero in her. But I couldn't. I find out in this hero process that some things she expects me to get, and some things she doesn't. I hadn't known that; I thought I was supposed to understand everything, which is why I tried.

She said I seemed overwhelmed by Doctor Dew Boys. And so she introduced me to Doctor Carver. She said I might understand him better, me being from the country and all. Since he is a farmer who turns into a scientist, she thinks maybe I can follow him from tomato plants to the laboratory. She told me he looked into the peanut and the sweet potato with a microscope. We had one microscope at the school, and she showed me what it does. Out of his own curiosity and initiative, she said, he picked up the crops from the ground. He took them inside to a laboratory, where he made new compounds. He invented things. She said he ground up both the peanut and the sweet potato. Remind me of the kitchen. Made things this country had a need for, but that no one else had figured how to get. From her voice, you could tell, she is proud of Dr. Carver. "Yes, I am proud of Dr. Carver," she answers me; "he is a Negro of great genius." According to Miss Pearson, This Country needs to see that there are many Negroes of great genius.

According to Miss Pearson, We need to pluck genius Negroes from the farms, and railroad flats, and shotgun houses. And We all need to know that We have our geniuses too. That if We look at what We do closely, We too will Invent and Discover and Be celebrated. Many more of us Negroes can be heroes, she believes.

Dr. Carver started out working with the soil. In farming there is so much to do, the demands of the land and the weather make you work, and notice, and understand. But, she says, she thinks that Dr. Carver—who was at that time just George—was paying close attention. He was practicing turning his mind to a thing because what he ended up noticing and what he ended up going after was specific and small. With studied attention to the specific and the small, he revolutionized science, she said.

Gloria Pearson got in the habit of being able to tell when I was vague about what she said to me. "I'll slow down," she said once or twice, and that gave me a minute to breathe in and start to concentrating fresh. Once I learned to breathe in and concentrate fresh, then I could also do it for myself, in the times she didn't say she would slow down.

MISSUS GLORIA PEARSON went to Livingstone College in North Carolina. She told me. I guess that's why she know so much about how to fix my English speaking. I wrote to Granma'am about Missus Pearson and Granma'am say ain't no reason I cain't go to a college, Livingstone or Hampton Institute, when I gets to be woman enough.

Granma'am say Hampton Institute cause she want me to come back to Virginia. I want to too; me and Granma'am feel the same about this. Granma'am say she got a little piece a money stored up in the house she can draw on when the time come. I don't exactly know how all that business happen but Granma'am say it's a grown folks' question. Granma'am say learn much as I can in Detroit, and then we can see about me going to college.

I DO ALL my work on the big kitchen table. In fact, the whole kitchen is mine. Nobody comes in to turn on the hi-fi, killing my quiet sound. Luke edward will not plop down on the couch, shaking it underneath me, or stretch his feet across to the coffee table so that I have to move my papers. In the kitchen, I don't have to use my back to bridge between their divan and the surface where I can write things down, what with all the papers I am stacking and restacking, writing on and reading through to learn.

The kitchen is also where I know everything going on. I know whether there are leftover chicken legs for Luke edward to snack on when he comes. Luke edward always goes to the icebox when he comes in the house. Big Jim says Luke edward holds the box door open like there's a hungry woman inside. I don't quite know what he mean, but I don't like the tone of it. What Luke edward really does is come in late at night, and check out the stores; he picks what he wants, and then he eats it, all. We don't have no rules in the house about leftovers. Big Jim and Luke edward and all us know, first to the leftovers, first to the leftovers.

When it's time to make the next meal, I just get up from where I'm sitting and move into my next set of things to do. I can look up words and write down definitions while the kidneys are parboiling. I keep a clean dish towel hung across the chair so I can wipe my hands from the cooking to my books and back again. I can hear anybody who calls me, or anybody calling anybody else. Margarete has to call through the kitchen for David or Luke edward. Sometimes they answer, sometimes they don't. When they don't answer, I can help things out and say, "Luke ed-ward. Margarete is callin you." I can even see the front door opening and closing from the place where I sit at the table.

MISSUS PEARSON PUSHED up her sweater sleeves. After some of the other kids start to leaving, she kept me and Josephus late as we could stay. Her arms write everything neat and lined up on the board.

Missus Pearson's interest in me, and Josephus's present pride, made me want to shine. I didn't have the time I could see it would take to prove myself to Gloria Pearson, but I worked with a fever, racing Margarete's baby to life.

It's funny and sad how I saw everything in terms of Margarete's child then. I think I thought there would be no life for me afterwards. I worked hard, hard, hard at Missus Pearson's lessons. At the same time, I resisted Margarete's.

MARGARETE SAID SHE wanted to clean out a drawer and look at my things. She had me clear out my grip on her and Big Jim's bed while she rearranged. She said she wasn't wearing much of nothing anyway, big as she was getting.

"Where the rest of your things?" she asked me.

"This all I got."

"What you mean, Neesey?"

"This all I got."

"You ain't got no clothes to wear to school?"

"Yes I do." I pointed to my blouses and skirts. "Four skirts and six blouses."

She picked up my two dresses and held them up to my shoulders. Then my skirts. "These skirts look mammy-made," she said, "and besides they too short. These dresses ain't much better. I can't believe this is all the clothes you got. What you do, leave the worst things at Mama's?"

"Yes," I answered, but I hadn't left much.

"Somebody hand these things down to you?" she went on.

"Yes. Lantene," I told her.

Margarete looked sad. "After I have the baby and get back to work steady, I'm gonna have to buy you a thing or two," she said. "I don't want you to be embarrassed about what you have to wear."

MISSUS PEARSON SAY she will teach us all the rules. She say English is governed by rules of grammar, and the rules, she say, go special with nouns and verbs.

Missus Pearson don't do exactly what she said. She don't tell us no rules. She start to asking us questions and wanting us to say the answers or write them down. I want to know about the rules. I don't have much time. I ask her, "Missus Pearson, which a these is the rules?"

Missus Pearson say, "Say, Which *of* these."

She waited, looking at me. So I say, "Which of these," and I remember the rest of my question, "is the rules?" She takes a deep breath, and that usually mean we got a lot to do yet. Shoot, I could of clocked myself on the head for making whatever mistake I made, but I didn't. Miss Pearson say I must express myself with English, not with gestures.

"Say, Which *of* these *are* the rules?"

"Which *of* these *are* the rules?" I repeat very carefully.

"Which *of*, two *of*, one *of*, six *of*."

"Which *of*, two *of*, one *of*, six *of*."

"On account *of*."

I am surprised. "On account *of*," I repeat very slowly.

"Can you think *of* other examples?"

I hesitate.

"Can you think of other examples of when you might use the word *of*, Denise?"

"Could *of*, should *of*," I say, looking up at her.

She blinks. "No, Denise." She picks up her chalk and says come up here to the board. She draws a swift line down. She writes:

Could have   Should have   Would have

Copy these phrases thirty times each, she says. I start to write, very slowly, so as to not screech the chalk.

SHE PUT UP on the blackboard Rules of Agreement, with fast and level lines under the words. Missus Pearson explain that the subject have to agree with the verb, and you use a different verb depending on your subject. I want to look at Josephus, see do he know what she talking about, but I also don't want to look away since Missus Pearson is talking right to me. I wonder will she explain it some more. "For example," she continue, "I is is not correct."

She ask us to repeat what she say, and we both repeat, "I is is not correct."

Don't make the first bit a sense to me. Then she ask us what is correct, and I think I need to know what what is, before I can even try to tell what is correct. I think we both just look at her. She wearing a pink sweater and gray skirt. She wear black T-strap shoes every day with stockings look like they fresh out the package. When she move round I smell counter-bought talcum. Her hair has loose waves and skirts her shoulders.

I wake up; her long chalk is writing on the board again. I look at what she is writing, and I wonder did I miss something important, like what this is on the board now. I had been wondering where she got her clothes from, see could me and Margarete go. The writing on the board say:

I am	We are
You are	You are
He or she or it is	They are

"Do you know these are verbs and pronouns, the present tense of the verb to be?"

Aw God, it's getting worse. I don't answer. "Say, I *am*," she tell us. We both say it. She ask me to read all the pronouns and verbs off the board, just as they are written. I read: I am. You are. He or she or it is. We are. You are. They are.

I can read pretty good. Granma'am had me read out loud all the time. I like the way I sound in the classroom, though, reading out loud with the big windows all round. Josephus don't read good as I do. I wonder if she know the "you are" is the same on both sides. I wonder what is the rule to help me understand this when it's not up on the board.

"Denise," Missus Pearson call me; "Josephus," she call him too. "I want you to start hearing these words." She tugs at her ears, and then points to the words on the board. "These are where you make your worst mistakes," she say, leaning toward us. "We will go over this, and over this." She go on, "You both must concentrate." She say, "Remember to form the ends of words, not just the beginnings. These words, and all others. Denise, say I am-m." Sound like I am-uh, and my mouth is screwed shut because she been leaning to me talking about my worst mistakes and I thought I done good reading out loud. "Denise," (clap) "say I am-m."

"I am-uh," I say.

"Josephus?" she call his name.

"I am-uh," he answers.

"Now, listen," Missus Pearson go on. "The next time you hear yourself say *I is*, know that that is wrong. Wrong. Wrong. Stop right then and say I am-uh. I want you two to really start listening carefully to how you talk. Listen to what you say when you talk and correct yourself immediately. This is so important.

"Again, be very attentive to the ends of words. If you say only the beginning of a word, that is only half the word. And since so many words begin similarly, you could be misinterpreted. Don't say fo', say for-r. Don't say a, say of-uh. Don't say gone, say go-ing-uh. Don't say 'gwon, say go on-uh. Don't say mah, say my-y. Don't say ah, say eye. Eye. Eye." She making me tired she think so fast. I don't really know what misinterpreted means but I guess it mean somebody cain't hear what I'm saying. "Don't say iss," she still talks, "say it is."

Dog. These is the rules and I ain't ready. I'm trying to get out my pencil and get my book open to a clean page. She say, "Don't say ast. Don't say ax. Say ask. As-suh-kuh." I don't get no rules writ down cause after that she clap on my name again with her voice.

GLORIA PEARSON HAS given me ten years' worth of spelling words—I go from one set to the next, and I am never idle. I am so grateful that she taught me to try to match the English language to what I was trying to say. Making a match between what I wanted to say and what is permitted in English is the closest thing I had then to religion. Although the whole of what she is showing me has yet to come clear, it's something I trust that she knows. I don't doubt what she tells me. So I open all my books, and get familiar with the red marks on all my papers. I check and recheck my spelling and try to make sure that the nouns and the verbs have the s's in the right places.

The walk from our flat to my school building was my time to examine my mind about things. I raked over my mind plenty, most every day. Lord knows life been kind as grace to me, allowing me to come up from down home and go to school all these months, learning about geography and maps, and math and English, and reading some poetry out loud. Here I am concentrating on proper English, and if I was still down outside Richmond, I never would of had a chance to learn it. And Missus Pearson, she such a fine teacher. She start to teach us the important things soon as she get in the classroom. Not like with Missus James, all us country kids sitting in the back and wishing half the time we was back home.

Missus Pearson taught me to diagram sentences. Put the subject and predicate on a straight line to themselves. Slant other words underneath the line of the word it modifies. In language, one thing precedes and another follows. That's what Miss Pearson said. Even though precedes seems like predicate to me, Miss Pearson say it is the subject that precedes and the predicate follows. When she said something that subject and predicate I could understand, I would reach out my hand, try to snatch it, and try to paste it correctly in my composition book. Late at night, while I waited for Big Jim and Margarete to come in, I would take apart the nouns and adjectives, verbs and adverbs, and get straight the words that had capital letters. By the end of all our time together, she had taught me appositives, and subordinate clauses, verbs of action and of being. She amazed me what she knew and saw in things.

I diagrammed the sentences she shot at me aloud. I wrote down the things I remembered that she said, and I would put them on their grammar lines. Do your homework. Purse your lips. Repeat what I say, Denise. Try harder.

The subject lines were mostly blank, and when I asked Missus Pearson about it, she was pleased to grinning by my question. She talked forty minutes about implied subjects and imperatives.

At home in our apartment, I wrote and wrote. At our kitchen table, or hunched over the coffee table, sometimes while I rocked Clara's bassinette swing. I looked up words in the dictionary, wrote their spellings and definitions ten times. Like formula, dismissed, perturbed, precipitation, barometer, proprietor. Used my dictionary for spelling and for meaning. I might put the baby to sleep, and then spread all my things out on the single bed I slept in in the room with the sleeping child. Or I might put the baby down and go back into the kitchen where I could smell that the kidney beans and neckbones were still cooking, about done, needing salt, or just about to burn. Me and Granma'am never ate as much neckbones as Margarete and Big Jim, Luke edward and David seem to. But I try to keep up with the tastes they have for things.

I FILLED A composition book a month studying on my own. The thick pages with my handwriting gave me something to show to myself for my days.

Missus Pearson said that it was my not knowing the English language that cut me off from a bigger world. But it was Margarete's baby that kept me in the house, that cut me off from outdoors, even. Well, I figured if I could feed and wash the baby, douse her with powder and lay her down, clean and sweet, then I could look up all the words I didn't know and write them down in my school notebooks and try to reach to somewhere.

I FIND OTHER things to do besides cook, clean, buy meat, wash bottles, and diapers. I practiced how to write answers to questions. Every time I went to school, I took in extra I had done.

At the end of the school days, I said, "Good afternoon," to Missus Pearson longingly. On the days I got my extra back, I felt better. The extra would be marked across the top: Look up Charleston (atlas). Look up Corsica (encyclopedia). Who is Valentine Kinsey? (your memory). Who is Lawrence and what about those brooms he made? How many times have you been to Richmond Center, and what did you do each time you went? And the bottom: Good. Very Good. Six, seven, eight, two wrong verbs. Correct and bring back. We got to the place where she stopped circling the wrong verbs for me. Just a note of how many, and I had to find my own mistakes.

SOME DAYS I walk with the carriage to meet Missus Pearson after she has finished the after-school work with other students but me. After me and J left, she stopped the after school at four when all the kids said they had to leave. I roll the buggy and she carries her papers and we go back to the flat where she lives. That's one thing Clara did for me, made Missus Pearson more than my teacher, also a kind of friend, for a time.

When there's time she invites me in, I mean, us in. I have made tea on her stove. Her stove is a small and friendly fixture in her kitchen, which is small too. Clara sleeps like the little exhausted baby she is; she sleeps in her stroller like it's a good bed. Missus Pearson's flat is quiet like a blanket that surrounds it. Missus Pearson lets me help her with whatever it is she has to do. The first summer I was out of school, I cut up two hundred and twelve paper bags and covered fifteen crates of school books for Missus Pearson's next year. The bag paper dried my hands out so bad. And it took me days because when Clara would wake up and start to bawl, Missus Pearson would not let me walk her up and down and shake her. Instead, Missus Pearson told me, the first time I tried to quiet Clara in her flat, that when Clara needed to play or cry or romp and grow, I should take her home and let her do it. She prefers children who can speak English and who are old enough for discipline, she said. I think I heard some amusement in her voice. I know I always hoped I did. Anyway, she left whatever I was doing—this time, the books, covered and uncovered—for me to finish the project on my own. Wasn't that nice?

She also gave me lots of things to write about, insisted I write about raising the baby. She read every page of my composition books, and marked them up with red ink. Never said a word about what I wrote:

Margarete does not seem interested in the baby. Clara threw up on my new sweater today. Big Jim wakes Clara up too late in the night. Clara doesn't seem to be full of Margarete's anger, not like Big Jim about Luke edward, not like I worried she would be, what with them arguing and the baby living in her belly. I am glad. Clara loves Luke edward like milk. Clara and me are the same in that way.

Missus Pearson was trying to cheer me up by letting me visit her apartment, and she tried to continue to teach me by letting me sit in the back of her class whenever I could come. Going to her house, I couldn't help but think: what must I look like, young, and with that carriage. I must look fast, and ruint too. Beyond myself. People must wonder where is my spoiler. They must think he gone.

APPLIANCES
SOLDIERED
ALL AROUND

IT WAS JUST after Clara was born that the rumble between Big Jim and Margarete ran out from their bedroom into the rest of the flat. I knew I had been hearing it in the night. It was like all the urgent, pressed exchanges that warned of surrounding disaster, that caused us women responsible to perk to the alarm, that caused us to reach under the bed to the money case and take out a few bills so carefully stored.

This is what time the train will be here, son.

Here is the money for your fare.

Do you have your bag?

Did you call on your mother?

Don't talk to anybody, and here is lunch in case you get hungry.

Do not get out of your seat until you get there and go straight to Harold Grayson.

If you don't drink anything you won't have to pee.

Luke edward, pay attention to what I say now.

In the light of day, it was nothing so secret, so romantic, so solved. It was a naked argument with a mute, a bad moment wanting to continue, just to hear itself be nasty. It was not what I fantasized, not what I might think an urgent pressed exchange would be. Margarete and Big Jim had an issue and it was Luke edward. And they wanted to see who it was could win, with only what-they-were-willing-to-admit as weapons.

The war showed so sadly on Margarete's face. She was very upset about Big Jim's continuing disapproval of her son. Her first line of fire was Luke edward's well being. "Jim, he ain't stealin, he ain't botherin nobody; I'm not about to put him out so he'll have to do all that."

Big Jim was not moved. "If you ain't gone put him out, Margreet, I will. You do not have to worry about that. Why should he be here, living carefree as a damn baby?" A pause breathes while Big Jim waits for Margarete to join his thinking; he doesn't wait long. "You better teach that boy somethin before he dies dumb as sin."

Big Jim just had no tolerance for Luke edward, mostly because Luke edward did too much nothing for Big Jim's taste. Funny to see a man so devoted to Clara, and so venomous like he was about his wife's other child.

Every evening Big Jim asked questions about Clara. Do she follow with her eyes? What she eat today? How much she drink? How long she been sleep? When did she start making that little grunt sound? Is she trying to make words? He looked down into the well of Clara's crib from his height. His standing at the crib left Margarete alone, to oil her skin and contemplate Luke. Big Jim was gently encouraging Margarete to lose the weight she had gained, but after he started in on Luke edward, she started to suspect everything he had to say. She accused him of thinking she was too fat, and he told her that she knew damn well he would tell her what he was thinking. And that what he was thinking she did not want to deal with. He was right about that, and Margarete didn't comment on Luke edward unless the whirring fight had her backed against a wall. Then she might say, No, Jim, I do not agree.

The two of them picked up their regular schedule over time: a week's work and a weekend's hard parties. Even when they stayed out late, Big Jim came in anyway to lean over Clara's crib side and look. Clara learned the smell of liquor from the crib side. Got to the point where I would stay up late on weekends, wait up, and write or read. So I wouldn't be startled by him, late, and me asleep. So I could watch and make sure he only breathed on the baby, and that the liquor didn't take anything else away.

Their argument continued. Came through the walls like a current in disrepair. At night, they whispered to each other, they jabbed the air with quiet blades. Margarete's voice low and tugging at the wires. Big Jim's voice solid, a machine at the end.

They did have all the gadgets. A nice shiny toaster that I used most every day, and a cake beater I used once a week. Margarete got Big Jim an electric shaver, black with a gold razor net on top. I have seen Luke edward using it too, but I don't think Big Jim knew about this. Margarete has brought a hair dryer from the shop, which you put over your wet head like a big hat. I like for my hair to dry in the braids, but sometimes Margarete insists, so I take the heat to satisfy her.

Like an appliance that has finished with its new phase and has settled into the hard work of repetition, the argument I hear rumbles in the wallboards. I can't tell top or bottom of the sounds. I wonder what they say to each other, so late in the night, while I am copying my extra onto a neat sheet of paper. Or rocking Clara to sleep: *Alpha beta gamma delta epsilon zeta eta theta iota kappa lambda mu nu xi omicron pi rho sigma tau upsilon phi chi psi omega*. It is a singsong alphabet Gloria Pearson taught me from the sorority she belong to. She said she wants it to remind me of how much there is to learn in the world. Clara likes it—it puts her to sleep right off. Missus Pearson told me if I want to join her sorority I probably can when I get more education, since the rules about color have been relaxed.

The rumble decided that the house is just too small.

It is late in the night again, and the rules and Greek alphabet are dancing outside my head—a future I might have. Big Jim, the fan, is whirring discontent, and Margarete, a thin and fraying cord, is draped across the floor, plugged in.

Luke edward is Margarete's favorite child and man. They act more like sister and brother sometimes than mother and son. They act more like husband and wife sometimes than mother and son. They are close in temperature, in humor, in separateness from me and David and Big Jim. They both sing. Luke in the front room, in front of the RCA, and Margarete in the bathroom or in the hallway coming up the steps. And too, they think many things are funny. I mean I'm not serious and sad, like David, but time I figure out what it is Luke and Margarete are laughing at, they have finished laughing and gone on to something new. I ask so many questions, trying to join the fun, that their mouths slack down in disappointment or exhaustion at the time it takes me to get with things. On occasion, when they want to, they can turn to each other and reignite. Or they get up and walk out, and whoop again in transit: Luke doubled over, Margarete wiping tears. Both glad to have my absent face behind them.

Margarete was nice enough to me. She was talkative and involved (for her) from the time she met me at the foot of the stairs. She was apologetic about the cot in the front room and interested when I told her that the knife was dull. She wouldn't let me go downstairs to sharpen it on the curb; said it was too late and that these the kind of knives she always used.

Granma'am wanted no parts a coddling Luke edward. She told Margarete that the child needed to be stood over until he could stand by himself. She told Luke more than several times he was spoilt and warn't no place for a spoilt Negro man in no world like this one. She told him that she didn't mind his earnin his little piece a change and buyin hisself a few things now and then, but he needed to learn to use his money to bake his bread first. She declared he didn't have the first mind for priorities and look like he just didn't care.

Margarete permitted him what she never permitted me. And what was the difference between us? Lots was different, as you can see by the end. I stayed inside the fence and inside the rules. Somehow that bought me some small freedoms. He was given all the freedoms and ended up caged. Even I saw it coming. I don't yet understand the paradox of it myself.

I don't think Margarete is going to win against Big Jim. Not as tired as she is.

BARBARA JEAN, MISS Macie's oldest daughter, came to take care of Granma'am after the stroke. Barbara Jean was so religious she seemed retarded. She made no decisions by reason, only by rote, having memorized what they told her God has said. She nods her head to my wail about Luke edward, and from inside the church of the upliftment doctrine, she says, "Don't you worry y'self none bout Luke, chile, the Master says the males shall be the Lord's." She is slow with her pronouncement, and she looks at me as if to see if I accept. Without a sign of recognition from me, she lapses back into eternal uplift-ment, and I continue to complain about my brother, who may disappear while we all argue. I cannot face no longer seeing who I know him to be.

My instructions were the bedrock. And they did not change in all my years down home. Fact, they were under my skin so, I had to stare straight through my berry brown to try to dig them up again. I just wanted to know what lectures propelled me. *Learn verses from the Bible and say them over meals. Sweep the house from front to back every other day, and sweep the room from ceiling to floor if you walk through a web. Wash all windows and walls in spring. Honor your grandmother and respect your elders, period. Go to sleep giving thanks to the Lord. Rise with humility, anticipating ser-vice. Do your schoolwork, read when asked—letters, news, instructions that came with packages. Be a good child, be a good daughter, never ever lie or steal. Come home before dark, don't track dirt in the house. And always, always close the gate.*

EVERYBODY IN DETROIT had their own money. Brenda Greenfield got allowance from her grandmother and aunt, and all during the week she walked into Peckway's before or after school, and bought what sweet or salty sour things she liked. One day she asked me what I liked. I had been in Peckway's with her by then enough to know the full layout of the store. She had given me a ball of gum, as she did most every day, and blowing the bubbles so big like she taught me had made me daring. I pointed my arm high up over the cash box where the boy who might have been Mr. Peckway's son was standing, hardly waiting to take money from some more little Negro chil-dren. He did not follow my finger, pointing. To him, we were nuisances with dimes.

ONCE UPON A time there were two brown and lovely dolls. Their appeal was their dark skin and real human hair. The dark dolls had not been seen in stores before. On the shelves of the market, they were the cutest things. Many women who shopped with or for whiteladies and who themselves had dark daughters, remarked over the two of those babies high up there. Because they were brown—different than most dolls—and because they had moveable hair, the dolls were more expensive than any toys should be. So, they lingered on the shelves and had only each other for company.

One doll, Nickel, was rotund and loved bubble gum. She was the one who discovered doll language. Sitting there one day, after yet another wonderful, doting grandmother walked sadly away, Nickel said to the other doll, Dime, "Hey, can you hear me?"

Dime was confused. She heard, just like she heard everything else, but Nickel had never spoken before. Should she answer? Could she answer?

"I hear you," Dime said. She almost fell from the shelf, chortling, exuberant to know her mouth could work.

They commented on all the women who walked by. The few men who came got remarks too. They learned from each other the places they had been; who put them together, who invented them, how rare they were: two chocolate doll babies with real human hair. Neither could figure how they got to Detroit or to the cold top metal shelf in the toy store. They discussed why it was that they cost so much, why it was they had to linger there. This conversation caused days of a lull in their talk. They were stumped.

Finally, it was taller, thinner Dime who resumed the conversation. "Nickel, if I'm a Dime, why are you bigger than me?"

Nickel answered, "I'm not bigger, you're taller."

Dime said, "Taller is not bigger, you're rounder, you're stouter. That's better; you'll get bought first."

Nickel thought quietly, another lull of days. "I don't know if either one of us will get bought. Or when. But I guess it is nice to be round. I guess that's what I get, because I am worth less."

Dime didn't know quite how to respond, although she thought there was something wrong with Nickel's conclusion.

And so, their discovery of language was concluded in this way. Neither one had anything else to say, having reached a limit, a doll's mind.

Brenda followed my hesitating finger, pointing up. Bolstered by my bubble gum, and feeling impish besides, I remarked around the wad, "I'ma get me some a those one day."

Those were white bobby socks that hung clean as just bleached in a store plastic envelope. There were several packages there, all white. Brenda asked to know how much they were, and the son behind the cash box stood up and looked over his head, pulled down one of the plastic envelopes, and dropped it on the counter. It had a little ring in it, for hanging on a store peg, and the son threw his voice at us: fifty-nine cents.

Fifty-nine whole cents. Brenda felt powerful and gleeful that she had gotten me to name a want. She calculated that it was Friday and she'd get more money on Saturday, so she said she was going to get them for me—that we'd pretend it was my birthday, and she was buying me a present. She counted out five dimes, a nickel, four pennies exactly, and pushed them with her neat brown fingers across the counter to the cash-box son.

"It's too much," I whispered past my gum into her ear.

"I still got a dime," she whispered back to me. "I never spend all my money." She had already told me about the dimes she put away, at the beginning of each week in the mayonnaise jar with a slit cut in the top that she kept in her bedroom closet. Peckway's son slid the bobby socks envelope toward her. Brenda picked them up and held them in two fingers. "May I have a bag, please?"

Every day Brenda performed some small ritual, solidly indicating she was familiar with purchasing. And today, buying this pretend birthday present, she was particularly puffed up and in charge.

She handed me the bag as we were walking out the store. I took it shyly. "It's not my birfday, Brenda," I said. "Why don't you keep these? They nice." I tried to press the small bag back into her hands.

There was humor in her eyes when she pushed them back to me. "No. It's your pretend birthday, we made it up, Denise." And, "Tomorrow my daddy will give me fifty cents, and we can have candy and cakes next week. Besides," she trailed on, "Grandmama gets my socks at Hudson's."

"Oh," I said.

We walked along chewing and listening to the scrunch of the bag swinging along until we got to where we took separate paths. "Will you remember I bought you a present and be my friend always?" she asked me.

"Uh-huh," I smiled, sincere, and young enough still to promise.

"Even when we grown and wearing stockings?" she asked.

"Uh-huh," I smiled, giddy; she was so smart. She went her one way and I my other, and I considered one thing carefully: she never spends all her money.

My brother David is like that.

DAVID WORKED MORE or less like a farm animal to pile up the money he collected, and then hid. Up early, in late, knuckles more swollen every day.

People buy furniture all the time and what they buy from King Furniture, he delivers. Sometimes he come home and say his hand was smashed, and you look at it, and you see early signs of Mr. Howell Jones, or Mr. Watkins, or Big Jim. Images of old Negro men would flap like a flag, me applying iodine to a cut on David's hand. He scarred: nicks and recollections of a dropped, too-heavy sofa, a metal door let go too soon.

My brothers are not looking up. Clap clap clap clap clap clap clap clap. One's vision is angling more and more toward the ground, and the other's eyes are veiling with frivolity. There is the sound of wood slats clacking in my head, trying to get my attention. Clack clack clack clack clack clack clack.

He takes his baths in laundry detergent. He likes Snowy. He'd come in at night, throw out whatever remained inside his chest, leftover from the day, as a greeting to whoever happened to be in the house. Usually me. Courteous in spite of it, he'd ask if anybody need to use the bathroom, and then he'd go in and start to running the hot water. He sure did keep a box of soap powder right there by the tub. He dissolved every day in the bathwater, a wash strong enough for agitating clothes. He says he is dirty coming home.

He concerned me, drying out his skin so bad like that. He had bad habits about his care over all. He snapped the bumps on his face between his fingers. I kept telling him don't handle his skin like it won't get marred. Serena told him I was telling the truth. She told him he shouldn't be pockmarking his face. She said if he ever wanted to change jobs, he was gone have a hard time. She said don't nothing scare whitepeople more than a beat-up-looking Negro man. She told him she would still love him, however he ended up looking, but he should really think about what we said.

I was not the future wife, so I didn't say much else about this. But Serena surprised me. What I thought she was gone say, with them religious skirts she wore, was that David should treat his body like a temple. Well, she didn't say that. She said that David's face was his investment in the work he did. It was not. David's work was hauling. Didn't nobody care how he look. Gloria Pearson said that Negro concentration in backbreaking labor came straight from slavery, but I couldn't talk about that any further.

Well, like I said, I was not the wife. So Serena inherited all these problems that me and Serena, not David, defined. Including his shrinking-seeming. His shut-more-than-yesterday eyes. His bent-more-than-last-week head. His fantasies descending, dissolving with his days.

"How you feelin, David?" I'd ask him when he came from out the tub.

"Tired," he'd say.

"YOU KNOW HOW to count, don't you?" The man at Hudson's who was hiring asked me this while he was writing my name down on the papers he had.

"Yes," I answered, careful to push my teeth square together at the end.

"Count to fifty," he said, writing.

After a minute, while I thought this through, I asked him, "Now?"

"Yes," he answered, impatience in his voice.

To make up for the time I had made him wait, I started counting and got to fifty quick. So many *f*s with all the fours and forties. Missus Pearson said I was still much much too heavy on my *f*s. I concentrated hard on getting off the *f*s quickly, and on not going too slow what with all my other pronunciation concerns.

"OK, go on over by the red door and wait."

The red door wasn't ten feet away from where we were, so I stepped quietly over to it and wondered where it led. Did it go out? Was that where I would be going? Was he gone give me work so I could help with Christmas, and is that where the red door would take me, somewhere where there was work to get paid to do? I was careful not to lift my foot and scratch my other leg. Maybe he could see me sideways out his eyes. He said to the next girl, "Well, can you count?"

He picked me and another older girl whose name was Carole. "Go see Myrtle downstairs on the first floor," he told us. We went down the stairs toward the back which was where his pointed finger at the end of his stuck-out arm showed that we should go. The store, that I had only seen from the front, coming in with Brenda or Margarete, turned out to have a whole back side. Two sets of stairs at either the right or left end. Depending on where you were going, you decided which steps to take. In general, the left steps was if you had to go down to the kitchen or up to the candy shop. Those were the two ends that marked that line. And the right end was really for if you had or wanted dry goods. That's the side I used to collect my pins.

Half the day, the middle half, I spent boxing pins and buttons in small clear plastic boxes that had Hudson's brand marked on it. The plastics were marked with Hudson's prices and the number of pins or buttons inside, except they were empty, and the pins and buttons came in bulk. So we had these flat boxes with thousands of hair pins, bob pins, curler pins, and black or brown buttons inside. Long boxes the size of cookie sheets, about two or three inches deep. Carole and I were to count the number of pins it said on the plastic and then shut the plastic up and put it in a display box. The display box was another clear plastic box, but deeper and long, like a roasting pan. We filled the display boxes with the counted pins and buttons. And then they took the display boxes out onto the floor and hung our plastic counteds on the spindles, Hudson's brand for sale.

Most of the pin packets had fifty. The bob pins, the curler pins, and the safety pins. The button plastics had six buttons, both for the big and the small. Because the button plastics were so many and the buttons inside were so few, they took the longest to package up. Carole decided she wanted to do the buttons, she didn't mind how slow they go. So I did all the pins. Roller clips is what the package called them; they were just like bob pins, but bigger. I did all those first, since they were for curlers that whiteladies wore. I thought I would get them out the way, so I would spend most of my time, or the last part of my time, working with things that sometime I might buy.

We packaged from about eleven o'clock till three o'clock. We had to be to work at eight, and we got off at five-thirty. During the week on the two days I went, I went in the afternoon, from two o'clock to five-thirty—and on those after-school days I didn't do no packaging at all.

"Denise, I thought you wanted to concentrate on learning," Miss Pearson said when I told her I had a job for the holiday at the downtown department store.

"I do," I said. "I mean, I am. Miss Pearson, I ain't doin nothin at that time a the afternoon except waitin for

Clara to get hungry. Margarete said she would like for me to help with Christmas and she don't have ideas for me to do things that much. She said I could go down to the department store with Brenda and get me a job, so I did."

"Brenda Greenfield?"

"Yes," I answered. I knew she would react like that. People always think that if Brenda Greenfield is doing something, it must be all right. I guess I ain't no different—I *am* no different I mean—because Brenda told me all about the job, and I was so excited, and I made arrangements right away to get down there with her and see if I could get one. Brenda works hanging slips and dresses and putting gloves and socks on spindles downstairs back of the first floor. She does just the one thing all day on Saturday, and she doesn't work on the weekdays because her grandmother says she has to concentrate on her high school work.

"What days does Brenda work?"

"Just Saturdays."

"And what days are you working?"

"Wednesdays, Thursdays, and Saturdays," I answer.

"What do they have you doing?" Missus Pearson asks me. She is the first one to have asked.

"When I first get there and before I leave, I clean the toilets, and in between time, I package pins."

Gloria's face is a storm when she turns around from neatly wiping her blackboard down. Her eyes are shuttered. She wonders why she can't teach my country behind anything.

"Miss Pearson," I rush, a torrent of a speech. "I am only gone have the job until the day after Christmas. It's just one month. I haven't had the chance to earn any money since I been—since I have been up here. Margarete's husband Jim gives me money but it's for the food, for the dinners and the lunches I fix. I'm sure him and Margarete would give me some Christmas money, but I don't want to ask them for Christmas money. I want to take the bus to the downtown store and earn my own Christmas money and buy what presents I want with the money I earned. When I was down home, I baked cakes and cookies for money at Christmas, and so for everybody that I didn't want to give cakes or cookies to—like Margarete and my brothers and my Granma'am—I had a few dollars to spend on them. I'm just tryina get a few dollars a my own."

Missus Pearson's face did not change much while my voice took on the singsong of a plea. Why was I pleading with her, she would have very little say—especially now that I had already started—and Margarete had said what a help this would be, and Margarete had already asked if I wanted to buy the turkey for Christmas dinner, and I had already said I would.

"You're excused, Denise." Missus Pearson had sat down at her desk and opened her teacher's notebook where she wrote down her grades and what she was gone teach on the next days.

"Missus Pearson, why you so mad? In a month I'm not gone have the job no more, and then on Wednesday and Thursday, I'll be home doing work again, and while I have the job, I will do all my work on Mondays and Tuesdays and Fridays. You'll see," I said.

Missus Pearson laid her pencil down in a diagonal across her teacher's book and folded her hands like she intended to say something calmly. She did not. "You will never get over being colored. You have no business down to that store," she said. The fault in her English was like a chasm in the ground. "They got you in there cleaning toilets, making you a good little negress, and your mother's response to it is that you should buy the Christmas turkey." Her face is pinched like a rodent's nose. "Well, this is certainly not what I intended for you, Denise. And I don't think it is what your grandmother intended either. Your mother is very shortsighted about your future; I have told you that before." She burrows. "You can be like her if you wish, but where you will find yourself when it's over will be very close to where you are right now. Now, when you lift your hands and face and nose from the toilets, you can come back to see me. Until then, you are excused."

I took my coat from Missus James off the chair and put it on. I picked up my few books from the front desk and tucked them into my elbow. I looked at Missus Pearson, who had slanted her back and head over her book. She leaned hard, at an angle, over her lovely wide brown desk. I blinked, accustomed to seeing her loving curve. I was clear, looking on, that she was waiting for me to leave. Although what was in the book held no interest for her right then, she would give me only the side of her face.

If there was anything I could have said to erase what she had said to me, I would have. If I could have changed the subject, I would have. If I had not gone through the toilet door with my youth and pails and rags, that would have been better. But now I wave the flag of dark and colored, and she and I witness it together.

"DON'T YOU WANT to know what they have me doing at the job?" Margarete and I were at the table with Clara, having string beans and cornbread for dinner.

"Yeah, what you doing?"

"Half the time I package pins, but first and then again before I leave, I clean the toilets."

"Yeah?"

"Yes."

Margarete looked up at me. Clara had held one string bean thirty minutes while we ate; she lives an infant's life. There was challenge in my face.

"It's not gone hurt you, Neesey," she said. "This is just a little job for you to have over Christmas. Ain't nobody touching you, are they?" she asked, and when I didn't answer, she went on, "We all do work we don't like; it won't kill you."

I had waited as long as possible to tell Missus Pearson about the Hudson's job. Waiting didn't do not one bit a good though, and it probably helped me do the exact wrong thing. And here she was mad as the dickens, acting like I was choosing Christmas money over her, which wasn't so. Fact, if I hadn't waited this long to tell her, I might have left Hudson's when she got mad. But by then, I had to finish what I started. Margarete was counting on the money and I had not planned another way to get any Christmas things.

A letter came to the house; it had that drawn, luscious, teacher handwriting. I wanted to open it myself, but if Margarete found out I opened her mail she would not be sweet.

December 19, 1965
Mrs. Starks,

Will you please help? We need to try to find a way to encourage Denise to study. She does have good potential to advance. I have learned that she is working at the department store for the holidays. We all can use the extra money that extra hands can bring. I am concerned, however, that Denise may get distracted from her studies, which hold greater promises. She does not have to face a future cleaning. Mrs. Starks, we have a shared responsibility for our children, and that is why I write you now. As her teacher, I am convinced she can have a good future. Negroes have many needs. She must devote herself to study and good practices, however. Do you and your husband agree? As far as I can tell, Denise understands all this and is trying, as she is able, to progress. Is there anything you want to discuss? Will you please stop by my classroom? If this is impossible, I will visit you; just send a message for an appointment by Denise.

Sincerely yours,
Gloria M. Pearson

Margarete does not like Gloria Pearson. She thinks she interferes. She thinks she is trying to tell her what to do. And who does she think she is anyway to try to tell her what to do? At least she didn't come over. I asked Margarete if I could have the letter; I had read it standing at Margarete's side. Margarete said, "You tell that teacher everything, Neesey?" and then, "No, you can't have it; it was addressed to me." She went into her room; I heard her pull out a bureau drawer. As soon as she left the next day, I located it, and read it again. I kept tabs on where the letter was for months, until spring; and then finally, I took it. Margarete had forgotten about it by then.

WE GOT PAID after two weeks, ten days before Christmas. I was so excited. The envelope was brought to me with my name typed on it! I happened to be packaging pins when the man brought the pay envelopes around. I put mine down at the bottom, under the sole of my foot, and slid my foot back into my shoe, even though Carole opened hers right away.

When I got home, I pulled out the envelope and opened it up. There was just a piece of paper inside.

I snatched it out and opened it up. PAY TO THE ORDER OF DENISE PALMS. What, What? PAY TO THE ORDER OF DENISE PALMS, and then below that, THE SUM OF FORTY FIVE DOLLARS AND $^{12}/_{00}$ CENTS.

I rushed to Margarete who was at the table with Big Jim. "What is this? What is this?" I repeat myself.

I have a temperature from confusion. I don't know if I should be furious; I don't know if I've been cheated. I know that I have not been studying. I have been cleaning toilets and dropping pins into plastic sacks, and in my pay envelope, which I have done all this for, there is a typed piece of paper and no money.

Margarete has calmly taken it from my hand, and looking up at me with my consternation, she says, "It's your Check, Neesey, you can Cash it Friday at The Store."

"What?" I say, alarmed. I pull a chair from the table, sit down in it. The paper, removed from the paper envelope, is between the three of us on the flecked kitchen table that I wipe off every day.

"Everybody gets paid with a Check, Neesey," Big Jim is explaining. "And you just take the Check to the bank, and they'll cash it for you."

"What bank?"

"To the bank you use, or to the store on certain days, or you can take it to the people who wrote it to you and they'll cash it for you too."

My hands are covering my face. I feel Margarete and Big Jim looking between each other, but Big Jim seems more sympathetic. I hate this way they have of not telling me the things they all so calmly know.

I feel like I been tricked. Duped. Why have they not given me cash money? They never said they wouldn't be giving me cash money. They never said: on the day we bring pay envelopes around, you will get an envelope with your name typed on it, and inside will be a paper with your name typed on it, and also typed on it will be the amount of money that the paper is good for which will be the amount of money we owe you, and if you bring the paper back to us, or to the bank or to the store on certain days, somebody will give you the money.

I have given them everything they asked me to. I have given them clean toilets twice a day and bags of pins for Christmas and the winter and the spring. I have not been studying, and what I get is paper. The paper I make from studying is more important.

"You just didn't know, Neesey," they both say in different words and different tones of voice, "but it's fine, it's fine."

I bake four dozen peanut butter cookies and barbecue two chickens, and it calms me down. I take the paper to a window in the basement on Friday, which is four days from Tuesday, and I get four ten dollars and a five. This is more money than I've had of my own, and I am happy about it, but my forehead still is creased because I don't feel satisfied by the paper they bring me and then the wait I have. It doesn't seem to me to be the correct exchange for my cleaning of the toilets and counting of the pins. I finish my job because I started it, and when Christmas is finished, I go back to Gloria Pearson's classroom and lessons. I don't bring her anything from the department store because, after thinking about it, I know she won't want whatever it is I can bring.

Two days after I'm back to her classroom, I am trying to hand her the paragraphs I have written about the four major United States religions. Missus Pearson says, "Night school starts at the high school at the beginning of February. We need to find a way for you to begin there."

She has not been as friendly since I came back from the store. I kept thinking I would win her favor again by speaking well and working hard. But she is dismissing me.

"No, I'm not dismissing you, Denise. You have dismissed yourself. You need more difficult classes, and you need to be around a more serious group of students. Working with me one to one has been fine, but now that you have competition for your time, you should go and study like an adult."

It is because of the toilets. I ignored what I had been trying to reach for, to stop and do something that only made my back hurt, and that chided every minute that I was a dark and colored girl. I AM SUPPOSED TO REACH BEYOND MY STATION! Missus Pearson had tried to interest me in Greek letters, and levels of government, and inventors. I had cowered and not worked hard enough and this is what I got.

I buried my hurt right at the top of the place where Gloria Pearson had found the core in me that could learn. Cooked, pressed, strained, and dark purple, it eventually gelled inside the Ball jar that I filled. Now the season of the grapes was past.

CANNING TOOK DAYS and days. We pickled hills of everything. Washed and peeled, cut off tops, and scrubbed the skin if it was being left on—like the carrots. Some things we cooked, and some we did not. We cooked the carrots and the turnips and the turnip greens. We cooked the corn. We pickled cucumbers, onions, and chow-chow. How many onions did I peel?

Mr. Watkins delivered new jars and rings. I counted out the lids we had and washed all the jars from last year.

Most of the cooking of vegetables Granma'am did, and I did most of the getting them ready to be cooked. I think we did the pole-bean crop for the whole town. The fat green beans with the seeds you could feel sat around the kitchen and back in crates. I got up in the morning, and me and Granma'am ate, and then I sat through the day feeling the fat seeds. Shucking loose the white caps. Stringing the bean. Snapping the bean in two. I made the snap as small as possible, so that none of the bean crop would be wasted. With either the first or second snap, I would try to catch the string that stitched the bean down the middle. If I caught it right, it would come all the way off in one swipe. Next to me on the table, I piled the snapped-off heads and the green pole bean switches. I wrapped all that up in the garbage.

It was also my job to hit the jars with a spoon after the heat had, finally, sealed in the fruit and vegetables we had spent our days preparing. Granma'am would sit the jars on tables round the kitchen using plenty towels and telling me to stay way. The glass of the jars was hot, hot. After things cooled, in batches, I went round and hit the flat tops and the glass sides with a spoon. You have to hit it right—with not too little but not too much force—to hear anything like a ring. Most jars rang, but some spit back a thud. I would move those to the kitchen table where Granma'am could see about them since the thud meant the seal wasn't right.

CHRISTMAS I MADE a turkey. Turkey is my favorite, and it worked out fine. Big Jim and David and Luke edward like dark meat, and me and Margarete like the breast. The meat was moist and everybody ate without wanting for anything. My gravy turned out smooth, and the giblets fell apart and floated nicely. Something told me to go on ahead and cut the meat off the bone after dinner. I did that between the time I washed the dishes and when we opened our presents. Good thing. Margarete and Big Jim's friends were over to the house round eight, and they didn't stop coming till New Year's. But Christmas night was very pleasant; I got more clothes for school. David kept the underneath the Christmas tree straight, and I stayed on the kitchen. I washed the dishes before the people came, and I remembered to pull out some paper plates so there wasn't too much more work made for me to do.

Charlie, Big Jim's best running buddy, wanted to know the outcome of the wishbone. Luke edward hadn't gone out yet, and he piped right in. "Yeah, Neesey, where's the wishbone?"

"Right there on the platter with the meat."

Luke edward went in and got it. Brought it back into the front, holding it in two fingers with his nails he files. "Who wants the other end?"

Big Jim got up and went right up to him and yanked the thing broke. I don't think Luke edward was ready. I think he expected that Big Jim would say, "Ready? Now." But Big Jim didn't say a word. Margarete winced and so did I; Charlie laughed; Charlie slapped Luke edward on the back. Luke edward didn't act evil, but his eyes shaded over.

I wish Big Jim could let Luke edward win some time. Stupid old wishbone, and he couldn't let Luke edward win. Luke edward's being left, in front of the company, holding the small piece of the wishbone—well, it kept me thinking on the wishbone for days after. I slid right in to thinking that that wishbone, it was like the life we lived. A wishbone life, with one stem and two legs. People yanking, trying to break a leg off. See who got the biggest piece. And this after being left laying on the platter with all the cut-up meat.

WELL, BIG JIM did not let up on Margarete. He wanted all us to be ready for the baby to sleep in Luke edward's room, with me. I heard him tell Margarete that we wasn't poor enough that I had to sleep on a cot in the front room. (Well, none of that was said before it was time to make space for his child.) And how long did she plan to let me just sleep on that cot? he wanted to know. Margarete told him I was all right. I couldn't even side with Big Jim cause he was being mean about my Luke edward, even though I did happen to be tired of that cot they bought.

Big Jim told Margarete to tell Luke edward to get out.

Margarete had a talk with Luke edward. She told him that since it was already spring, wouldn't he move to the sunporch and let me get the bedroom ready for the new baby. It needs painting, she said. And Neesy needs to get settled, she said. And he would be warm all spring and summer. By fall, she would figure out something. Maybe we could move, she said.

Luke edward listed his mouth to one side, handsome and embarrassed, and said he knew he wasn't gone have that nice room to himself long.

He moved a bunch of his things in crates and drawers to the sunporch, which was still much too cold for sleeping. He stayed out late like always, and when he came in early in the mornings, he would just take off his shoes and socks and fall asleep on the couch. In the morning in the bathroom, you might see his shirt and sweater draped over the towel rack. His shoes and socks would be in front of the couch. His coat might be thrown over the chair. He would be long and snoring, and I would be sleep in the bed he had had.

Big Jim said to Margarete, "We don't have room here for that boy."

Margarete cried.

"I'm putting him out, Margarete," Big Jim said.

"You gone leave my son alone is what you gone do," Margarete answered him, weary, teary, tired of his pushing, but firm.

"Who you married to, Margarete?" he rattled, like a stick that had been stuck in the gate of the fan. Big Jim let the blades run over and over it. Tat-a-rat-a-rat-a-tat. Br-rat-a-tat, br-rat-a-rat.

"What you mean," she rattled back.

"You married to that boy, or me?!"

Margarete sucked her teeth and turned and left the room, the house.

They had words and more about it. They fussed and fumed and rumbled, and looked surprised and evil if I walked up on them. Big Jim finally got exhausted from having to argue with his wife, and he left out then, his turn. He stayed away a whole few weeks.

Margarete didn't remark on anything except that the bills kept coming. At every night's mail, Margarete sucked her teeth. She counted and recounted in her wallet. She never sent me out to pay anything—maybe because of the light company. Some mornings she'd say, "Going to the gas company, going to the phone company." Then at night, she rubbed her head and was quiet.

MAMA LOST A lot of weight the year my daddy died, and one Saturday, I caught Miss Lena trying to spoon-feed her grits. And then the lights went out. Mama was a mess, and she forgot.

I woke Luke edward up to take me to the bathroom, and he fussed, saying I had walked to the bathroom a million times, and I knew the way. "But it's dark, Luke edward," I said.

Mama sent me and Luke edward to the light company with money. She gave the money to me. We stood in line for a little while, I remember, and when we were just about up to the desk and to the man, Luke edward asked me to see the envelope. I gave it to him, and he took half the money out and told me he would be back in a few minutes. "Where you goin with Mama's money, Luke edward?" I tried to sound stern, seven years old.

"Stay in line," he called back to me, and he was out the door.

I went up to the desk. I handed the man the envelope with the address marked on it, and whatever money Luke edward had left inside it. The man at the desk asked me who was here with me, me with my head hardly a foot above his desk. His mouth was moving, open, but the words came out scrambled. What I heard was: we're going to box your brother's ears, your mother will never be all right again, and furthermore, you don't have money, you don't get lights. I jerked my ears back in line.

Luke edward was gone, the lights were off, my mother was skinny as a found chicken. I had no explanation, my daddy was dead, and David had gotten silent too. The man behind me in the line started talking to the man at the desk, talking about the young ruffian who had run off with the money. Who was this man? Why was he talking and why that tone of voice? I turned to look up at him and kicked him hard where I reached. At least this way, me and Luke edward were the same in everybody's mind.

Now I heard that tone about me from the man I had kicked. A curious look from the light company man. Then Luke edward came back, in the midst of this, and he told some lie about money for two bills and asked wasn't that enough to turn the lights back on. The desk man hesitated, and then Luke went on: our daddy, he said, he died. The desk man wrote a note about the Next Payment Due, and Luke had something inside his coat. He was back, though, protecting me; I felt much safer. That nosy man in line behind us shook his head.

First, Mama smacked me, and then she smacked Luke edward. She said I need to learn to hold onto my money. Mama was recently widowed was how she called it, and she needed help. David said he understood, and Luke followed so did he. Well, why did you take and, smack, go play with my money, smack smack, Mama wanted to know from Luke. David stood by, a witness, while Luke took his licks. Before long, Mama was heaving dry and choking, back deep inside the ruins Buddy left. David, in sympathy, started to hold Mama's hands while she cried.

Luke got the big box of light-money candy he had bought that afternoon and offered to share it with Mama and David. Mama pulled Luke edward and David toward her, rubbing on their nubby heads. "Promise Mama you'll be good," she asked Luke edward. And Luke edward promised, stuffing candy in his mouth.

Miss Lena came by as usual that night. I don't know what she saw.

I USED ALL the leftovers and salvage from the icebox. I hadn't seen the shelf metal so bare since I'd been back. It was sad, so I washed the box out with hot water and soap powder. Might as well clean it while it was empty.

Most of the stored food we had I used too. I told Margarete when we got low on milk, but other than that I didn't say nothing. If we had creamed corn for dinner, then we had creamed corn. We had canned spinach with oleo one night and peanut butter and jelly one night too.

Margarete put three dollars on the table. "Go get some neckbones and make sauerkraut," she said, "or beans." I bought two pounds of neckbones and two pounds of limas. I drank the bean liquor in a cup. I fed the bean liquor to Clara with a spoon. Lima shell casings floated in her bowl; I avoided them, afraid they might choke her.

On Thursday, Margarete's late day, J rang the bell. I thought it was David or Luke edward finally, and I was gone give them what for about the veins throbbing in they mama's head. "Hey, J," I said, and he patted Clara, who was sitting on my arm where she always sat. "What you doin comin by?"

"Anybody home but you and Clara?" he asked me.

"Naw," I said, "you want to come in? Margarete still at the shop," I told him. "You want some lima beans? Ain't no cornbread."

"No thanks, how you?" he said.

I told him how we ain't seen Big Jim. Or Luke edward either, for that matter. I told him Luke edward was supposed to be sleeping on the sunporch, but since then, it's like he only comes here when he ends up in this neighborhood. I told him Margarete is a mess, and I showed him the gray metal shelves in the icebox that I had cooked clean and then washed clean. They were still clean empty.

He said he came by to bring us some money.

"What you say, J?"

He said he came by to bring us some money. He counted two hundred dollars in twenty dollar bills out on the table. I couldn't touch it. What you talking about, J? I wanted to know. Where you get all this money, J? I wanted to know. What you mean you brought it for us?

I didn't let him out till he explained that Big Jim had brought the money to him and told him to bring it by today while Margarete is late at the shop. What should I do? I asked J. Just give it to Margarete, he said. It's the first of the month, he said. I was so tempted to take twenty dollars and go buy a lot of food. But J said he was happy to give me five dollars of his own, so I bought food with that.

Margarete came home and I reported all the things that happened. She asked me did I see Jim, and I told her no. I asked her about the money and she said she had to sleep on it, and she did. In the morning, when I'm best, I asked Margarete was she scared.

"Scared a what," she said, not looking at me.

"Well, scared Big Jim won't come back?"

"Neesey, you sad as a funeral, I swear. You always want to talk about the ugliest things in life." She got up from the table, and leaned on her hands and looked at me. Her bitterness hung like a veil. "This is how it is, Neesey. Get used to it. This is how it gets. Who do you know my age got a man?"

BIG JIM DID come back. He had a new baby, after all. And plus, Luke edward had come and taken all his things over to Christine's. After a time, they unplugged the electricity between them, and it got easier to walk around the house.

For extra, Missus Pearson tells me to write a paragraph, in good English, about a current problem. I turn this in.

March 19
Our flat has a tremble like the machines that pass the road. Big Jim has left on a count of Luke edward. So Margarete is alone again. I made her and the baby a big pot of chicken and dumplings. She has eaten them all. I said to Margarete in the kitchen the other day. Margarete, is you feeling alone? She says back to me, this is what happens, Neesey. Who you know my age got a man?

The next time I saw her, Missus Pearson gave me a lecture. First, though, she asked me a question. "I have a question to ask you," she begins. How am I going to explain how Margarete acted without lying? "Once you said that somebody told you everybody wanted to leave Virginia where you lived. Remember?" she asks me, and I turn a corner in my mind. "It is time for you to think about why all the people want to leave. Now, why do they?"

I parrot Luke edward, "They want to get someplace better."

Right into what she has already decided to say, she launches: "Yes, Denise, that's an idea. It may be that you find the people you know want to migrate from one place to a place they think will be better. Of course, never having been to where they say they want to go, they don't really know how much better or worse it will be. Now, do they?" I look on, in awe of how she thinks about things; mygrate, I write down. "But what I'd like you to consider, and think deeply about it, is that we Negroes have been forced to live in temporary places. We have been made to consider, no matter who of our family and friends may be with us, that any day could bring an edict that we be split up, sold. We are accustomed to separation, splitting up, losing members. Our families are the families that slavery made."

I pretend I am a rat. That I can nibble with speed and ferociousness through whatever slices of pasty or dark or stale or crusty bread I find myself sandwiched between. Slathered with mayonnaise, or mustard, or shame.

CAKE IN THE OVEN

MARGARETE USUALLY CALLS me into the bathroom to wash her back. Before Clara came out she needed help in the bath in general. After Clara because she was used to it and it felt good. Before Clara was when I first got a good look at her belly with the baby in it. Margarete would call me, "Neesey, will you come in here and wash my back?"

I would say OK from the kitchen, next door. I would go in the bathroom, close the door quick behind me, and Margarete would be sitting on the cold side of the tub with only her feet in a low layer of water.

"Margarete, why ain't you down in the bath?" I asked.

"Ain't good to sit in water while you pregnant."

"Oh," I say, dipping her washrag in the few inches of water round her feet, rubbing her back with soap, rinsing the washrag, rinsing her back, wondering about that baby in control of everything, not even born yet.

Margarete trained me in the bathroom years ago. The bathroom is where her religion lives. First, special soap. Saved. Used once or twice, then let to dry completely, then wrapped in wax paper and stored high up in the medicine chest. "See, Neesey, don't it smell special? We

226

won't use a lot, let's wash with regular soap first. Then we'll wash with this, and then the smell will last." Then creams and oils and lotions next, different bottles and jars for the different parts of our bodies. Perfumes and powders. All things from different places. Some from stores, some she made, some concocted by her friends, some stewed and boiled by Granma'am. Some things they have exchanged at Miss Sally's. This goes on your hands, and this goes on your feet. This cream goes on first and then this oil. You rub this in your hair. And you shake this powder in your panties, and under your arms. Last she paints her face. She dusts me lightly with the powder from her compact so I don't shine. "Don't say nothing to your daddy," she whispers. "It's our secret." And it is.

She pulls on stockings from a package. They are thin and see-through and come out of the package shaped like a leg. I like looking at the curved foot part. I stow the cardboard insert with the top of my pajamas. I will draw a picture on it for my daddy, later on.

I pull on my white socks with lace around the edges and slip my feet into my new white shoes. They are patent leather with one strap across. Mama and I both leave the bathroom in our slips, and when we open the door, the scent of woman rushes.

We meet the wall of roasting ham in the kitchen.

NOTHING COMES TO me these days; not the stomach part at least. If the stomach is _____, then it's a girl. If the stomach is _____, then it's a boy. One position is high and pointy, and the other is midsection and all around. And no one in Detroit was talking about the high or low of it.

Every day—more than once usually—I raked my

mind and tried to remember, what with Margarete's belly weighing so heavy on my next few months and years. She just got bigger and more pregnant, and nothing to help me came from my raking. The idea of her baby to come took up all the space in the house that wasn't already occupied by furniture, or men, or me and Margarete. And I couldn't remember how to tell what it was. If I could have boxed the wondering up and taped it shut and put it in the closet until the baby came, I think that would have helped me. I like it when things are neat and ordered, a place for everything and nothing out of place. But I couldn't put the questioning away, and every morning, it seemed, Margarete's baby in the belly was a heavier weight. So I rushed to get dressed, and then rushed out the door into Detroit's cold air. On the way to school I want to know from myself: Is the truth about the stomach gone come back to me? And why can't I remember so plain a thing?

Of all Margarete's and Big Jim's friends, and Luke's friends too, who visited, who were in and out the house; they all looked at her belly, but no one said, like they would have down home, *High as Margarete's stomach is? You know iss a* _____.

My thirteenth birthday comes and goes. Margarete is seven months pregnant and I still can't read her belly. This failure of my recognition taunts me. *It is low and all around*, I think to myself, but this still meets a blank in my forehead where I expect the meaning to live. Margarete has forgotten my turning thirteen, what with her belly jumping to life. When I was down home, I usually got a package from her with something in it from Detroit. Must have been my being away that made her remember, and now that I was there, I was forgotten. Lantene would double over with jealousy in front of me about whatever had come in the mail from Detroit. If what Margarete sent could be worn, Lantene would ask to borrow it and would near stretch it out of shape. Granma'am said I can't let Lantene borrow nary another thing my mama sends.

Harold brought by a card and thirteen dollars from Granma'am. I put the card up on the table, and then I got a flurry of presents. Two skirts and blouses that looked adult from Margarete (and Big Jim); I put the clothes on and looked in the mirror and looked like her. Two of the same white button-down sweaters from David and Luke edward. When he saw them both, Luke edward took his back and brought me blue. I don't think David knew about their same choices, because he left the box for me, and I thanked him, and that was the end of it. J sent a card through the post with Denise spelled the American way on the envelope. One afternoon, I take the money Granma'am sent and go down on Woodward. I buy myself a necklace that looks prim like Miss Pearson, and I decide there is a girl in Margarete's belly. How could there not be? Granma'am has sent the potion, and look at me, here, hovering, ready to raise. I don't know the first thing about raising no little boy. Neither does Margarete.

SHORTLY AFTER CLARA came, I was feeling sick like I had been for almost a week, and knowing it was because all hope for my after-school progress had ended and seemed like I would be busy with the baby for the rest of my days. Waiting on Margarete, washing linen and diapers, listening to the little noises the baby made, telling Big Jim everything the baby did while the baby was in my sight and not Margarete's. And after he finished listening to me and eating his dinner he would go in the room if Margarete was in there and sit with Margarete and the baby, and ask Margarete about everything the baby did while Clara was in her sight and not mine. The three a them cooed together; I would hear it in the kitchen after I had finished running the water and before I started rinsing the dishes I was washing. I admit it, I would strain to hear. If I hadn't been straining, I'd of rinsed the dishes not all at once like I did since Margarete didn't care about my using up the water. But I wanted to hear everything I could; this was a straining time.

Like I said, I had been feeling sick about the whole mess the house was in. And two weeks after Clara come, about eleven in the morning after the child is back to sleep for most of the rest of the day, and Margarete too is napping, I go into the bathroom and close the door with my geography book. I open it to the section about Turkey and sit down on the commode. The shocking spread of red blood on my pants is stretched between my knees directly north of the map in the book.

First, I am immobilized, and then I groan. "Aw, na-a-aw." Maybe out loud, maybe not, can't remember. I feel the tears trying to ball up there where they first start to choke, down in the core of my throat and back between my mouth and jaw. Nothing to do but go tell Margarete.

I breathe in, then I let myself lean forward to the book. I slide it forward to cover up the sight of the blood, and I gently lay my forehead in the crease of the pages. *Alpha beta gamma delta epsilon*—I singsong the whole thing in my head, and when I'm finished, I am wishing for two things. To be able to talk to Granma'am about this bleeding mess, and to be able to visit Turkey.

When Margarete wakes up from her nap, the chicken wings are soaked in gravy, and I have a neatly folded bandanna between my legs and a clean pair of drawers on. I have used hot hot water and have not been able to erase the first blood; I have a hard time deciding whether to throw those drawers out, or to ask Margarete what works to clean blood.

"Margarete," I say, going into her room because I have heard her moving around and she has not come out. So I go in and say, "Margarete, I started my bleeding today." She looks at me sympathetically—I appreciate that—and she sits down on the side of the bed. "Lord, more blood," she says. What she means is all the bleeding that happened with Clara has probably made me bleed too. That's when I remember, like a goof, that it's cold water that gets the blood out the linen and will get the blood out the drawers I have stuffed in my pocket. Well, turns out I had already boiled the blood in those forever, but my next pair of drawers that got blood on them weren't ruint like that. I threw the first pair away in a garbage can cross town. I got a fright about leaving my blood so far away from me, but as preservation I determined that even if the stain wasn't gone, I had boiled myself sufficiently out. All that was left could be left cross town.

Margarete says, "Look in my drawer and get two dollars." I get up and cross the room and get the money. She is reaching in her bedside drawer. She pulls out a big Kotex napkin and says, "Put this on." There are two pieces a tissue sticking out from each end, and Margarete holds one a them out in her fingers. "You thread this part through the clip in the belt, and you do the same with the other end," she says. "Now, go on down to Peckway's and get yourself a belt," she says; "it ain't gone be but a dollar and some change. And put these in the bathroom." She pulls out a whole blue boxful of them napkins.

I walk up and down Tireman to Scotten and back

three times before I get up the nerve to go in Peckway's. First I pray that that old young boy ain't in there. And then I realize that that's ridiculous he is always in there. And then I start to practice what I will say and do: I will hold up the two dollars and say, "Gimme one a the belts that holds up a Kotex, please." And then I start to wonder is there someplace else I can go. I look up and down the street to see if anybody is there I can ask to do it for me, but everybody I would know is round the school of course. I have a quick thought about Luke edward, but now that he's sposed to be sleeping on the sunporch, ain't no telling where he is.

Deep breath. *Alpha beta*. I get to the door and see him through the glass. *Gamma delta epsilon*. The address of the store, I never noticed before, is 561. I push the door in and go up to the counter. I hold up the two dollars and say, "Can I have one a the belts that hold up a Kotex, please?" He looks straight at my moving lips, and it takes more than a minute for his to curl just a teeny bit up. He is laughing at me, I am thinking, and though I expected this, the two dollars in my hand start to shake. I put the two dollars down on the counter, and put my hands down by my sides, but I don't move my eyes. I glare at him like he is completely responsible for the predicament I'm in. Take that money and get that belt, I am thinking. I don't mind smacking the both of them, I am thinking, I can smack this whiteboy and smack Margarete too.

He responded to my glaring. He reached up to a place I did not look at. I concentrated on directing his simple butt. He brought the belt down to the counter. He put the belt in a bag and dropped some change in the bag too. He put the bag down on the counter, and then I picked it up.

I left the store slow as I could.

My walk back to the flat was direct and I was burning up, and so the walk was short, but it gave me plenty of time to think on some things. This could not possibly be all Margarete was going to say on the matter of my bleeding (but it was). And how often would I change the big Kotex napkins: because of their size, I started with morning and night. Nope, four times a day and once again, if I woke up during the night.

I HAD TAKEN a photograph some months before leaving, at Mrs. Valentine Kinsey's suggestion. We were expecting Mary Kinsey, the Kinseys' oldest daughter, to bring the photograph over to our house anytime. But the photograph didn't arrive before I left. And, in the dismal gray of going back, I forgot about smiling-me in front of the Richmond lights.

Mrs. Kinsey invited Granma'am to have me take the photograph. She and her husband had a car. Mrs. Kinsey was one of the rich ladies at Calvary, our church; she was invited to participate high up in every function because of her donations, and her list a friends was part of what made a Ladies' Day successful. The whole town had heard I was leaving; it was a subject of parlor talk—the same as the lovely bows that had decorated the church at Ellen Coles's wedding or the carved wood truck with moving wheels that had come by mail for the pastor's son's birthday. Neesey Palms is going back to her mother in Detroit.

Mrs. Kinsey had a piano and three children. She was taking her children to the photographer's visit in Richmond center. They were having a family sitting, which they tried to do every other year, God willing. When Granma'am sent a cake over one Saturday, Mrs. Kinsey sent back a card, which I read out loud to Granma'am. *Mrs. Martha Dambridge*, it said. *May the Lord continue to bless you and thank you for the delicious cakes you make. I am taking the children to R. center for a family portrait on Saturday August the 4th. I have heard that Neesey is going to her mother this fall—you must be grieving, she is such a good child. I wondered if you would want me to take her for a portrait. Two copies could be arranged, one for you and one for Margaret. I am sure Margaret will be surprised and happy. I am meeting Mr. Kinsey at the train. We have room in our car for Neesey. The cost is $3.00 each portrait, since Mr. Kinsey and I have already paid for the sitting. Since this may take all day, Neesey is welcome to stay the night with the children, and we will all meet you at first Sunday. Sincerely, Valentine Hall Kinsey.*

Valentine Kinsey's handwriting was beautifully curved, so well drawn. Granma'am got six dollar bills out from her grip under the bed. She had me write a note that the Lord blesses, even when his children don't know what is next. I tried to imitate the handwriting best I could. Granma'am looked over it for neatness and noticed my imitation. She rubbed my hair. "That's right," she said. "If you gone imitate people, imitate the best people. The people like the Kinseys what got nice houses and professions. It never does harm to imitate whitepeople either, what have lace curtains and inside heat and educations." She had me carry the note over the next morning, before school.

The Kinseys were the people Granma'am preferred to be my friends. They were good churchgoing people. They lived in a house with an upstairs. And Mr. Kinsey did business in Richmond and other places. The children had different kinds of clothes to wear. These things were all the more reason for the friendship, as far as Granma'am was concerned.

Granma'am upped and sent the picture by Harold; I had been in Detroit four months when it came. Margarete said I look older already, and Luke edward laughed. David liked it, and so did Harold Grayson. I was surprised that the camera could show my nervousness like that. I could almost see my knees shake.

Granma'am noticed. Down home with Granma'am, there wasn't a feeling could cross my face Granma'am didn't notice or some other kind of way feel. I guess it's because she raised me. With the photograph, there was a note from Granma'am, written by Harold Grayson. "Neesey," it said, "I see some sadness around your mouth and eyes. You too young to be grieving, child. The Lord got a life planned for you. Grand Ma'am," it was signed. Two words, that was funny. And then at the bottom: "It is a very nice picture of you, my dear grandchild. I have put it on my bureau to remind me of you."

Hearing her words read back to her, Granma'am would add encouragement. She always wanted me to have what I would need to go on.

I only had two good dresses, both for church. And Granma'am washed and ironed them both. Hung them high up on the rod over the dresser in her room. They hung there five days. Granma'am chose the white dress over the blue. I knew she would pick the white one all along.

I was well behaved, as usual, in the car. With the Kinsey children, I was always the example. That was the ladder of instruction: Mrs. Kinsey would imitate whitepeople and Granma'am would imitate those things Mrs. Kinsey might have learned that Granma'am had not had a chance to yet. I would imitate the both of them—Granma'am and Mrs. Kinsey—and Mrs. Kinsey's children would imitate me and each other.

Mrs. Kinsey's children were much younger than me. Her oldest daughter, Mary Lynn, was nine when I was twelve. Age was why we weren't closer friends. Well, also, ease in life makes you seem even younger than you are. So Mary Lynn never seemed to catch up to me somehow.

Mrs. Kinsey had her children dressed. Both girls had their hair straightened and hot-rolled. Clothes so new they still smelled like the boxes. It was terrible Virginia-hot that day, so the smells of hair grease and new clothes and Granma'am's good soap singed in the air. All four of us children had on white; the baby boy, short pants.

The Eboline stained the back seat, I know, because all of us were greased to shining. On the walk to the Kinseys', Granma'am had me wear my old shoes with everyday socks and carry my white socks and good shoes in a paper bag. She told me not to put them on until I got to the photographer's place of business, and she told me several times to make sure to ask Mrs. Kinsey to make sure my socks was straight.

Granma'am said every inch of me would show in the picture, and we all would look at it for the rest of my life, and my children might have it if it last that long. "Fix y'socks with that on y'mind," she told me. As I was closing the gate she added, "And don't wrinkle y'dress."

The man who took the picture had a lot of equipment—lights, curtains, cameras, tissue to wipe down the Eboline. The Kinsey family went first, I waited. I asked Mrs. Kinsey to check my socks soon as I put them on. She checked them again after their family photograph, while the man who took the picture was telling me where and how to sit. Where my hair was fuzzy and short around the front and sides, she rubbed it back with warm, sure hands. She dabbed some of the pressed powder from her compact and brushed it on the tip of my nose. Her busy smell of mother.

J ASKS ME can he come over to Margarete's to see me. This is after he quit school and started the job he got. He is already over to Margarete's visiting when he asks me this, and I am deep in my book covers half listening to him. I ask him from where I am where is he going. He doesn't answer back right away so I look up at him. I can tell by his silence and his face he is saying something that I should ask him more about. I simply ask him, "What you talkin bout, J?" He and I both know from the false high of my voice that I am stalling, and I am; I don't want to talk about new things. I want to keep on doing what I'm doing. I don't want to be interrupted.

His face crumples a little.

Well, dog. What exactly is he asking me? I take a deep breath; there he is looking at my hair, I guess. He says the way I braid it reminds him of home.

"I cain't answer you, J," I say. I am the only one calls him that.

"How come?" he asks me.

"Cause you asking me," I dodge, "about Margarete's house."

"Oh," he accepts.

Huge mistake. J had been educated in the Arkansas school of whatever this was he thought he was doing. He sent his uncle Jump over to ask Margarete.

I didn't think nothing of seeing Jump at the house them few days later, so I have to say I might of opened the door on this eruption myself. Big Jim and Luke edward and Margarete teased me enough to burn clean through. For a while, I was so heated up by all this off-color attention that I took a clean dive into the cool spring of my lessons. I tried not to think about J and his boyfriend girlfriend silliness. But the teasing made me kind of mad.

J did come by, a couple weeks after his uncle. First thing he said: "Cain't my uncle Jump make anything happen!" Grinning. I could of slapped him. Instead, I cussed him out. Shocked at my roiling, he asks, "Whassa matter, Neesey?" and that pitiful piece of heather branch he brought me dropped with his arm from behind his back and ruined his surprise.

"Everybody looks at me like my hips are spreading!" I shot at him, my eyes full to snapping with all the dis-agreement hanging. He looks foolish and uncompre-hending.

One after the other, they had each got me privately. They teased me in public, but they all felt like they had something more important to say. First David came, then Margarete, then Big Jim, and then Luke edward. Keep your dress down. Keep your dress down. Keep your dress down. Keep your dress down. They all said exactly the same thing. Except Luke edward who said keep your dress down and your underpants up.

My next birthday, my second in Detroit, when I was turning fourteen, only J and Luke edward remembered, and only J on time. Though he had been as persistent as a farmer, and come by once a month, I was curt with him until my birthday was forgotten. Just like my family helped me get mad at him, they created the vacuum that let me know he really was a good somebody to have around. J sent me a card and came by the house after work. By the time he arrived, my mouth had turned down the way I hate and the way Margarete's does when the bills ain't paid. I was not glad to see him, and I was shamed of my feeling, and then he commenced to showing me a box wrapped in birthday paper.

My day changed, late as it was. It wasn't a real big box, but that didn't matter not at all. It was wrapped in birthday paper, and he grinning, "Open it, open it." We had some coffee in the kitchen, and I opened my one box slow. Inside was some long-arm kitchen mitts. I squealed. J explained, "They industrial. For all-the-time cooks, like you."

I had put them on while he's talking, and up to my elbows was covered in silver quilt. I got right up and went to the oven and pulled the pan of lamb chops I made for myself for my birthday, see did I feel any burning heat. I didn't. I basted the chops while I was up, see did I have any trouble working with a spoon with the mitts on. I didn't. J had got up with me, and said, "I was wonderin how you cooked em. They sure smell good."

"You hungry? They done."

"You got enough?"

I felt defiant. There were leftovers in the box, and any of these late Negroes who forgot my birthday for the second time, well, they could just eat what we had yesterday. I put two lamb chops and a mound a spinach and a mound a potatoes on his plate. I fixed a plate for me. "You want some gravy, J?"

"Yeah," he said.

"What you want it on—the meat?"

"And potatoes," he said.

I laid my mittens neat in the box and poured us some ice water in my lovely tumblers. We sat down and had a birthday dinner. While we was eating, J asked me did I know the rhyme about Mary had a little lamb.

I nodded my head yes. Miss Pearson had reminded me when we went to Hudson's cafeteria and had tea and mashed potatoes that I must never never never talk with food in my mouth. Mrs. Valentine Kinsey had said the same thing to me all the time down the country, but Mrs. Kinsey said it mostly so I would teach her children good manners, I thought; Missus Pearson really cared about how it made me look.

"What about it?" I asked him when the murky mixture of tender lamb and soft spinach had slid warm down my throat. I wiped my mouth with the paper towel I had laid our silverware on. I liked talking to Josephus. (Even though the way his schooling was handled made me mad—in the nights I had had to wonder if I was only mad cause their ignoring him in school meant he left me there alone.) When he talked he said real smart, country-wise, foretelling things. "What about it, J?" I repeated, when he took too long to answer me.

"Well," he started. "Mary had a little lamb, little lamb, little lamb. Mary had a little lamb. Its fleece was white as snow. Everywhere that Mary went, Mary went, Mary went, everywhere that Mary went, the lamb was sure to go."

And then sometimes, he made not a whole lot a sense. He shoveled more food in his mouth after reciting, as if the break to say the rhyme had starved him.

"J, I don't know what you talkin bout," I said. Not understanding things puts me in a bad mood, usually. I didn't want to get in a bad mood when this was my only little birthday celebration. If he didn't explain hisself, I was gone be mad, and I was gone be mad at him. He had about five minutes. I started to pull together my dishes and things like I was gone get up. And like you might expect, that put fear of God in him.

"You think it has to do with the Bible?" he said.

See what I mean? He may be country, but he is not dumb. And I am very fond of curiosity, I love questions.

"What you mean, J?" I said, happy.

"Well, Mary," he said, emphasis on Mary.

"Yes," I said. I have finished with my food.

"And the little lamb could be Jesus," he said.

"Hmmm." I said. "I ain't never heard it bein bout the Bible, J," I said, "but that don't mean it ain't. You could be discoverin somethin," I said, and then I did get up to start on the dishes. I didn't want to sit over no food scraps, chatting.

J asked me what was my best time this year and I remarked about all the crates a books I covered for Missus Pearson over the summer. How it took me all those weeks to finish the job, and how Missus Pearson just left it for me to do. How that was a real job that wasn't cleaning or cooking or something else that need to be done day in and day out. How when it was finished, I could look at the books stacked up, and know I had lasted through all that was expected of me. I love schoolbooks, anyway, I said.

"We all know that," J answered, smiling broad.

J asked me, well, what about the baby I'm raising so nice. I had finished all the dishes in the sink. Me and J went and looked over the crib rail at Clara. Clara is eleven months. Clara has a big appetite. J wants to know what I feed her. I tell him she eats a half a soft-boiled egg with a half a piece a bacon mashed in it in the morning. She likes just a spoonful of applesauce for dessert. Dessert of every meal. I give her a little prune juice in her bottle when I come home from school, and Saturdays and Sundays at eleven. For dinner, she just has whatever vegetable I fix—I mash it up for her—because she's so distracted by Margarete and Big Jim she'll eat anything at dinnertime, no trouble.

J is seventeen, be eighteen in the summer. I think from his questions he gone say something stupid about babies and make me want to send him home. He whispers, "Ain't we gone have birthday cake?" I tell him no, I ain't got no cake. It's bad luck to bake your own birthday cake, I tell him. J says he sorry he didn't know that before he came. I tell him that's OK cause those mittens he brought sure will cut down on my scars.

J left to take the bus across town, home, and I felt better. I turned off the oven and let the food get cold in the kitchen. Nobody was hungry when they come in even though everybody remarked that I didn't say we was having, what's that they smell, lamb chops.

In the morning, when the kitchen got light, my mittens with the birthday paper could be seen. Everybody was sheepish, and I got presents the day after.

J called on the telephone and had a conversation with Luke edward. I wasn't home, didn't know nothing about it. I had been to Missus Pearson's, and she gave me a box with cotton gloves for the spring. Off-white gloves with tuck seams down the back of the hand. They were wrist length and in a glove box. I was thrilled near to a faint.

I didn't have such a good time that visit, though. Margarete had woke up late that Saturday and, rushing to get to the shop, passed all her agitation on to the baby. So Clara was cranky, and Missus Pearson was happy I was fourteen but thought this was the time I needed to start paying more attention to how Negroes act.

She wanted to know if I saw what was going on in this city. If I was noticing how rambunctious Negroes were becoming.

Rambunctious, I think.

She started to talk about the fires on this and that side of town. And in other cities too, she waved a newspaper at me.

I used Clara's crying as my excuse, and I took my gloves and left. Missus Pearson could outdo herself, talking about Negro weakness or laziness or failure to understand about the world. (Clap, clap.)

But the gloves made me smile all the way home. And at one red light, I took the box out of Clara's stroller and looked at them again. When I got to the house, I had my hands full so I rang the bell. No answer. It was hardly twelve noon, Saturday morning; I knew Luke edward was in there, probably sleep.

"Luke," I hollered, and it made me laugh. It was just like when I was in Detroit when I was little, and Margarete would send me out to get them boys, and I would holler and holler till my head ached, seem like. And I would still have to walk all the way up to their faces, and be big and strong and bold. A mama representative. "Git in the house, Luke edward, time to eat. Git in the house, David, Mama wants you NOW."

"LUKE, LUKE," I hollered. Finally he came down to the door.

"Hi, Buddy, how you?" I said. "Help me with this stroller." I lifted the baby, Clara held my glove box, and I headed up the stairs. "How you get that flour on your sweater?" I asked.

"Where you gettin them hips is what I want to know," he said. He bumped up the steps with Clara's Cadillac.

I smelled cake. Clara saw J inside and called to him in garble. He came and took the baby from my arms. He had flour in his hair.

I walked straight into the kitchen, which you know was a mess. Nine cookbooks open, flour and eggshells everywhere. The cabinet doors a-gaping.

"It's a cake in the oven," J beamed.

It came out a little lopsided, but it came out. When Margarete and Big Jim's friends came over, everybody got a little sliver—just a little sliver—and we had a birthday party, rowdy, for me. J stayed half the night and walked home happy.

It was clear from the beginning that J would take care of me. Before he started at River Rouge Plant, he kept me from being by myself in all my country ways. He encouraged me to keep my head up when the baby was coming down like a guillotine. And he always asked what I was studying, said I should keep my mind alert. After Margarete had Clara, he came and visited and hauled the big stroller down the front stairs for me while I hauled the baby behind. I had got mad at him before, and for good reason, I think. But after that birthday, I forgave him, and he noticed. He felt better. So when Clara is finally toddling—and can be left with other people from time to time—J says he wants to make out and is it OK. I think it is probably time.

We go to his bedroom on his birthday; mine is long past. The men get they birthdays off at the plant. His uncle Jump has told him to have a good time, and because I don't want to know, I don't ask if he told his uncle Jump I am coming over.

We have been to have hamburgers and french fries and milk shakes at suppertime. We walk back; J knows I like to walk. J's room is neat and orderly. He does not have a closet, but he has hammered up two long boards at different heights all along one wall. On the boards he has put nails, and on each nail is a hanger or two with his clothes he wears. His shoes are lined up, and his feet are big.

J asks me if I want to sit on his bed, and I sit down at the edge. He kisses me behind my ears a number of times. He seems to be taking care to be soft, and I appreciate that. All while this is happening, I am telling myself I am near fifteen, and this is time enough.

J asks me if he can touch my titty, and I stop thinking about my age long enough to tell him, yes, he can but not hard. I am surprised when he reaches inside my sweater to touch it, but he doesn't pull it hard and it feels nice. I look at him out the side of my eye, and he is being so careful and looking at me so hard that our eyes lock like hangers caught together at the hook. I have to laugh cause I'm nervous; something in the caughtness of this hurts a little bit.

He laughs with me, and we talk for a little while. He promises me that his uncle Jump is not coming anytime soon, and he tells me that his private is big. He asks me do I want to see it, and I tell him no. He asks me do I want to take off my clothes, and I tell him no. He asks me can he take off his clothes, and I tell him no.

Then he asks me if he can kiss me in the mouth. I just lean forward, except I close my eyes shut. He kisses me in the mouth and it's nice, and he puts his hand inside my sweater again and I am happy.

We do this for a long time, and then J presses me down on the bed. He does not press me down hard. He doesn't push me either; it's kind of like the sway you see in the movies, and because I have seen it in the movies, I know what to do. J squirts some lotion into his hand and reaches for his private. I don't look.

I just lay down there and kiss him back, and J hoists himself up on top of me. I don't complain because I'm not taking anything off. Anything spills will get on my skirt, and that's that.

He is strong as the dickens, cause he is moving his legs and everything around, holding himself up with his hands. I don't want him to fall down on me, thinking he will break my ribs, and then what will I say I was doing? He doesn't fall down on me, but this holding himself up lasts a while, and I am shocked by the whole thing.

Yes, J is using the lotion and rubbing himself up and down on me. He breathes hard. I open my eyes and his are squeezed shut, and he is calling my name. His ramming his hips has hoisted up my skirt, and he is moving like he's got a motor. I am alarmed, and I call his name. He answers calling mine, but doesn't stop moving. Well, I never! The bed was just a-shaking, up and down against the wall, and my legs is spread open to go round the space his machine hips is taking up. I realize I have thrown my arms up, to kind of hold on, and I take my right one and throw it down between my legs, when he's in a up motion. I just want to make sure my panties is in place. My hand knocks against his big knuckles of one hand where he rubs and rubs.

I don't think he even felt me move, but he started to shudder about that time. Thank you, Neesey, thank you, he is saying. He opens his eyes, and I am looking at him. He smiles at me, thank you, Neesey.

He moves off me to his knees, and pulls my skirt down as he goes. He lays his head on top my skirt, and rests there, kneeling. I know he does need to rest. I touch his nubby hair, cause I like him, and cause I can reach, and cause I don't want to be alone after this short but true alarm. We lay there until he gets up, and I notice his private is flat again in his pants.

First thing he says, "Is you all right?" I tell him yes. We sit quiet on the side of his bed. I guess he is probably thinking, like I am, that this is a curious business. After some time when we only breathe, he stretches out, smiling. "Neesey," he says.

I leave him all the space to go on, and turn my head to him.

"This my best birthday," he smiles and tells me.

"This *is*," I say.

JOSEPHUS TOOK TO coming by for me some Saturdays, to spend part of his weekend off from work at the plant. At first, I was mad at him for involving Margarete like he did, but he stayed out my way for a while, and in time, of course, I missed him. I missed school, I missed activity. I missed everything but diapers and mashed food.

Saturdays was Margarete's long day at the shop. She got a regular customer at eight o'clock who liked to have her hair done before she did her shopping. Close to the baby's birth, the eight o'clock wasn't no problem, cause Margarete was home and resting. But when Margarete and Big Jim started to go out again on Friday nights, then Saturday morning got to be a groggy mess with Margarete rushing around on not enough sleep and me trying to keep the baby's morning sweet.

Big Jim slept a little later on Saturdays, but by nine he had seen Margarete out, had two cups of dark coffee with three spoons of sugar in each. Granma'am had told me that if I had too much sugar it would give me a tick, so I was sure to have only two sugars in my coffee, but now I drink it every day, and I didn't used to.

Josephus would come by around eleven or eleven-thirty. I would be home by myself and by then would have put the baby down for her nap. I closed the door to Luke edward's room so the noise wouldn't travel in, and I would play Luke edward's records and talk to Josephus about how it was at the plant that week, and how much money he had saved, when is the last time I saw Luke edward or David, or whether I was tired of taking care of Clara, and whether he wanted to eat what I had left over for lunch.

Josephus always asked me what I had done that day with the Missus Pearson work. That was my favorite part of his visit. I would take and show him from my books and notebooks all the knowledge I ran behind. Josephus let me teach him. If I had not had that to look forward to—a set of wondering, attentive eyes and ears—I might have started the long walk down home, back to where somebody would recognize me. And left the baby with a bottle in the crib.

After Clara woke up and I fed her again, I would wrap her up in her outdoor things while Josephus would haul the Cadillac stroller downstairs. Josephus and I would walk all around the ways he learned between where he lived across town and where we lived. He would help me push the stroller, and more and more he took me to walk near the big high school. On Saturdays, the school was closed, the air was cold, and the yard was full of boys practicing their exercises for the football games they played, and girls cheering, majorettes. J and I pushed the stroller all along the high fence.

MY DREAM CALLED Clara before she arrived. I usually dream like a spectator. Usually I dream about other people, and I watch what they do, like I'm sitting on the edge of a fence, and the people I'm watching are play-acting on the field. This time, I was really in the dream, and that's how I know it had bearing on my real life.

Josephus and me was closer than we are by then. Or maybe I was just over his house playing like. I didn't see no legal papers hanging up in the dream, and all country people have that legal paper hanging in a frame, if they got it.

I was loving shoes! I was picking them up all over the place we lived in and rubbing on them as if they each was alive and needing love. I was kind of sick of myself, doing all that. And I was only finding one shoe at the time. I would hold it, sit with it, rub on it, and then put it away, lay it down on the floor of the closet. After that I would find another and do the same again.

Other than the shoes, the place was clean as the kitchen at midnight, so that's how I know that I'm in my own flat. Josephus was out working, though I won't know ever what shoes he could of been wearing, many as I was picking up round the place.

Here's the beat-all: Margarete come in. She walk right into the front room where I am holding a black shoe. Margarete looks direct at me, and I hold my breath! Margarete's hair is gray-white, and thin as new onion. Her big stomach what was full with the baby is flat in the dream, gone. She smiles at me on that one side like she do, and asks me ain't I glad she taught me how to love and take care of my children. What is she talking about, I'm thinking, these ain't children, they shoes. I'm considering that her eyes getting limp as her hair. I looked down at the shoe, and sure as afternoon, it was a drooling baby child, a girl.

I jumped up and went abruptly to the bedroom closet to investigate. I dropped the shoe baby I held. There they were, a whole brood of drooling babies, lined up on the floor, cross from the bed. All of them girls. I had been putting them away—shoe baby girls—all afternoon. I counted: seventeen.

I rushed back to see about the one I had dropped. There, still in the front, was Margarete and the child. Both of them cooing and bald.

And that was the end of it.

Of course that dream was just what it seemed. Margarete's new baby girl, Clara, come in the next two weeks. She changed the whole way I lived.

So Plain a Thing

MARGARETE SAID, "I'MA have the baby in the bed in your room."

I was quiet, listening; the baby was here practically, Margarete was confirming it. Now, I had just moved into Luke's room, sad that my brothers weren't in the room they had had so long, and glad to be out of the public front of the house. Why did Margarete want to have the baby in there? Was she feeling like she wanted to be in the place Luke had left? Did she want to be near me, thinking this baby coming might take a long time? Well, should I just help her get in there? What's on top of the beds? I wonder to myself. Oh, I better go clean the clothes off the other bed. "Margarete," I say, "let me just clean the other bed off, it's some clothes I folded on top."

She is already lifting her heavy feet, getting off her bed and into her house shoes. "Let me go head now, keep this room clean for Jim," she says.

Things fly through my mind like thrown hardballs. I am remembering Granma'am's rhythm: "You be sure and he'p y'mother, now; be sure and he'p y'mother." Obediently, I move toward her bed to walk Margarete to my room.

Margarete puts her arm around my shoulder, and leans. She smells like fertile ground. "Neesey, thank you for comin up to help me," she says. You can hear her feet slide now. "I'm too old to be havin a baby," she says. Slide, shuffle, say her house shoes in between. "You should be havin this baby, not me," she says. I avoid the hardballs with my head.

BIG JIM HAD exercised some forethought, though, and he had borrowed a car from one of his buddies, so when it was time to go cross town for Miz Alma, he swore to me he would be back in a hurry, and I believed him. Big Jim told me when he left that I should start all the big pots of water to boiling, and make sure Margarete was OK. His nervousness hung in my head like a family portrait, in between my filling the pots up near to the top with water, and walking them to the four burners on the stove. I was thirteen years old, and had been dealing with pots for at least five of those years, hard. Still, I remarked how heavy it all was. As I hauled the full pots from the sink to the stove, the weight pulled at my inside, I noticed.

Margarete babbles her way through our wait, and her water, and the boiling pots of water in the kitchen. I turn the burners down, and cover them with lids, to keep the water hot, and just to have something to do.

"Neesey, come sit down here by the bed," Margarete calls, not feebly but raspylike. I look again for the blue car while I think where to sit.

"OK, Margarete," I call back, "let me go get a chair from the kitchen." I go back to the kitchen and close up the instructions for the order of operations. I slide the closed book carefully to the very end of the table, in case the lady Big Jim brings needs to use the table space. But the book will be there when she comes, in case they don't need me, and I can have the kitchen and try to understand what the instructions say. I pull the chair out from the table—the chair I have been sitting in. Before I take it into the bedroom, I decide to check the boiling water. I start with the cast-iron pot because I worry that the water will damage its season. I dumbly grab the pot handle with my fingers—and just like that, a scar.

I do go to sit by the bed with Margarete. I take a cold rag and ice to nurse my burn. Margarete babbles and embarrasses me. Of course, Big Jim has not yet returned because Margarete must say what she says. So I listen and do not repeat her babblings ever, and hope that she will be finished by the time he arrives, hope that he will come with the lady before I have to be responsible, hope that Margarete will not want to be closer to me because of what she tells me, if she remembers.

"You remember your daddy, Neesey?" Of course I remember my daddy. I tell her "of course," in a soft voice with a clean *f*. "Your daddy was the best man," she goes on. "He took me from the country like I was the first apple to fall from a tree he shook. Every gal down home wanted your father, Neesey. He was strong and fine and had been so many places. We came to Detroit together. I got so full of dreams between the time he asked me to marry him and the time when we left for Detroit, I gained weight." She smiles, she looks caught between memory and now. "I wanted to come up here and try out as a singer. Me and Evelyn Ownes had that plan. Evelyn can actually sing a little better than me, but I had a higher voice so I could sing the lead parts. Made my singing a little easier to appreciate than Evelyn's, I think, but Evelyn has the better voice. Do you know any of this, Neesey?" she asks me.

"Yes," I answer being sure to close my teeth, "me and Lantene talked about you and Miss Evelyn down home."

"Do Evelyn smoke?" Margarete asks me.

"Naw," I say, "but she use snuff."

"Snuff!" Margarete snorts. "Lord, we gettin old. Where do you think Jim is?" I don't answer because I want to bawl, myself. "Well, see Evelyn's voice probably still better than mine, mine has crumbled like a old wall behind these Chesterfields I been smoking. Your father loved to hear me sing. I sang to him all the time. I came up here, and found a job in a shop right away. Actually got a friend a Buddy's who had a club to let me sing in there one night a week. Had a little following too. Men who worked the rails, all Buddy's group of people, would bring their ladies in and stay and listen to me sing all night. And order enough pork chops and pigs feet to reassemble the hogs." She laughs a little. And calls out, Lord, from the pain. "Your father wanted children, and I had them. I didn't have no luck with the singing, but Lena told me that's cause I was waiting for somebody to come in and get me like Buddy had. She said all the people came there was coming for dinner and cabaret, that discovery was beyond their means and their minds. I always liked that saying she made up, their means and their minds. She kept telling me to take myself to the door of somewhere where discovery meant something practical, but I just had children, and got good at cro-quignole. Men want children, Deneesey—it's in them. Remember that. What our men think they passing on, I don't know, but our men just like the rest of men—they like to have babies."

MARGARETE MOVED BACK into her room with Big Jim soon as she could, and I rushed from home to school and back again while Clara came to life. I didn't see Missus Pearson for any extra at all at first. Seem like I spent all my time cooking and washing, and toting Clara. I didn't mind so much, but I was surprised by the hill of diapers always need attending—either washed, folded, taken off or put on the baby. Thank the Lord for Margarete's wringer washer. I used it every other day to wash the twenty or thirty diapers that Clara either wet on, poo-pooed in, or that I slung across my shoulder for her to drool or spit up on. I would put them all in the tub and let the automatic machine shake out all Clara's messiness, and then I would run one or two diapers through the wringer at a time. Margarete showed me how to be careful that my hands didn't get stuck, so I would guide the white, bleached baby things through the wringer rollers and end up with white, flat, waterless diapers, clean and ready for the line. The clothesline Jim had strung up to go out the kitchen window, across the yard, to the roof of the shed was perfect. I would open up the window wide, and roll the line after I clipped the diapers to the line with clothespins. I got better and faster at getting all this done. Got so I could wash diapers in the morning, feed Clara, and then go on to school. This was the way it should be, so the diapers could dry in the glory of the sun.

Summer came, and then school was finished. After school was finished, I didn't have nothing of my own to miss or to rush to.

PERIODICALLY, I WALK through the front room and look out the window down the street. I am looking for the blue car Big Jim borrowed to come back with the lady Miz Alma in it. I walk light because I don't want to disturb Margarete. If she is handling this anything like me, she hears all my movements as if her ears are thumb-tacked by the narrow part to the floor. That is how I am listening to her in the bedroom. When she turns, and I am looking out the window down to the street in the front, I can hear the change in the direction of her breathing. I decide that it is the difference between breathing into the wall, or breathing out into the rest of the room, that I hear. I want to go in and help her, if there is something I can do. The blue car is not coming; it is a watched pot.

WHEN JIM TURNS his key in the knob the ice has melted from my burn, and I feel like I have been pressed flat into a big cardboard doll of a girl. I am folded, of course, in the chair. Jim rushes in to Margarete who I hope will not continue her stories. And I introduce myself and take the coat from a woman who says she is Alma Jones. She is as big as me and Margarete put together. Miz Alma Jones has her head tied with a big white cotton cloth, and her mouth is slack.

I am happy to see Miz Alma, as you might know, and I am happy to take her coat and hang it inside a closet because I'm sure we won't be needing it for some time. When I come back, Miz Alma is in the kitchen and she has turned up the flames. She sees me favoring my hand and picks up my arm to look at the burnt fingers; they want to swell up, but I have been beating the swelling back with the cold of the ice. I do not intend to do any more with the pots. "You burnt y'self on dese here pots?" she asked me. She says it like "boint."

"Yes," I answer.

"You through wid dat rag?" she asks me. I have the rag I used with the ice in my hand.

"Yes," I say, "but we got plenty rags."

"I'll take dis one, hit's already used," she says, and she takes the rag from me. She squirts snuff from her mouth into the rag, and turns and opens the window over the sink, and drops the rag out, down to the back yard. I reach under the sink and pull out a stack of rags I have washed and folded, and I follow Miz Alma into the room where Margarete is. Big Jim has propped Margarete up more than she was. "Forget dat burn," Miz Alma Jones says on the way.

Miz Alma seemed a little light in the head. I didn't know whether she was; I allowed that it was possible that she has things in her head that I don't know nothing about yet. And so I could think she was light in the head and be wrong, easy. Big Jim went way cross town to get her, he must know her marks: I decide I should be listening to the things her talk held, light in the head or not.

Once Margarete is settled and Miz Alma is in charge, I go directly to my math. The book says: In the order of operations, multiplication is first. Division is second, addition is next, followed finally by subtraction. When equations contain more than one operation, as many equations in new math do, select operations and perform them in this order, unless otherwise instructed by parentheses.

CLARA'S MAMA HAD her right there in the bed in the room that me and Clara shared; Clara was born in the bed I sleep in now, that Luke edward had slept in before. Big Jim was excited. He wanted a girl, and he got one. He come clomping in the house and to the bedroom door in those filthy work boots of his. Filled the doorframe where Margarete's labor had her screaming. After Clara was out and living, Margarete didn't make much more noise.

Miz Alma had me go out and tell Big Jim the baby girl ain't come yet and to get on away from that door. "Fact, tell Jim to git on out this house," Miz Alma called from the valley between Margarete's legs. "He kin come back in three hours." First time I ever said anything to Big Jim about what he should do or where he should go.

Miss Alma stayed at our place a country day, which is from daylight to daylight again. She talked me half to death, just like Margarete had, but that was OK on account of I was real scared about whether I could of taken care of Mama by myself. I was so relieved when Miz Alma arrived. Miz Alma told me Mama ain't need much taking care of, specially by me, on account of Mama had laid up with me just like she laid up with this here baby girl.

Dog, she knew right off! Miz Alma come right in Margarete's birthing-room door talking about the baby girl what's coming.

Round two in the morning, I guess, when sleepiness was threatening to make me look like a child again, I sat there half nodding half dreaming about school; Miz Alma had taken a break in her going on about the babies she had birthed in Biloxi. She had told me about her daughter Bereneice who had five children now. According to Miz Alma, Bereneice had made herself a nice piece of change washing clothes up here in Detroit. Only had to leave her house once a week or twice a week in the summers and near holidays. Now some of Bereneice's girls was getting to be nine and ten and so was getting old enough to help with the washing. Miz Alma was real proud of Bereneice, say she got a good machine and twelve rope lines outside in the yard. She say that they been saving together all the years since her son Mack died. Soon, she told me, her and Bereneice gone buy the family a home up here.

I ASKED MIZ Alma what happened to Mack. First she told me every question wasn't the right question for a young lady my age to be asking. I dropped my head and she didn't speak again for some time. Fact, I had given up on finding out what happened to him and was thinking bout something else totally when she said, "Po chile, dis heah city took 'im quick."

I suppose if Miz Alma hadn't of just now told me to mind my place, I'd of spoke right up saying, "Whatchu mean, took him?"

Or if it had been Lantene listening, instead of me, she might have asked, "Exackly what de city do tuh him, Miz Alma?" I sure did miss Lantene and how good she was with nosiness: I am clumsy with my questions and slow to know what's good to find out. Miz Alma went on on her own after a time.

"Be glad y'mama havin a girl baby. Ain't nothin harder dan bein mama to a son, paticuly a son whas good at somethin." Miz Alma sat right there in that hall chair and explained how the first thing went wrong was when the boy start to drinking corn liquor like God was taking corn. "An I mean takin it all tomorra," she went on.

She say he got a job in a filling station, hadn't been up here forty-five minutes seem like. The man what had the filling station had Mack getting underneath the cars changing oils and fixing things. Say Mack was like many another colored man—could fix near anything just putting the tips of the fingers God gave him up against whatever it was was broke. I knew she was exaggerating, but it could of been the late hour or all her hard work with Margarete made her spin like that. "Dat boy got paid once a week, reglar. Even wid helpin out wid de rent an Bereneice's chillun, de boy still had too much money fo' somebody from de country once ain't had none."

Miz Alma was quiet again. "I don't think dat child seen five dollahs in a month down Biloxi, an he was sweatin fuh de money, cuttin yards an trees, huskin cotton, sellin scraps he pickt up to de factory. Tryina help out de fambly. Came up to Detroit an got fifty-five full dollahs every week de Lawd sent.

"He give half a it to me, every week, an I kept fifty cents a every dollah he turnt ovah. He was gittin to be a grown man an was earnin the money hisself. I didn't wanna take it from him. I knew some time he be able to use it. Ain't a soul in dis worl cain't use a dollah when it come.

"Lawd Jesus, if I didn't spend alla dat money on mah baby's buryin." She stopped another minute. "Got a lil piece lef, gone put it in de house."

Well, Miz Alma sure did talk forty miles and didn't tell me what had happened to her Mack. I was disappointed, but I didn't dare ask again. I wondered if he drunk himself to death.

Miz Alma finally told it that he start to running with these fast-butt city folk, and she couldn't hardly get him in the house to eat good. She say he ended up going straight to work from wherever he happened to spend the night, and if she wanted to see how her baby was, she had to walk her skirts down to that gas station and see bout him. "Ain't no kinda way fuh a mama tuh have tuh live," she said.

She say she left him and Bereneice down Biloxi for three years. Then she brought Bereneice up first, ain't had no intentions on bringing Mack. But he begged and begged to come, and she missed him like she missed black dirt. "Once I let him come up here, I knew it was a mistake. I shoulda lef mah boy in de country, leas till he was full an grown.

"Well, I'd walk downa that station an see him, once or twice a week. He be grinnin, happy to see me, smellin like a still.

"I tole him every time, don't make no sense boy. Y'mama gotta walk down to a outside fillin station see how her baby boy is doin. I tole him I'se gone send him back down home, but wasn't really nothin I could do, and he knew that, he just said, 'I ain't goin back home, Mama, now come on here, look at dis beauty I workt on today. I got it runnin sweet, Mama, sweet.'

"Usually I brung him a meat san'wich, or whatever we had an he sit on de ledge an chomp it down. I'se so worried bout his eatin since I couldn't see him much. 'Hi is Bereneice?' he always ast.

"Lawd. He was a good boy. I guess I sho did know dat since I couldn't control him no mo, I wasn't gone be able to keep him. One a dem fast-butt people he was runnin wid come knock on mah do one day tellin me tuh come down tuh Juniper Street and git him from dey house. Dey's mighty sorry, dey said, but he got sloshed dey callt it and fell out in the back yahd a dey place. They didn't notice he had gone out back, thought he had gone out front. Dey thought he went home, dey said. He froze."

CLARA CAME A lovely baby. Divine. She was all baby smell and bundly. She was all healthy and all brown. Margarete said, after Clara's hair grew in, that her hair was growing in hard. Otherwise, she was perfect. A good-humored little girl.

MISSUS PEARSON LEANED her hands on her desk. "You can come to my classroom anytime, Denise. I will give you work to do, and I will correct whatever work you give me. But if you find you have to stop studying seriously, it will probably mean I won't be involved in your life." She looks at me—I believe it is a sympathetic look—to see how I am taking this. I take it fine, I reach for whatever she offers like a weed tearing ground.

"If you must stop studying, find a serviceable job," she says. "You can add and subtract. Count money. Do errands. Take care of an old lady, or man. Roll change at the dime store. There is learning that can happen there. If you are not studying, then you have to learn to get paid." She leans more forward, toward me. "And don't let your mother make you idle, or housebound," she says. Then she hands me a dollar and tells me to go home.

I leave somber, not knowing what else to do. I wished I could figure out a way to stay, but it takes me a long time to figure out what to say behind the fancy lectures Miss Gloria Pearson gives me. In a day or two I will have a response, but now I just have to leave or stand silently. She has dismissed me, so I go on home. I put Gloria Pearson's dollar in my grip underneath the bed.

I absorbed what she said. I have replayed it many times.

I went and sat in her classroom after school whenever I could until Clara was near three years old. Margarete and I tussled about this, but there wasn't much I could explain. I just stayed focused on what I was trying to learn; I couldn't give up anymore. Gloria Pearson's remark DON'T LET YOUR MOTHER MAKE YOU IDLE, HOUSE-BOUND, rang in my head loud like the school bell, and just as long like they hold it, insisting you come in.

EVERYTHING HAS FALLEN

BUT THE COLLARDS

THE WATKINSES' CROWDED shelves and narrow aisles were as busy as Patuskie had to say for itself. The warped, wide floorboards creaked under the town's shoes and needs: more flour, bags of rice, pounds of dried red beans, lima beans, black-eyed peas, cornmeal, the children's hopes for raisins. All the goods waited between the sunlight and the colored store like hand-made gingham curtains with curled ruffles. The matching ribbons of the Watkinses' class buttoned the curtains back, and let the world in.

Luke hated the place. Not because it didn't entertain him. It entertained him in some small ways. I think he hated the ways it was the same. It was the same as it had been, every summer when we came. The porch of the store was its greeting and its permanence. Clear and swept and sunwashed in the morning; you could look at it and have second thoughts that it was the dilapidated small center of the colored town you knew it was. Ladies going to wash or clean would stop to say a word or two to May Belle, and would drag their wide feet and flapping shoes up the porch stairs, and back down in more of a hurry. By noontime, especially near the end of the week, the young girl helpers of the women—wherever the women worked or if they worked where they lived—might be sent on a dash to get a few pickles as a supper surprise, or some more bicarbonate for somebody whose stomach ached that morning, or if you sat for monied children like the Kinseys'—like I did—you might be sent for some already cooked cornbread that May Belle had worked on in the morning and set out in a basket between napkins to hold in the escaping heat. The shoes —like mine—scraping up the six steps and across the porch would be industrious, excited about responsibility.

Luke hated the place because for all its busyness, he was bored. There was nothing for him to do. He did not sit for children or tote food. He was not interested in fabric or other dry goods. Watkins never gave him anything to make, hardly gave him the time of day. It wasn't because of Luke, really. Watkins thought himself to be just the busiest man. Him and Eisenhower. Everything Watkins gave was by example, and everything he took was hard, like cash or baskets of fruit.

The last summer Luke was down Patuskie, he must have been fifteen. I was about nine and already living down home with Granma'am. Didn't Luke come down there that summer and try to steal from Watkins? Lord. Made one of those memories that make you shudder, even when twenty years have lodged between. Started the whole country town to talking about Mama's unraised city boys. "Margreet," they called her, "sho got hell in dem chillun, specially dose big ole boys."

One of Macie's million minion run up to our side door to tell Granma'am what had happened, long before Luke edward got home. I don't think I'll ever forget it. When she got to the side screen hollering, *Luke edward done got in trouble,* I got up from the meal I was helping

Granma'am make and stalked to the screen like I was Mama.

"What you talkin bout, Mae Rellen?" I demanded. I did not open the door; she blabbered from the dirt side of the screen.

"What you say, Mae Rellen?" Granma'am took over.

"Miz Dambridge, Luke edward done stole some'm from Mistah Watkins." Mary Ellen rushed to tell it. Granma'am's joining me at the door gave importance to the situation. Her presence also washed away my itsy-bitsy authority.

After the tale had finished being told—I just wished it was a lie. I followed Granma'am to the front, feeling little, not knowing where else I should go. Granma'am fussed and talked to herself, didn't turn up the parlor light at all. Granma'am was always saying she didn't see so good these days, but she let the parlor descend right into dark. I knew why, I had seen that her eyes had cracked. Thick sliding tears came down, like egg-white slather, after the shell gets slammed on the bowl.

WATKINS COME IN cause Granma'am invited him. That's how country people do, even if it's some bad news coming, or maybe some enemies being made. Country people start out by asking each other in. After that they get to sweating and tussling, and get they lips poked out. Sometimes, like in Granma'am's case, they part mostly friends: patting each other on the back, tipping they hats if they men. Leaving out the door with the parlor lights off, to keep the place cool, and smiling at each other to keep relations warm.

Watkins walked to the house with Luke, he was trying to lecture: all us being Negro and living in a hard world and living in a world where nobody will excuse nothing we do and he's sure Luke must know this from living up there in the city where at, in Detroit, wasn't it? Luke was quiet, letting the man talk. A head taller than the man already, Luke just let the little man talk.

Mistah Watkins wasn't never so tall—Miz May Belle Watkins was taller than him—plus, Mistah Watkins had already started to shrink some on account of him gettin old.

Luke was a good listener even if they said he was a thief, and I'm sure he didn't answer no provocations. Luke don't pay none of them no mind, I know that about him. "All these country people talk is Bible or what's growin, don't none of em know dishwater from bath-water, Granma'am included," Luke once said.

I drew in my breath at the nerve he had to say things.

People down the country was always trying to raise David and Luke edward; Margarete thought it was nobody's job but hers, and Granma'am thought she couldn't possibly do it. Especially not alone. "Iss no way Margarete can handle dem big strappin boys by herself, jes herself," they all said, "specially up dere in dat city where everybody seem to think dey wiser than us home folk. Look like dat's what Margarete's boys is growin up to think. It's jes a shame bout dem kids." They was all saying it, the same things.

So Luke and his stealing gave people a ready excuse to talk about what not having a daddy does to boys. They just can't become men without a strong man around to whip they butts. Can't become good strong men, no way.

The complicated lot of our sons.

"Dat Luke," people said. "Gone git hisself cut up dere in Detroit." They had all heard that in cities there was stabbing, one bad Negro to another. I was still young and seemed a good girl—people said about me. "You'll probly be all right, a good Christian girl, but understand, dear, dat yo brothahs, wid dey big selves and dey bad ways, ain't to be imitated." They just kept on talkin about my brothers, to me, around me, to each other.

"You know these silly country folk, they got things as figured out as God," Luke edward had said. And they was just a-telling me how to handle myself with respect to my brothers; I heard but did not listen. Watching was more important, cause let me tell you, that summer Granma'am was fit to spit.

Sometimes when Granma'am went out to funerals or to some place she had to travel to, she put on a wig Margarete had brung her. The wig was dark brown like Granma'am's hair, and it went more forward on her head than when Granma'am fixed her hair herself. When Granma'am put it on, it looked more like a hat than a wig to me. Shining like a beetlebug shell. After Macie's daughter left from the side door where she had dumped the news, Granma'am went fumbling into her room; she surprised me coming back out into the parlor; she was wearing the beetlebug wig and her outside shoes. She had buttoned up her housedress all the way to the top.

MISTAH WATKINS WALKED Luke straight up to Granma'am's front. Granma'am and me watched the two of them come in the yard and up the path. Granma'am had gone to sit in the front room and wait for our big boy, Luke, to come back. She mumbled: "Comin down here makin embarrassment for me where I got to continue to live wid people, down here where I been livin for more'n fifty years an where his mama was born and still from. I don't know what's a-matter with dat boy but he ain't gone steal an he ain't gone mess up my relations."

Mistah Watkins, he tipped his hat. "Well, Miz Dam-bridge"—he drew it out, seem like—"me and this here granboy a yours got some bad news to dis-skuss witcha." Luke was not looking direct at Granma'am; he better not. Granma'am do not allow you to look directly in her face unless you old as she is or you got something of great importance to say. You better not be looking at her, spe-cially if you wrong. She don't allow not one suggestion of disrespect. I was looking at Luke edward, and Mr. Watkins was steady slow-talking. "Well, boy, you wanna tell y'granma whatcha been up to t'day?" Luke did not speak, of course; he stood in the parlor pitiful. So there me and Granma'am were in the dark-almost front room waiting on and now listening to the men. We waiting for Luke to tell what he did, confess, take the heaviness of Mistah Watkins away. We was waiting for him to make drawling Watkins leave, what with him standing there breathing like a old hyena. And Watkins went on, saying we all hoping that Luke would still grow up to be a man. (Is that what we all hope?)

I wondered if Granma'am had expected Luke to come home alone. I did. My chest was getting constricted from the deep parlor darkness. My chest was getting heavy, family-flat.

I start to follow the whine I hear in my head. Luke, why you disappoint Granma'am, why you got this man standing here talking about you like he talking about you when he know and Granma'am know and I know and you know, he talking about Mama, talking about our mama straight to her mama's face, saying all the awful things the whole town wants to say about our mama. Everybody in this town still talking about our wild fast mama and here you is back here after all this time and everybody talking about her bad-ass boy. They don't know us like they try to, saying her husband done died, probably from living too hard. They saying I'm too young to help really, and ain't it a shame good Christian Miz Dam-bridge has such a hard time with the young'uns, specially them boys of Margreet's.

All of a sudden, seem like, Mistah Watkins says to me: "I say, little Miss Deneesey, I hope you don't think all lis bidness is funny; I sees you sittin dere teeth just a-shinin. What is you grinnin like a chessy cat bout? You know dis big brother a yours ain't done no fine thing, comin down here tryina steal from us. We's all workin, we's all tryina make our own lives, and we cain't, naw, we cain't be stealin from each other. Is'at the way ya'll do up dere in dem cities?" His voice wheezes up like an engine warming.

Why is he talking to me! Is he just planning to talk up all the space to anybody till some other thing happens? And what am I supposed to do with his questioning, should I answer since he's grown? I decide I won't say nothing, that there's nothing for me to say.

He just talks. "If dat's de way y'all do I don't know how y'all be livin wid each other at all, dat ain't no way to respect a man or his family or yo' neighbors or yo'self. Ain't dat right, Miz Dam-bridge?" He drawls on, ain't getting the first answer from nowhere, looking for agreement from my Granma'am who would rather Luke edward act different, but who would not exclaim her feeling in front of company. "I jes hope you ain't sittin dere laughin at dis sitya'ation." He is still trying to talk to me. I can't believe it, and he go on, "Cause dis is vereh seryous y'know."

Salt rolled off my face onto my teeth by then; guess Watkins had good eyes for a old man. He don't have bullseye sense, though. Teeth showing like that ain't no laughing all the time—teeth showing ain't even no smile all the time. Fact, it was my imitation and my recollection of my mama's stretched mouth, my mama's teeth sitting out there trying to figure out what the hell to do about the child got her standing there front of the authority. *What I'm gone do with these kids? Lord have mercy.* That's the teeth Mistah Watkins was seeing in my face in the dusk, he just didn't know it, I guess. He ain't seen my mama in so long, ain't no wonder. Or maybe she ain't never been yanked in front of him like this. Or maybe my mama Margarete don't see him like the authority he making of himself this evening, in control of my brother this way. Mistah Watkins, he don't know how much my mama's child I am.

Granma'am, she know, and maybe she hear the salt and snot melt together, my faceful a worry for my god, Luke edward. Maybe Granma'am hear me try to draw it back in my nose and down my throat quietlike. My Granma'am, she know me, she know what's happening cause I been living with her these past few years, and she always say how come I can't separate myself from the boys. They almost old enough to be a different generation from me, she say. But I'm their sister and when they on the fry I am too. When I get to the front of the line (which I will do), I want David and Luke edward right with me.

Granma'am interrupt Mistah Watkins, and I'm more awake now but I'm still stuck with that crazy almost-grin on my face, calling it a grin according to Mistah Watkins cause I just don't know how to eat the salt of shame without the corners of my mouth jerked back. Not yet anyhow.

So Granma'am interrupt him: "Luke," like thunder, "whatcha got tuh say fuh y'self; we gone send Mistah Watkins here on his way. Whatcha got tuh say fuh y'self, Luke edward?"

"I stole a handful of cracklin from Mistah and Miz Watkins today, Granma'am," Luke edward answered, a manly voice from a boy's shoes. He knows the rhythm of this dance. He only comes in when it's clearly his turn. Luke edward has been a good dancer since we were little in the bottom-floor flat. He was a long drink of water for a young Negro boy, and the ladies would just rub his head and the men and my daddy would say he's gone be a killer.

When one song is over, a new one starts.

Granma'am stood up: "Well, you know, Willyum," to Mistah Watkins, "I am terr'bly sorry bout all this. I'm a come by there tomorrah an pay you an May Belle for whatevah we owe y'all. Lemme jes take care a this young man here. Thank you for stoppin in." Granma'am talked her city proper talk, she thought, and so we knew—I knew—she had the fury in her. She opened up the screen, an Mistah Watkins turned and tipped his hat and said, "Now, you know, Miz Dambridge, dis ain't no kinda reference to what you might owe. Miz Watkins and I is jes concernt bout dese chillun. Alla chillun belong to all us, you know."

"Well, thank you again for stoppin," Granma'am repeats. "I will come by and see bout things, just the same." Granma'am can't hold the door no wider, so Mistah Watkins finally walks through it.

I breathe again cause Watkins was back out on the dirt. Luke continued to stand up like he knew he had better; you don't sit down in Granma'am's parlor no way, and you sure don't sit in it when you wrong.

Granma'am shut the door, and I missed the distraction of old nasty Mistah Watkins right away. Granma'am, she just walk out the parlor, straight down the hall to the back, where the light of all our working was lit.

"Come heah, boy," she called back behind her. Luke drug his pitiful long self along, and I got up and followed him this time.

I think my head was tipped to one side, that's how I carried it stoved up with things; I still hadn't looked my brother Luke full in the face. The shadows had kept me from it, but Luke wouldn't have looked at me no way, not boxed in all that trouble he was in. He mutters, "Wish I didn't have to come down this place ever again."

That was his last summer there down home with me. After Mama heard from Granma'am about Luke's going to pot, Mama decided that Luke was dog on uncooperative. She stopped sending him down home. Now we had two escaped and often recollected beauties in the family, Margarete and that handsome young devil of hers.

GRANMA'AM CALLED LUKE when she was in the middle of the hall, and he followed her and I followed him. Granma'am still wearing her beetlebug wig. Luke edward seemed gangly and lanky and unrepentant even in this fresh moment. I had my mouth pressed shut, head tipped to the side. Granma'am went straight into the slop closet. As she was closing the door behind her, she said: "Luke, go out in the yard and bring me a wet green switch. Neesey," she kept barking, "move that tub out the way."

I could not believe Granma'am was about to switch Luke edward. She hardly never switched us anymore. Besides, Luke was big as sin, bigger then than Granma'am, I recall. I also remember that this is when Luke started to make his famous walled-up face and blank eyes. He was only beautiful when he was not that way. Anybody went ahead and yelled at that boy would only get a look at how dammed up he was.

I lost myself: I don't know what I was seeing, or what I was tasting rolling off my face. I know there was a sightlessness stealing off the little painful parts. The night was like a punctured black wall. Luke cussed and muttered about dirt religion and I think I heard him calling Granma'am this and that witch. Luke went out the back door as Granma'am hollered from the slop closet that she didn't hear no movement out there. I started pushing the big tin tub back behind the stove where we kept it when nobody was bathing, or going to bathe soon, or had just finished they bath.

Luke come back with a switch courageous. Hadn't taken him two minutes to get that thing, long as a rope almost. I wouldn't never want to be hit with nothing so like a whip as that.

He was standing there with his switch for his trouble and his lips was poked out. I *know* Luke edward; he was my god, especially then. I know that daring poked-out mouth he gets. Like when somebody at school would mess with me or one of my friends, and maybe he would get a chance to fight. He would walk up in the screaming circle and beat up some fool, protecting me, with his lips poked shut like that. Mama never got on Luke about that because she thought it was manly, told him it was his job, told him he was like his daddy; yes, he should watch out for his little sister. All the time I went to school before I got sent down home, not a body ever put a hand on me, on account of the threat of Luke edward, and how quick he showed up with that half-perturbed half-smile.

I was still looking at the switch courageous—I get stuck in my tracks under duress—when Granma'am come out the slop closet with a newspaper pulled between her hands. She put it down in the middle of the kitchen table, and I liked to fell out. It had a huge mound of movement on it, brown and high-piled for the few minutes Granma'am had took to make it. I ain't never seen no pile of movement like that before, less it was from a cow or dog or some other such unconscious thing. I like to got sick: how would I have my grits on this table in the morning what with the movement on the table this evening? This was the table of my breakfast, the table of my pumpkin, the table of my entrance to the day. I knew I would always see that mound there, whenever I looked. Was that what Granma'am aimed?

I drug my hanging open mouth and my bucked eyes up, away from that mess so I could see some faces, get some clues about what was fixing to happen here. I wondered where was David, outside and this rain coming.

Luke had the trepidation now. "Gimme that switch, boy," Granma'am said. "Whachu know bout stealin?" she start right in, not a second worth of wasted breath. Lawd, Granma'am, please don't start askin Luke no whole buncha questions, you know he ain't gone half answer you an then you gone be madder an less steady than you are already. I know she knows he ain't gone answer and besides Luke stared hard at that movement on the table like anybody with sense would. He was wondering too. I know it. We didn't have no experience with this. "I ast you what you know bout stealin." The room thundered hell, and Luke's judgment rocked over him in the person of the old woman whose face sweat and whose legs tripped around the table in a dance of condemnation, some wicked ritual of salvation, her wig slipping ever more to the side.

Four rivers salted my face: eyes and nose both let loose in his honor. Luke started to taste his own salt too, I think. He wasn't answering Granma'am, she hit him hard cross his long skinny arm with the switch.

"Whachu know bout stealin, you no-count little boy?" She was stroke mad. Lawd a mercy. Luke took one hand and put it over the place where the switch had hit. I knewed there'd be a welt there in a second. Right where those fingers were, Granma'am struck Luke again. Her beetle-wig sliding. "I don't know who taught you so wrongly that you could decide that you only answer when you feel like it, but I'm your elder!" she hollered. "I asked you whachu know bout stealin and I aim tuh git a answer out you shortly." I think she had hit him enough for all his future by then. "Whachu know bout stealin?" Her screaming belched. She was mad as a bear on fire.

"Nothin. I don't know nothin bout stealin." Luke edward finally backed out of his cocky courage and backed into his youth, what with being on the ugly end of a beating and in the face of wild control. He whined and he whimpered and he cried. "Nothin."

What did he know about stealing? Why was he stealing? Why didn't he just lie if he had to, and say Granma'am said he could have the cracklin? Was it more than three cents even? Had Luke been stealing before? Why didn't he ask for what he wanted, didn't he know that he could have? What was Granma'am gone do with that newspaper on the table? Luke looked at it hard and he simpered, that way we do when we scared.

Granma'am just kept to whacking him—I wondered if Luke was feeling it anymore. "Well, if you know so nothin whachu doin up in Willyum an May Belle Watkins' sto' where I sends you for everything I needs to feed y'all here in this house, stealin some'm an havin him bring you back heah like you a dead body or lost child, cain't git yo'self honest back where you live? Whachu doin, boy? Whachu doin, boy? Whachu doin, boy . . . ?" Granma'am looked broke like the broke record she sound like. Her shiny wig had so slipped that you could see her real braided hair on one side, sweat had beaded in her moustache, her eyes had clouded with her disappointment and her crazy rage. Seem like she kept asking the same nothing. Luke already done answered much as he was going to.

I had moved the tub like she told me, and she moved herself round the table in the space the washtub took. I don't know if she expected Luke to hop, but he didn't, and she moved herself around hitting every side of him. Seem like she kept trying to hit his hands, which I guess makes sense cause if you steal, whether you get what you tried to take or not, it's your hands that's the problem.

I never learned whether Luke got the cracklin he tried to take. I could just see him stretching his long arm down in that barrel, anticipating the crunch and the brine. Luke always did like salt. Those barrels were high and rubby-brown and many on the Watkinses' floor; they invited you to reach in and help yourself. He bought pork rinds for five cents from the store in the city. For just a little bag fried somewhere else, in a bag with crimped edges from the factory. Nowhere near the good taste of the cracklin from the Watkinses.

Down home, you could get a ton of cracklin for five cents. Plus, Granma'am had a bill she run; Luke could of just said Granma'am said he could have it, then he would of just been lying, and not stealing, and maybe it would of kept a secret of his fall. The whitepeople and the Negroes in authority seem to make sure all the Negro boys fall in public, somehow. I'm still thinking today about why that is. But here Granma'am was participating in it: about to have a stroke, running round this gangly

Negro child of hers, trying to hurt him with that switch got broke off a Virginia tree.

"Turn aroun at the table, boy." Look. Luke had got hisself twisted in the chair.

Luke and I both looked straight in her face. I don't think Granma'am knew I was there any more than Luke seemed to know that what all this was about was the wrong turn he seemed to be making at so exactly the wrong age. It was the future taught me that, of course. In this moment, Granma'am just looked straight back at Luke and she was breathing hard, hard. "Turn around at that table, boy. WHY DO I HAFTA REPEAT EVERYTHING I SAY TO YOU? Lawd, have mercy." Crack crack. Crack crack crack. Switched from the back to the shoulders, right across the side of his head. Look at Luke turn round, hang his head; see his lip hanging down.

"Thieves and murderers have filthy hands so you go right on ahead an get y'hands dirty," she wheezed. "I want you to remembah dis."

Granma'am holds her back where it pinches. Luke jerks his neck around and looks straight in Granma'am's face again. I wished I could see his eyes. She raised the switch, raised her voice: "Lawd Jesus, why I got to repeat myself to dis boy, what happened to dis boy, dis misunderstandin granchile a mine? Show him what little he got is what he got."

Granma'am wailed, Luke turned, the switch come down again and hit the back of his neck. Luke sat still at the table with his head down. The sound of Granma'am's awful breathing replaced her wailing on account of she was tired, I guess. Luke edward was quiet too, collecting hisself. When he picked that head up again, I had moved closer to his commotion, and his face was rock.

Granma'am walked around the table a little bit so she

could bend down and look Luke edward in his stony face. She didn't put her finger under his chin and push his head up like she would do sometime. She didn't rub her hand across his summer red-blond-brown. She put her hand on the table, her wrinkled fingers curved from age and her fingernails opaque like door glass. She stooped low to look under Luke's bent head, and you could see she was tired, sweat on more of her face, especially her lip where her old-lady moustache sat like a tag. "Put yo' hands, both of them, right in that dung, boy."

Granma'am's plate of false teeth slipped, and she talked real close to Luke's face. He didn't move and she sprung up like youth, wailing "Lawwdd." Did Magdalene and Ruth and the other Martha wail this way? She must of hit him then for all the Negro boys whose lives she feared for in this young and lanky man. She must of hit him for all her fears and all their futures. I wondered what kind of lie this would become. Probably just silence, which is its own kind of lie. Luke's hands finally shot out and went in the top of the pile of fresh brown shit. Hands in the dung on the newspaper on the kitchen table while I looked on and Luke edward backed more into his secreted self. Granma'am commenced to holler again: "Squeeze it, make a fist back an forth, put yo' hands in it good. You thievin."

Look at Luke, he does not move. Me either. I am in a stupor watching the grandmother make this punishment. Create it like a recipe, ingredients from history and the self, invention and the yard. Luke edward tries to follow her orders, but he looks confused: his face goes from rock to babychild and back again. He was fifteen then, sixteen in the fall, and his grandmother, who seemed like she was ninety but I know now she wasn't, was trying to make him squeeze her excrement at the kitchen table in front of me, and he my darling brother.

Luke jumped up from the table, tormented, his hands covered not like his own. Was I gone hate this woman here? Why didn't she think she would destroy him? Where was David to help us? And help us do what? Look at Luke, banging out the screen door, the back door. Look at Granma'am drop the switch, heaving breathing heavy.

An old embattled woman sat down in the seat Luke edward had just nearly knocked over. She looked like a slave with a lampshade on her head. And the wisps of my brother's spirit, left in the chair and in the kitchen behind him, fold her in his bitterness like cellophane I see through.

Sealing in the Meat Scraps

SHE TAKES ONE corner of the newspaper and folds it across the pile. She begins to make a roll and folds a second corner in. It could have been chicken bones and the snapped-off ends of string beans scraped off the plates after everybody was full, the meat scraps already fed to the dogs. She pulls the whole bundle toward her, and rolls the paper into a log over the mound, sealing his fingerprints away. Then she folds in the two loose sides over top of the roll, first one side and then the other. Then she rolls the rest of the paper over top of the folded-in sides. The package is closed, kitchen garbage. It looks unspeakably ordinary, everyday. No flies in and no maggots out: Granma'am had taught me how to fix the garbage. Bundling garbage was my job after supper any night.

I am a century old in this evening's kitchen. Alone now with Granma'am. I don't know where Luke edward or David hide, but I have seen Luke edward more than naked and less, I think, than a baby. Where was David— why didn't he come? And where did Luke edward go— what is he doing now? I am convinced he will never be lighthearted again. I'm convinced I will never be light of heart again.

Granma'am picks up the heavy pail from under the sink and half fills it with water, grunting as she lifts the water to the stove to heat. Is she grunting about Luke edward, or is she getting too old to hoist the weight? Tears wet her face like a dunking. I watch her bend over and pick up the switch from the floor there where she dropped it. I watch her bend the green branch into small pieces: it is just too green to break. She puts the switch in the trash on top of the folded newspaper. It springs back alive. When the water in the bucket is hot, she pours a quart off into our old cleaning bowl and drops a rag down in the steam.

"Here, Neesey," she whispers hoarsely, "clean off the door and the floor there where your brother dropped his memory." Her words come across the room to where I find myself, sitting on the floor in a corner. My head leans back on both the walls. Immediately, though slowly, I get up, and walk over, and take the hot rag gingerly from the bowl. I add my elbow grease to the wet heat Granma'am has made for me. Familiar motion and the smell of bleach.

I didn't mind cleaning it up. What have I learned, if not to clean up behind them and wait for them to come, or to return?

Granma'am makes a cleaning bucket for herself, and then dumps a lot of hot water on top of the table, where we did have fatback and grits the next morning. Luke edward ate only a little, stubborn, silent, and bruised; David ate everything offered to him, looking knowing.

Granma'am scrubs the table a long time, slow, in preparation for this next day's meal. The ammonia water drips and drops to the floor. Then Granma'am went over the door I had cleaned, dousing with ammonia the trails of bleach I'd left. Granma'am sends me to bed without excitement, early. When she says go, I do. Awake a long time, I listen to the sound of Granma'am's rag mop washing, washing the floor. This is the sound I finally fall asleep to, and neither of my brothers is inside.

YEARS LIKE RIOTS

LIKE ALWAYS WHEN he settled one thing or another, we had as a group breathed a sigh of relief about Luke edward. He had finally gotten another job after having laid around with Christine and their son Jordan for a year. We relaxed too soon. And with the kind of giddiness that I have learned by now precedes a tragedy. One weekend during break when I was off from school, Luke walked off from the gas station. All the roll of money he'd collected was in his pocket instead of in the cash drawer at the store. That's what the man who owned the filling station said. He was some transplanted peckerwood who we hadn't seen before. He was at Margarete's door Saturday morning before the birds flew.

Luke edward had moved away from Margarete's, again, so she could tell the truth about him not being there. But hers was the address he had given the station man, so that was Problem Number Two right then. Margarete told the man she was sure there was some explanation. Margarete looked like she would start to plea in a whisper. Big Jim told Margarete don't ask him nothin. That was after she closed the door.

Would have been nice if they could have kept Clara

out of it, but when I caught my ride back down to Hampton and to school, I had to leave Clara morose and in the middle. Broke my heart to see her like that, and then again to go.

MARGARETE AND CLARA and Christine and I went to the courthouse. I had not been in one since David married, and then before that when Granma'am and I had traveled to Richmond, taking the children from our outside Richmond school to see government. Here we were, Luke edward's team of women. Except Christine had Jordan in her arms. He wasn't walking yet.

On our way, Margarete insisted we stop for lunch first. She says we have left in plenty of time, that she planned this, that we should sit down and calm our nerves before we go. She is smoking.

Christine says it's a good idea; she says if she gives Jordan a bottle now, he'll be sleep.

We stop at Dot & Etta's. Margarete gets shrimp and she has her fork in her hand. Christine gets a crabcake sandwich, and she holds Jordan's bottle with one hand, a french fry in the other. I become the mother. "Clara, will you bless our food?" I say, and I put my hands together. Clara puts her hands together and she rests her thumbs on her collarbone. I bow my head. "God is gracious," she says, "God is good. And we thank Him for our food. By His hands we all are fed. Give us, Lord, our daily bread. And God, please bless Uncle Luke," she said.

In the middle of the meal, Margarete says to nobody in particular, "Don't y'all worry about my child. God gives the mother the last word."

I say nothing. I stare into the mist of her pronouncement.

MARGARETE TOLD THE judge some long story. I was stone-faced. Furious. Concentrating on my courses in my head. I saw other boys we knew, waiting for their names to be called. It was a roster of a kind. Anthony Lawrence Junior Blake John Dwight Midwood Cyrus Luke edward Palms. Now this was before they were guilty or innocent. This was when they just went up and were verified. Every five minutes they were called.

My lips have tightened into a straight line.

I stood there in one of my best skirts and blouses. Margarete had said to dress up. I thought about the first time I had met Christine. I had been convinced, new arriving, that Luke edward was seeing Miss Tip. She had to be a bad influence on him, in my mind. I had been surprised and pleased about Christine.

Now what good had she done him? With her sweater unbuttoned and that child so right away.

"I WANT YOU to meet my girlfriend Christine," Luke edward says; he is walking me to school.

"Who is she?" I ask. "She wasn't over to the house."

"She's my girlfriend," he repeats.

I wonder if I should say I thought Miss Tip was your girlfriend, but then I see the city block of school building. "Is she pretty?" I ask him, just to keep the conversation going. I get inside my nervousness about this day ahead.

"I think so," Luke edward answers.

"She dark?" I go on.

"Nope," he answers.

LUKE HAD TAKEN me to hang around with him; he thought it would be better for me than being in the house cleaning and cooking all the time like a maid, he had said. I tried my first cigarette at his friend's card party. And Christine, the first time she saw me, said she would adopt me as a little sister. She unbuttoned the top two buttons of my sweater. She told me I shouldn't be so tight-stitched. I was uncomfortable for her to open my clothes like that, but then I was distracted by the boys competing for my attention. Luke edward kept saying *Keep it distant* to the boys.

I only stayed a couple of hours because while I practiced on a third Lucky Strike, I choked so loud it stopped the party. I could not calm down after. Luke edward walked me home, and left me there with my scraped and burning throat.

MARGARETE TRIED TO talk the judgers into believing that Luke edward was a good boy. I don't think they believed her. Christine cried onto Jordan's crocheted baby sweater. I don't think they believed her either. I say nothing. Everything in my head takes up all the space of sound. It's crazy-making. My god Luke edward, my studious man of the lamp, Lena's darling, where will we have to leave you, fallen? Lord, I was in a mood. I tried to calm my nerves and talk to Clara. I asked her about school, second grade, one of my favorite subjects. She was irritable. I told her all about Hampton Institute. Some of what I said I had written to her in letters, and she whined. She told me she already knew these things. Her eyes were glassy with disappointment. It was just exhausting, the wait.

LUKE ONCE SAID the people in Patuskie ain't no different than tomato worms. It was near the end of one summer, and it was cool that night. Luke edward was prone to up and say the most critical things. Me and Granma'am both suck in our breath. I'm wondering where Luke edward will go with this; the room quiets around his remark. Granma'am leans over a pail in the sink, cleaning dirt off collards, and she doesn't turn around, which is good. Luke edward sits at the wiped-off kitchen table with me. He is picking his teeth with a twig.

"How you mean, the people like tomato worms, Luke edward?" I ask. I don't really want to know. I am that way about some things Luke edward talks about. It is because I think he says some things just to get people's back up. But I know Granma'am will want to know about this. She is who Luke edward is talking to, anyway. Granma'am says you have to know what's in the children's mind. I see expectation rising in her back. And so, again, I ask: "How you mean, the people like tomato worms, Luke edward?"

"People trying to work these raggedy farms like worms be borin through tomatoes," Luke edward says. "Stick their tongues down in the dirt and eat whatever's down there. Act like it's good, like they thankful."

Luke edward is really being clever. "Most people wanna leave here, anyway," he says.

"Most a the people like who?" Granma'am says from far away where she stands at the pail. The collards pile up. Clean green leaves in a stack for our dinner. The stems on the waste side, whisked in one swipe. I decide that it is disappointment rising in her back. Or maybe it is anger that I see. Luke is preoccupied with his teeth. Plus, he is turned the wrong way in his chair.

I already have three ham hocks boiled, and I get up from the table to lift the lid and look. Ham hocks do not need to be checked on ever, especially before the vegetables go in, but I am trying not to see what's in Granma'am's face, when or if she turns to look at Luke. Rather smell the pork steam. I can see Granma'am standing bent over the sink, out the side of my eye. She wears all her history across her shoulders, like two buckets on a broad stick kept for carrying. Full buckets. Maybe full with milk or with water for boiling clothes. Maybe full with wood chips from the torn-down house her father built. Maybe full of other salvage from her past.

"Lantene wants to leave," he says.

Dog. Lantene is *my* best friend, and I wish Luke would not bring her up. Luke edward does not hesitate to involve me in his disagreements, and I really do not like it. He goes on to name Price Green and his girl, and Nathan and Jacob, and Ethel Moore and her sister, Leroy Davis and his cousin, and all the Macie Fleming kids.

Granma'am finishes cleaning the collards before she talks again. About the same time, Luke finishes with his teeth. "You say you, Luke edward? I didn't hear you say, Luke edward wants to leave."

"I don't live here," Luke corrects her. I am aghast. "Plus, I'm going home next week," he says.

Granma'am has taken her knife: she chops up about half the tough, pale-green stems and she shreds the collard leaves. The minced collard stems will flavor the pot liquor, while I wonder where is David. Must be out running in the woods.

MARGARETE FINALLY GOT tired of Granma'am's foretelling, and she got tired of Luke's bald stares. She said to Luke edward, "Dog on it, sixteen is old, young man. Too old for me to be spendin my little piece a money tryina give you fresh air in the hot summer. Why can't you open your mouth and talk? Why would you cause Mama such embarrassment? When I was your age I damn near had David, so you better believe I was grown and actin responsible. If you big enough to act ugly, then you must be big enough to figure out what to do with yourself all summer. I don't know why you can't be down home and act like you got some sense. Lord," she says, walking out the room, "Mr. Watkins done had that store and been selling Mama goods fifty years. And here you come. This bad-ass boy of mine."

Finally, it doesn't matter, how Granma'am wants to hack at Luke. Or how Margarete tries to be mean. Like I said, the boys stopped coming. So Granma'am's hand in them was done. And Margarete's mean attitude for Luke edward had about ten minutes of life in it, and that's all.

I THOUGHT MR. Jenkins was just a light Negro. He had the other store, right at the edge of the colored section of town. His store had more canned and packaged things than the Watkinses', so some people preferred Mr. Jenkins's store for that reason. The cans and packages cost more money and so he let folks run bigger bills. Granma'am did not allow me to shop with Mr. Jenkins. We went to the Watkinses, and that was that.

Turns out, Mr. Jenkins is not a light Negro but a whiteman passing for colored. Whoever heard such a thing! Lantene told me all about it, and if I called her a liar, and I probably did, I had to take it back.

"Granma'am! Lantene says Mr. Jenkins a whiteman."

Silence.

"Granma'am? Mr. Jenkins white?"

"Yes."

"What?!"

Silence.

"Well, what's he doin married to Miz Irene?" Miz Irene Jenkins was as colored as me and wore her head tied up.

"They married, and been married since before you was thought of."

"Granma'am."

Silence.

"And, Neesey, I mean what I say. You stay way from the Jenkinses. If you need to get somethin, you go to the Watkinses, you hear me?"

"Yes."

Lantene filled me in. Told me Miz Irene was faster than everybody. Including my mama and hers. Said Miz Irene had planned her husband-hunt, hard. She talked all the time about her intention to go to somewhere she could find herself a light-skinned husband. White be even better. Lantene said her mama said that after Margarete left with Buddy Palms wasn't nobody left for none of the girls. Not even to hope on. Said her mama and Miz Irene thought they would never get nowhere else but where they were then.

Well, Mr. Jenkins spent so much time on the colored edge of town. And their somewhere else was too imprecise. So Miz Irene put on her best dress on a dare and went up to Mr. Jenkins. Told him she give him anything he want for all his life if he would marry her. Lantene's mama say he laughed. Said Irene knew right then she had him. Everybody know whitepeople laugh from nervousness, not just cause they think things is funny. Said it wasn't nothing funny bout her proposal, so if he was nervous, that mean it hit on something somewhere. She talked to him through some liquor that night, and told him try it out for a month. Keep it secret. At the end of the month, if he had one complaint, they would be finished. She would go back to her colored life, and he to his white.

They been married. Been married.

"What's his first name?" I asked Lantene. She went and asked her mother.

"My mama don't know," she reported back to me.

EVERYBODY DOWN HOME knew my mother and all her stories. When she planned to visit, they wanted to know when she would arrive, exactly, and would one or both the boys come with her this time. When she visited, they waved and grinned and wanted to talk about how the City was treating her, and wanted to know what new things she had brought for Miz Dambridge. After she left, they wanted to talk to me about how wonderful things seemed to be for my mother, and how much I had to look forward to.

At the same time that all this present talk happened, history was reviewed in detail. If I didn't know the ways I was the same as or different from Margarete Dambridge Palms Starks at any age, there was somebody round Patuskie to tell me. It was repetition that lodged my mother in my backbone. I grew tall around her lore. But underneath how I walked there was drilling. It was as simple and as straight as that. Legend made her out like sky to me. I reached for her heights. But how we were and who we were was altogether different. We were less like two dream girls and more like fry cooks, flipping meat. Testy with each other in such a small, hot space. Mad and serving food.

MARGARETE SAT AT the kitchen table rubbing her hair-dresser's fingers across the pain in her head. "Neesey," she said, hysteria warbling like a caught bird, "guess we better get on over to Christine's and warn Luke the owner been by." *We*, I consider, as I watch Margarete's tired fingers run the grooves in her forehead, and as I consider the distance between the old shirt of David's I had slept in and the clothes I would need to go out. "It's a good thing you here," she trails.

"What you want me to do, Margarete?" I asked. She lifted her head. We two are alone in the kitchen. Four dark elbows on the flecked kitchen table. Of course she wants to snap at me. And she does: "I want you to get some clothes on and go warn your brother, Neesey." I watch the bitters fly out of the red flush tunnel of her mouth. I wonder if I am woman as she is. My hair has been cut, and is rolled to style. Whether or not I show it, I know how disappointment turns the lips down. I am as shaken up and worried as all us women who attend. Doesn't this make me grown?

She does not have to repeat herself. The reflex to obey says I am still a child. The child me trails the woman me. Like a bride's lacy net, it is near weightless and drags prettily on the floor. Absently, I pull the rollers from my flip and walk toward Luke edward's closet. My clothes take up so little of the leering space.

I smell his pomade and cologne seeping from the wood. I come quickly to my senses. I forget about Margarete and start to worry like a bomb about Luke.

I scrape the hangers across the naked rod. Looking for my blue-checked skirt. I pull out an ironed white blouse, and I feel silly buttoning the long sleeves. Who has all this time? This, this is emergency.

The owner will find him. The owner might take him somewhere, from us. *Move, Neesey.* I scold my ownself now.

I lunge for my shoes underneath Clara's bed where I put them when I visit, as a prayer. Of course, I knock her awake in the haste I manufacture. She starts and turns a few times. Then she jerks up. She has always been the kind of child for whom the mornings are a misery. She has that part of Luke edward in her. I lie, "It's OK, sweetie, sorry I shook you." I leave her for Margarete to fetch.

"AIN'T YOU GONE yet, girl?" His mother worries. It is not a question she asks. It is not one last admonishment to get me out the door. His mother yowls. Or howls at least. She is a yelping soul in the doorway, watching me try to dress. I pass her and go to grab my coat, from a hook in the front hall.

Clara wants to know Mama what's the matter.

"Tell Luke exactly what happened," Margarete impresses. She walks over to where I hold the door open, listening to what she says. She sticks her hand into my coat pocket and puts her dwindling few dollars there. My pockets are shallow, so I put my hand over her money. I go out the door and do not look back. Why should I look back? I know all the nicks in that door. I made most of them with the stroller, bringing the baby in for dinner.

Margarete has pushed the door shut behind me, and inside, Margarete talks to Clara who is tired and will not be becalmed. Margarete is slow to turn back into the flat because she knows just like I do the look on Big Jim's face, all of us in turmoil over Luke edward, and so early in the morning.

I rush forward. It is a fifteen-minute walk to where Christine and Luke edward live.

ONLY EARLY BIRDS are up. Sanitation workers, maids and us. And I am cold, as usual.

I catch myself wondering if J is up and gone to work yet. Be so nice for him to walk me, so I don't have to think about where to go. Be so nice for him to help me through this mess, so I don't have to try to take care of things plus summon up sense of my own. But he is not with me, and in my disappointment and my embarrassment to catch myself thinking about his company, I rush him out of my mind by checking that the dollar bills are still crumpled in my pocket. It's time to start looking for that big brick house on the corner where I need to make a right.

I HAD PUT my own money pouch in the bottom of my drawers. I hadn't wanted Margarete to know about the money I had. I sneak behind a hedge and take the pouch out. I put it in my pocket with Margarete's money. I put my hand over all of it since, like I said, my pockets are shallow.

I wonder should I call David for his strongbox money? No, I decide. First I will go to Luke edward. He is out here vulnerable, and if I don't get to him fast enough, I will be blamed.

HOW LONG WILL Luke edward continue to cause all this confusion? No doubt he is over there half-drunk or half-sleep, dancing, playing cards or doing who knows what with Christine and their friends. Their apartment is a flophouse, and Luke edward is King Flop.

The brick house should be coming soon. I shouldn't act like Luke edward ain't no good; it just isn't so. You had to know him when he was young to know what I mean.

When the Owner Man came to our door, we had all headed toward it in our hazy phases of sleep. We all recognized the knock, it belonged to Luke edward. The question was, who knocked? Was it him, with his long, suggestive fingers? And what long story would he tell?

He hardly came by anymore since Jim had taken his key away. Or was it someone else, about him? Someone with shorter less beautiful hands. Would they say he was dead, or just in trouble? What kind of grief was at the door?

The Owner Man says one of the other boys knows where Luke stays with his girlfriend. Has the Owner Man gone to wake up the other boy? The other boy is probably a man, like Luke edward. The Owner doesn't believe the other man did anything, so he probably won't go wake up his family like he did us. It may be that I will get to Luke edward first.

The man has to know Margarete lied about not knowing where Luke edward lives. Anxiously, I pull the money out of my pocket and catch a ten bill caught by the early air. Three tens and a five. Thirty-five dollars. There is one hundred ten dollars in my pouch. I take one of Margarete's tens and push it down into the bottom of my shoe. Something to help me start again. I look down the block in front of me and behind me for the white house with the black gas lamp that is across the street from the brick house where I make the right turn.

All around me are houses with high-shaped hedges. Damn. I have walked clear across town. How many times have I walked to Christine's! If I could yell at myself, I would. J would be running his mouth, me running mine. He would be tugging my arm as I walked straight past the brick house and he turned right. Only alone would I get so turned around.

I don't think twice about what to do. I turn on my heels and walk double speed in the reverse direction. I am so disappointed; I jam my hands into my pockets and recrumple Margarete's remaining dollar bills. That's when I discover my carelessness with my coat. I have buttoned it wrong and so one side hangs incoherently below the other. I am so concerned with protecting Margarete's money, with protecting Margarete's son.

WHEN I REACH Dexter Boulevard, the street Christine lives on, many things have happened. People are out being swallowed up by buses. I hurry by. They stare at my anxiety and pinched face. They see me walking fast on my way. They don't know how dumb I am about directions. Not even for her brother's sake can she find her way around. Alone, I feel conspicuous on the street. The barometer in my panties quivers. All this frenzy and this fear. Five or eight blocks back, the ache in me erupted. J has taught me what this feeling means, but I am confused and displeased by it now.

Turns out, I had not missed a turn. In the long ago of my leaving the house in the hurry and stupor of door-banging and huddled, crumpled money, I had made the turn and forgot about it. Once I recognized where I was, I rushed ahead and clambered up the steps to 78 Dexter, my panties and Margarete's money both nearly wringing wet, the one wrung from worry, the other wet from breaking open. I had to knock hard to rouse the house. I called and knocked on the window, a nervous woman with thin knuckles: "Luke edward, Luke edward, Luke edward." No answer. I didn't leave, didn't go round back; I stood stock still yelling on the porch. Christine pulls the door open just a little, sees it's me, opens it wide. Her eyes are nearly plastered closed and her hair stands every which way. "Luke edward here?" I bellow. Out of breath but arrived.

"Yeah," she answers me, and we both walk to the bedroom where she rolls his top half, and I shake his naked and protruding red-berry legs.

"Whatsa matter?" he wants to know, recognizing me in this his other house.

"You in trouble," I tell him and rush on. "That man owns the gas station came by to find out where you are. He say you lifted some money last Friday night." Christine wilts. I see it from the corner of my eye. It is sad.

"What you talking about, Neesey?" Luke sits up in the bed and the sheet he had swirled around him fell. His swathe, his holy rope.

Christine props herself up against the wall. She sits in a small chair. Her hair is an irate halo.

Luke edward sits up in the bed. He alerts a smell of musk and last night's dance and today's ferocities all around us in the room. He is a man, and the breath of his sleep-mouth insists, "Neesey, stop dreaming and tell me what happened." I wish this unpleasantness was sweet. The hair on his chest is soft and straight and reddish-blond. Fine like something on a baby's butt. Both his feet break the color of the bedclothes: they are long and well-shaped and neatly kept. His veins and thin bones make a nice map across the top of his feet.

Abruptly the sheet jerks back, and the long, red-sienna man with cherry-blond hair steps out of bed. He reaches over near Christine to grab his pants. The belt buckle clinks. I realize by his sudden movement that I have been silent, stumped, transfixed. But if I was transfixed then, I am cast, a statue now. Mouth an O. I have not seen Luke edward without his pants and shirt and socks and shoes since we all got into the big washtub one after the other down home. Then, he had no hair on him. His peter did not swing; it was not plum. I imagine I hear it flap and smack against his thighs. I turn myself around and sit down at the foot of the bed. Luke edward is a man.

He comes around and squats to face me. He is bare-chested and earnest. He persists. "What happened, Neesey?"

I repeat all the facts. "The man who owns the gas station came and woke us up early this morning. He banged so hard on the door we thought somebody round was sick or dying. Margarete answered, but me and Big Jim were standing right there with her. He says last Friday before you quit you took money from his register. You were supposed to put it in his safe. He says you planned to take it, that's why you quit so fast. He says you slipped and mentioned it to one of his other boys. He says he can have you put in jail." I looked dead center in Luke edward's face. He did the same to me. Luke edward, did you take that man's money? My voice is pinched up high. I can't tell whether he looks hurt. I mean I can't tell why he looks hurt. I can't think. My sobs are breaking rain. This is when I melt into Margarete.

My eyes dart across Luke edward's face in a frantic search for truth. It may be now that I do the melting.

Christine joins the conversation. "You steal money from the gas station, Luke?" she is asking.

Luke stands up from in front of me and continues to dress.

I want to yank him back to where I can watch and try to pry an answer from his refusing again to talk. Why does he refuse to talk? I remember I had decided before that it has to do with activity. It must. The way the boys are at war with activity. Their urges to move around always win. That is why they are so word shy, and book shy, and school shy. They can't sit still for the time it all takes.

"Don't swallow everything whole," he says.

I can watch out for myself, Luke edward. I have found my way here to get *you*.

"Margarete told me to bring you this money." I expect him to respond to my tone of voice. He does not turn toward me.

"Luke edward, do you want this money Margarete sent?"

"I don't need Mama's money, Neesey."

"It's one hundred twenty-five dollars, Luke edward."

Christine says, "Luke, what you gone do?"

I think I see them decide to get rid of me. At least I think that's what they decide. I try to think should I pull the money out. But it is too pitiful, even for me to do.

I want my Luke edward.

Luke has buttoned up his sweater and rubbed his hands over his hair. He pulls a coat from the closet and leaves a hanger swinging. "Come on, Neesey," he says. Where is he going? Wherever he is going he thinks I'm going with him. Well, I'll go with him. But not very far. I am as tightly stretched as a slingshot set to spring.

I have to take my mind to think on something soothing. Even as I stumble up the road. I recall myself learning. I remember when that sky opened up. I feel the new sensation of lightness over my head. I explore this endlessness that seems to be a part of the whole thing. I smile about all those many discoveries, new words. I learn to identify humidity and to predict the coming rain. I reach to where the freedom is. I put on an old coat and run out to the yard. We need greens for Sunday dinner. It is my responsibility to get them. There are not many rows to pick from at this time of the season so I do not linger choosing. By now, everything has fallen but the collards.

NEW YORK, 1994

THE GOOD NEGRESS

Questions for Discussion

QUESTIONS FOR DISCUSSION

1. How does language — diction, idiom, syntax, spelling, and punctuation — show how characters grow and change? How does it show where they come from? How does the way we *use* language go beyond what it is we're actually saying?

2. Why did Margarete, Denise's mother, choose to take Denise "down the country" to Granma'am, while she kept the boys in Detroit with her? What are the differences between the expectations for girls and boys? How are Luke edward and David treated differently from Denise?

3. What is the dynamic of the Palms family? What impact does not having a father have on them? How does Denise romanticize or idealize the memory of her father? What were Margarete's choices as a widow?

4. When Granma'am punishes Luke edward early in Luke edward's childhood, why does she choose that method of discipline? Has Luke edward transgressed in an alarming way? Does Luke edward deserve the punishment he is given?

5. Denise idolizes Luke edward, her older brother closest to her in age. What are the main differences between Luke edward and Denise's oldest brother, David, and why does Denise feel so connected to Luke edward? Who is someone you have looked up to in your life and why?

6. What is your impression of Gloria Pearson, Denise's teacher in Detroit? How does she communicate with Denise? What was the behavior that suggested Missus Pearson was interested in Denise's ultimate success? Or, could Missus Pearson's behavior toward Denise be considered discouraging? What might be the most appropriate behavior for encouraging and educating a student Denise's age with Denise's social background, skills, and intellect?

7. What does Missus Pearson mean when she says, "Our families are the families that slavery made" (page 225)? How does slavery loom over American history in the 1950s, when the book takes place, and today? What are several examples from *The Good Negress* of behavior or conditions in the African American family that have continued or evolved from slavery?

8. *The Good Negress* is set in the late 1950s and the early 1960s. These years were segregated times in America. What are some similarities between Denise's era and now? In what ways do the challenges Denise faces still exist today?

9. Denise is pulled between being homebound with her mother and studying with Missus Pearson. Have you

ever felt torn between your loyalties—and if so, how did you cope?

10. What kinds of hardships do the men in the book have? What kinds of hardships do the women have? How are they different? How are they similar?

11. By the end of the novel, Denise surpasses her own—and others'—expectations for herself. What are some examples of moments in your life where you have exceeded your own expectations?

12. How does Denise grow throughout the course of the book? In which ways does she stay the same? What does education and language bring to her life? What are its limits?

THOMAS SAYERS ELLIS

A. J. Verdelle is a novelist, essayist, and working mother. Verdelle won a Whiting Award for Fiction and the Harold D. Vursell Memorial Award for Fiction from the American Academy of Arts and Letters for her novel *The Good Negress*. Verdelle has taught at Princeton University, the University of Kentucky, the University of Vermont, and in summer programs at the University of Iowa, the Fine Arts Work Center, and the Carnegie Center for Literacy in Lexington. Verdelle currently teaches undergraduates at Morgan State University and in the low-residency MFA program at Lesley University. Verdelle lives with her daughter in Washington, D.C.